For Mum - Bette M
spread her wings and flew to New Zealand
with Dad, the lad she first spied doings his
newspaper round in Liverpool over sixty-
five years ago.

Compendum of Liverpudlian words

A ntwacky
 Old fashioned or out of date

Bootle Buck

A hard-faced lady

Queen

A woman

Divvy

A stupid person

Belter

Describing something positively

Ozzy

Hospital

Cob on

To feel angry, agitated or irritated

Prologue

The child vanished on a stifling Liverpool summer's day in late August.

Up until then, it had been a perfectly normal day with no hint of what was to come as the young woman pushed her small child in the fold-out umbrella pram up Bold Street.

The eclectic mix of tightly packed two, three, and four-storey buildings loomed over the duo forming a higgledy-piggledy montage either side of the street and the bombed-out church at the end was a watchful sentry.

As the young woman moved forward with the pushchair, she noticed the child had undone the straps, again.

'What have I told you?' she huffed, veering out of the way of a woman in a pink sari. She'd a hand-knitted sweater thrown over the top of it to ward off the awful wind whistling down the street.

'Don't like it, Mummy.' The child wriggled in an attempt to avoid being buckled back in.

'Stop that right now, do you hear me? Or there'll be no chocolate bar when we get to the station.'

The wriggling stopped.

The shop beside them had a 'To Let' sign in the grimy window and an empty lager can along with a collection of cigarette buts littered the doorway. The woman wrinkled her nose because she was sure she could smell wee.

She bent over the pushchair to click the strap back in, jumping as a piercing wolf whistle sounded. The culprit was a fella with longish hair leaning out the passenger window of a white van as it sailed past.

Pulling a face and pretending to be annoyed, she tugged the hem of her skirt down. Then, ignoring a group of lads with Mohicans in every shade of the rainbow, studded dog collars wrapped around their necks, and scrawny white arms protruding from Union Jack singlets she weaved around them and spied the familiar striped awning framing Tabac across the street.

The cafe was a source of fascination to her because it was a great spot for celebrity spotting and the food was good. She was too skint to call in for coffee or a bite to eat today but she could veer past and see if anyone of note was dining in there today.

She waited for a break in the stream of cars and when it came bounced the pram across the road, coming to a halt under the awning to gawp in the window. There were no diners whose lunch was worth interrupting to ask for an autograph and so, with a disappointed sigh, she hurried on.

The sign for the wedding shop tucked between two larger buildings a short distance ahead caught her eye.

It was the boutique where one of her old school mates had chosen to have her wedding and bridesmaids dresses made. Brides of Bold Street. Her mouth tightened. She hadn't been asked to be a bridesmaid.

The irritation that still rankled at the snub disappeared however as she saw the newsagents where she'd called in to buy her monthly magazine treat just a week ago had gone.

In its place was a shop with posed mannequins in the antwacky gear her mam might have ponced about in. Retro was all the rage these days she thought. Not that she'd be caught dead in clobber like that.

Her eyes swung out to the road. *How weird.* There were nowhere near as many cars as there'd been a moment ago and the ones tootling up the street were similar to the old banger her grandad had refused to part with.

The air had changed too. It felt thick, almost as if she were wading through tepid soup. She came to a halt. The sensation wasn't dissimilar to the time she'd stood at the top of the Blackpool Tower and her legs had threatened to give out on her.

'I'll just close my eyes for a second,' she mumbled, having decided she must be having a funny turn of sorts.

The whoosh of people carrying on about their business as they passed her by continued as if there were nothing at all odd about her standing in the middle of the pavement with her eyes squeezed shut, clutching the pram for support.

The familiar smell of exhaust fumes and a trail of cigarette smoke saw her cautiously open them once more. She blinked rapidly to assure herself things were as they should be.

Only they weren't.

The blood turned to ice in her veins as she realised the pushchair was empty.

Part One

Chapter One

Liverpool, 1981

Inside the workroom down the back of Brides of Bold Street, Sabrina and Evelyn were sewing in companionable silence. Separated from the shop floor and partially hidden by the wall behind the counter where they were seated now was where the magic of dressmaking happened.

A mannequin wrapped in a calico toile posed in the corner of the industrious space and against the left wall was a row of dresses with plastic covers protecting them. All the gowns were tagged with their bride-to-be's name. This was how Sabrina and Evelyn thought of their dresses. There was the demure Catherine, the slinky Margaret, the frothy Lucy and so on. All of them their finished handiwork waiting for collection.

The shelves out the back here were laden with cotton spools, sequins, rolls of ribbon, packets of lace, needles, thimbles, several tape measures and a jar of pens because pens in Evelyn's opinion had a mysterious habit of vanishing. You could never find one when you needed it. Hence the jar.

A roll of paper stood to one side of the cutting table as Sabrina had been trained by Evelyn in the draping method of pattern making.

Their brides could choose from the collection of books housed in the shop featuring patterns from the latest Parisian designs, from the selection of readymade styles on show on the shop floor, or have a bespoke Brides of Bold Street gown designed.

The design side of the business was left to Sabrina these days. Evelyn maintained she couldn't be bothered with all the fussing involved with creating a wedding dress from scratch anymore. Her days of tuning in to what the client had in mind which more often than not turned out to be completely different from what they'd initially thought they wanted, were done and dusted. She'd passed that baton to Sabrina.

The truth was Evelyn's eyes weren't as sharp as they used to be thanks to years of threading cotton through needles and working under weak lighting. Not that she'd admit to this failing, insisting instead it was Sabrina's turn to channel her creativity of which she'd plenty.

A transistor radio was tuned to Radio Merseyside on the cutting table with the volume just loud enough to hear it above the thrumming of the old Singer machine at which Evelyn spent her days.

The Singer was older than the shop itself but she refused to do away with it. She didn't need to see well to work it. Sewing a seam at her machine was something she could do with her eyes shut.

The finer needlework she left to Sabrina but she was still a whizz on that machine. She could manage to coax it into life even on its most temperamental days and her feet made the motion of pushing the treadle down even when she was sitting in her chair enjoying her evening smoke.

The sign on the door to the shop had been switched to open for an hour now and Sabrina and Evelyn each had their customary brew in front of them. They made a good team.

Sabrina drank her tea from a pottery mug she'd picked up in a thrift store. She'd immediately been drawn to its slightly misshapen shape and had thought it needed a home. She also never took her tea without a biscuit to dunk in it. She liked to say the need for a bicky was on account of her low blood pressure but the fact of the matter was she had a sweet tooth.

Evelyn however, refused to drink her tea out of anything other than a delicate, bone china cup and saucer. She was adamant her English breakfast tea tasted tainted in anything else.

Sabrina found her easy to buy for at Christmas and on birthdays because just as some people had a shelf full of books, Evelyn had her china cup and saucer collection. Indeed, a shelf behind the counter was laden with the pretty patterned sets she'd brought her aunt over the years. Evelyn Flooks would never be short of a teacup.

As for the counter, well, it had once served as an antique oak table but had been painted white and repurposed when Sabrina gave the shop a makeover. These days instead of plates and cutlery it was home to their till, telephone, index card filing system, notebook and yes, more pens.

Evelyn had said painting over the oak was sacrilege but secretly she liked the way it brightened the place up. Sabrina had a flair for that sort of thing. This was why she'd given her free rein over the old place when she'd decided to follow her into the business upon leaving school. That, and she'd wanted her to put her stamp on the shop she was to be a partner in.

Sabrina had worked wonders breathing new life into a boutique that hadn't changed since the late nineteen twenties when Evelyn had opened her business.

For a woman who'd been born and bred in a tough part of the city, Evelyn spoke very properly. There was no hint of the Scottie Road where she'd been raised about her.

When Sabrina had asked her why she said things like, 'How are you today?' Instead of 'Ahright, luv?' like everyone else around their neck of the woods. Evelyn had told her it had come with practise, 'yars and yars of practise'.

She was a woman who ran a business, she'd gone on to say. She was at the helm of a respected bridal shop, dressmakers. Call it what you would but either way, it was a business and it was hers. She'd built it with hard graft and sheer determination. She'd not failed where others had and she'd proved wrong those who'd muttered she'd not stand a chance.

She'd seen her business through a depression and a world war for heaven's sake. A woman like that *should* speak properly. There'd be no ta-rah, luvs or ahright, queen? on her watch thank you very much.

It always made Sabrina smile when her aunt would forget herself and drop a Scouse clanger into her conversation.

It always happened after the match on Saturday if her team lost.

Evelyn was football mad and so far as she was concerned her boys who made up the Liverpool team walked on water except when they lost.

Every Saturday for as long as Sabrina could remember, her aunt would turn the sign in the shop window to closed, pull her red beanie on and wrap her red and white scarf around her neck. Off she'd tootle to catch the number 17 to Anfield Stadium.

Her one and only indulgence apart from the ten Woodbine cigarettes stretched out over the week was a yearly seat in the stands.

Now, she was squinting despite her heavy glasses as the Singer stitched a seam.

Sabrina hummed along to Bonnie Tyler's *It's a Heartache*. She was perched at the cutting table where she could keep an eye on the boutique, hand sewing delicate Irish lace onto a gown.

'Give me Cilla Black any day,' Evelyn muttered pausing to change the angle of the fabric under the Singer's foot. 'Voice like an angel our Cilla.'

They both started when the door to the shop jangled open.

Sabrina watched as a hard-faced woman carrying a large bag urged a younger girl to hurry up before closing the door behind them.

Abandoning her stitching, she stepped into the shop. 'Good morning, how are you today?' She smiled from one to the other hoping she didn't have biscuit crumbs stuck to her lips.

Evelyn carried on pushing the treadle.

It was the older woman who stepped forwards and placed the bag on the counter with a thud.

'We'd like you to alter this, wouldn't we, Susan?' Her tone brooked no argument.

Susan looked to be in her early twenties like Sabrina and her nose was red and chafed. She sneezed.

'Bless you,' Sabrina said automatically, thinking what gorgeous hair she had. She was always wistful when it came to curls and this girl had a mane of them. The colour was an unusual shade too, it made her think of whisky. Not quite blonde, not quite red.

Susan smiled her acknowledgement taking the hanky from the woman. 'Ta, Mam.' She gave her nose a good blow.

'I'm just getting over a cold. Change of season ones are the worst.' She stuffed the cotton square in the pocket of a boxy, navy blazer and looked at Sabrina with watery blue eyes before turning them to her surrounds. Her gaze was contemplative as she swept the shop.

A white stand rested against the grey wall, housing thick pattern books, and next to it were rolls of enticing fabrics in shades of oyster, champagne, cream and white. They begged to be unwound and admired.

An ornate chandelier hung from the ceiling and near the counter was a pink velvet-covered blanket box upon which were a display of satin heels. To the right of the counter was a rack of readymade dresses inviting her to come and admire them. The plain wedding hues gave way to vibrant bridesmaid dresses in varying shades and styles.

The fitting room was located next to them, framed by plush, pink velvet drapes. Inside she could see a stool for belongings to be placed on and a full-length mirror.

Sabrina was enjoying the girl's admiring stock take. She'd worked hard to give the boutique a romantic feel with her palette of pink, white and the soft grey which had reminded her of a fine mist.

Susan's eyes had settled on the dress on display in the window and Sabrina was pleased. It was exactly what she'd hoped for when she'd dressed the mannequin after having put the finishing touches on the gown. She poured her heart and soul into all her dresses but that one had been an extra special labour of love.

The older woman had opened the bag and was holding up a dress which, although beautiful, had long since had its day. 'I think our Susan will look a picture in it if it's nipped in a little around the waist, the hem's a tad longish too.'

'It's lovely,' Sabrina said noting Susan's stricken face as her attention swung away from the window to the gown her mother was clutching. 'It could do with a little modernising though. Perhaps we could change the neckline and shorten the length a little, add a ruffle that sort of thing.' She shot a reassuring smile Susan's way.

Hope flared on the other girl's face.

'I don't think so,' her mother sniffed, and Susan's eyes dulled. 'That dress has been handed down through the family and me poor auld ma would turn in her grave if she knew it was being snipped away at.'

Sabrina willed Susan to speak up. It was her day after all. When she didn't say a word, she decided to take matters into her own hands.

'I saw you admiring the gown in the window just now Susan. You'd look lovely in it.' She smiled her encouragement.

Susan seized the opportunity. 'It caught my eye. It's exactly the sort of dress I'd love to wear. Look, Mam.' She moved over to the window and gestured to it.

It was exactly the sort of wedding gown Sabrina would like to wear were she getting married. The dress was white, and almost Georgian era in its simple style. It spoke of Jane Austen and Mr Darcy but the lacy sleeves added a touch of modern glamour.

There was no chance of her wearing it any time soon though. She'd need a fella for that! Her track record wasn't good either. The last fella she'd gone out with, Dave, had been a proper divvy.

He'd wheedled his way into a date with her at the Swan Inn where she'd been catching up with her self-proclaimed bezzie mate Flo. The pub was stumbling distance from the boutique's back door onto Wood Street.

When she'd relayed to Flo after her night out at the flicks with Divvy Dave that she reckoned he'd eaten a raw onion before meeting up with her, her friend thought it hilarious. By the time she'd finished telling her he'd talked all through the film and had a habit of starting his sentences with words beginning with 'H' just to be sure she got plenty of oniony blasts throughout the evening, Flo had crossed her legs and was bent double, crying laughing.

'It's not funny,' Sabrina had protested although she was grinning. 'And I'm sworn off all men for the foreseeable future.'

Sabrina watched the wonder on Susan's face as she admired the dress. It assured her she had the best job in the world.

Susan's mother however was having none of it. 'It's a family tradition, our kid,' her nasal voice insisted as she flapped the dress at her daughter.

Susan dragged herself away.

Sabrina watched as her shoulders slumped and made up her mind. She'd do her very best to ensure the dress made Susan feel every inch the beautiful bride by the time she'd finished with it. It wouldn't be easy but she'd work her subtle magic and her mam would have no cause for complaint upon collection.

She owed it to Susan to make the gown work because together, she and Aunt Evie stitched the dreams of the girls who passed over the threshold of their boutique on Bold Street.

Chapter Two

'I tell you, Flo, she was an old Bootle Buck if ever I saw one and the wedding dress she brought in wanting altering for her daughter was proper antwacky.' Sabrina spoke over the top of Gerry Rafferty crooning *Baker Street* from the jukebox. She raised her glass to her lips and had a sip of the ale. Her lipstick left its mark on the rim.

Florence Teesdale who was seated with her back to the wall, a black and white print of bygone days hung above her head, was Sabrina's oldest friend. Their friendship had been cemented on their first day of school when Florence had taken the shy little girl on the scene under her wing.

For Sabrina's part, she'd enjoyed the boisterousness of Florence's terraced home which was far too small for all the people squeezed inside its walls despite her older brother having left home.

She'd two younger twin sisters. Shona and Teresa. They were surprise babies, ten years younger than Flo and although she made out they were the bane of her life because they were always nicking her stuff, she was fiercely protective of them.

Flo's mam, in Sabrina's opinion, made the most belter scones in all of Liverpool. Mrs Teesdale put raisins in them and always let her pick the burnt bits off the tray.

Her dad had an allotment and his prize-winning veg was his pride and joy. He was football mad like Aunt Evie only he was an Everton man. This was something Evelyn had grudgingly decided not to hold against him for Sabrina's sake.

Sometimes the friends would lament their lot. Officially in their twenties now and still living under the same roofs they'd always lived under but the alternative, a damp flat, held no appeal. Besides, it wasn't as if either of them needed their own pad so as to entertain their fellas. They'd have to find some first although Flo most definitely had her sights set on one.

Now, Florence giggled at the image conjured up of a po-faced woman and her mutinous daughter before shovelling in a handful of crisps.

The air was smoky but the ashtray on their table empty. They'd tried to get the hang of smoking cigarettes around the back of Flo's dad's allotment as teenagers after school. Sabrina had pinched a couple of her aunt's Woodbines but after much coughing and lurching of their stomachs had decided it wasn't for them. Aunt Evie had never said a word about the stolen cigarettes. She'd probably figured Sabrina's green face when she got home had been punishment enough.

'Poor girl,' Florence lamented once she'd finished her mouthful. 'Me ma's dress was full-skirted, tea-length. Can you imagine my calves poking out the bottom of that? It'd look like two milk bottles or bowling pins trotting down the aisle.'

Sabrina smiled at the silly remark and helped herself to the crisps.

Florence swatted her hand away. 'Oi! Get your own, girl.'

Sabrina was unrepentant, licking the salt off her fingers.

Florence's pretty, round face with milk chocolate eyes that could never keep anything secret grew serious and she thrust the packet at Sabrina. 'Here, go on, finish them off. I'm supposed to be on a diet. I've a Weight Watchers meeting on Monday night and I'm determined to beat Bossy Bev when we step on the *scales of doom*.' She used a dramatic movie voice overtone for the latter part of her remark.

'Ta, I only had beans on toast for tea.' Sabrina took the packet from her but before she popped more of the salty snacks in her mouth explained, 'Aunt Evie was having her usual Saturday night salmon steak and I wasn't keen on smelling like a fish all evening.'

Evelyn was of the firm belief her weekly dose of the oily fish kept her heart beating strong as an ox and had the added benefit of giving her a complexion that couldn't be sourced from a bottle bought at Boots.

Sabrina was of the firm belief that were she to partake of said salmon she'd be guaranteed to remain single for the rest of her days and, unlike Aunt Evie, she rather liked the idea of a man she could share her life with. Even though after her experience with Dave the divvy she was beginning to despair of ever finding one.

'Aunt Evie came home in fine form. Liverpool won.'

'Dad will have a cob on then. I feel sorry for me ma,' Flo said.

Sabrina remembered her friend's comment. 'Who's Bossy Bev?'

Florence rolled her eyes. 'Beverley Jones. She's an old school pal of me ma's and she's an awful know-it-all. She's always giving me helpful tips on weight loss that aren't helpful, they're annoying.' She put on a mock falsetto voice, 'Eight glasses of water a day Florence, *or* portion size, dear, it's all about portion size.'

Sabrina giggled.

'I want to lose more than her this week to shut her up.'

'You're too hard on yourself, Flo. I don't know why you bother with those silly meetings.'

'Easy for you to say.' Florence dipped her head glumly and the light shone on her recently cut, chestnut hair.

It was Sabrina who'd come up with the term 'chestnut'. She'd seen it on a hair dye box and thought it sounded much more glam than medium brown.

Flo's hair had always hung long down her back but she'd had it cut to a chin-length bob and her fringe had been teased into spikes.

'I don't need her tips because I could lose ten pounds just like that.' She clicked her fingers. 'If I didn't like food so much.'

Sabrina belly laughed at that along with the woebegone expression on her friend's face. 'Flo, you're funny, beautiful and I love you just the way you are. I don't want you to change.'

'And I love you too, Sabs, but it would be nice if Tim Burns would love me too.'

Sabrina knew there was no point telling her Tim was only worth having if he liked her for who she was and not because she fit into a size eight mould. It was a conversation they'd had more than once and one that always fell on deaf ears.

'Speaking of whom.' Florence dug into the pocket of her Calvin Klein jeans. It took a moment as they were rather snug but she managed to produce a crumpled piece of paper.

Sabrina watched curiously as she unfolded it and smoothed it on the table.

'What's that then?'

'This, queen, is the map of my life.'

'It looks like it was ripped out of a magazine.'

'Cosmo to be exact, every girl's bible.'

Sabrina grinned. 'Come on then, what is it?'

'My stars for the year, that's what. Well, for September onwards anyway.'

'Did you manage to pull out Scorpio's?'

'I would've but I was at the hairdressers when I saw this. I only had a split second to rip it out while Cassandra checked on a perm.'

Sabrina shrugged; she wasn't sure she believed in all that stuff anyway. 'Fair enough, let's hear what's in store for you then.'

'Well,' Florence puffed up excitedly and stabbed at the paper. 'Capricorn,' she traced her finger down the page to the month of September. 'It says I need to take a break from climbing the corporate ladder because my focus on my career could be taking away from my personal life. Close friends might be feeling neglected.' She looked over at Sabrina alarm on her face. 'Am I neglecting you?'

Sabrina snorted. 'No, Flo, I haven't felt pushed aside while you try and advance yourself in the secretarial world of shipping.'

Florence who worked as a typist for a shipping firm down by the docks grinned. 'Yes, well, one size doesn't fit all, Sabs, you have to take the relevant bits from it.'

'The bits you like the sound of, you mean,' Sabrina smirked.

'Oh, shurrup and listen. Here it is! This is the part that matters.' Florence scanned the type before reading aloud, 'Look out for an encounter with a man who is passionate about music.' She glanced up. 'Tim likes music.'

'How do you know?'

'Because he puts money in there each time he's here.' She waved over at the jukebox as though it were glaringly obvious before dipping her head again. 'Further down it says I'm very compatible with Taurus the plodding bull. It also says I'm a sure-footed goat—I don't think I'm goaty at all do you?'

'No nothing goaty about you at all and definitely not sure-footed either. You tripped over the cobbles walking to the pub tonight.'

Both girls giggled at the memory of Florence's impromptu dance to stay upright.

'I wonder if Tim's Taurus?' She'd a daft dreamy expression. 'Do you think he'll be here tonight?' Florence scanned the packed pub in case she'd missed seeing him walk through the door.

They were on a stakeout at the Swan and had managed to find a table that gave them optimal viewing of both the entrance to the public house and to where Mickey the barman with a gold tooth and a heart to match was pulling pints.

Sabrina thought they should raise their sights and try and to get into the Steering Wheel upstairs. They could mingle with Liverpool's VIP's, footballers and celebrities instead of sitting here waiting for Tim Burns and his biker pals. Flo wouldn't have a bar of it though.

The chatter around them was loud but shortly the music would crank up and the area in the corner of the pub where the jukebox was would be transformed into a dance floor.

'He usually is on a Saturday night, Flo.'

'How's my lipstick.' She puckered up.

'Perfect.'

'Hair?'

'Gorgeous, super shiny like a shampoo advert.'

'Is my fringe still spiked? I put half a tube of gel in it.'

'Check.'

'Teeth?'

'Don't do that you look like Aunt Evie when she's checking her falsies are in properly and no, there's nothing stuck in them.'

Florence breathed out happily and the sight of her expanding bosom under her satin shirt made the lad at the next table flick his ash into his pint accidentally. She was oblivious as she launched into a story about Carol, the other typist at her work, having met a fella last Saturday and how she'd been going on about him all week.

'Honestly, she's driven me potty. It's been Roger this and Roger that. I mean how can you compare the colour of a person's eyes with a filing cabinet?'

Sabrina shrugged.

'I don't know either but she did. What I'm saying is, if Carol can meet someone nice then there's hope for—' her eyes bugged. 'Oh my God, girl, it's him, he's here.'

Sabrina grabbed hold of her pal's glass. 'You nearly knocked that over then. The sight of you looking like you've had an accident would have caught his attention ahright.'

Florence wasn't listening though; she'd a lovelorn look slapped on her face as she tracked Tim Burn's path to the bar.

Sabrina glanced over in time to see him swagger past, motorcycle helmet tucked under his arm, and flanked by his usual entourage. They'd all got their Liverpool scarves on and she was betting they'd been at the match and were clearly in the mood to celebrate the win.

She sat up a little straighter in her seat as she gave one of the lads she hadn't seen before the top to toe.

She liked his hair. She watched as he roughed it up. It curled at his collar and was so dark it shone blue under the light. He looked good in his leather jacket which was battered just the right side of cool and undone to reveal his club shirt.

She continued her inventory. The denim of his jeans was faded to a sexy hue; he wore them well. Unlike the sandy-haired, shortish fella next to him whose denim was so tight he could surely hit the high notes better than Barbara Streisand herself. How he managed to cock a leg over a bike without splitting the arse out of them was beyond her.

Moving back to the fella she was checking out she fancied he didn't have that arrogant air of Tim's. Tim expected the ladies to come running and they usually did.

Women, Flo being one of them, loved the bad boy aura he oozed but it left Sabrina cold.

It was a kind-hearted man she was after. Yes, a steady Eddie with hair that curled at the collar and shone blue-black would do her nicely. The sort of fella who wouldn't take the corners too fast were she to ride pillion on his motorcycle.

Her cheeks flamed as he turned and caught her gawping. She ducked her head feigning fascination with the contents of her glass as she waited for her heart rate to slow once more and for the beating wings in her stomach to settle.

'What are you acting all shy about?' Florence demanded, dragging her gaze from Tim's backside as he stood ordering a round, back to her friend.

'He's someone new with him tonight. Not that I'm interested and don't look so flamin' obvious!'

Florence stopped searching through the cluster at the bar for who Sabrina was talking about.

'Leather jacket?'

'They've all got leather jackets on.' Sabrina pointed out the obvious.

'Hang on, Liverpool shirt, jeans, black hair?'

They all had Liverpool shirts on too but Flo was looking in the right direction. 'Shiny hair?'

'Very.'

'That's him,' Sabrina confirmed. 'But I'm off men, remember.'

'Mr Onion Breath, I remember, and he's tasty but not as tasty as my Tim.'

'It's a good thing we don't have the same taste in fellas,' Sabrina said, finishing off her ale which had gone flat. 'I'm desperate to spend a penny.'

'Go. I'll see if he checks you out on your way to the lav.'

'Now, I'm liable to trip over or something. Ta very much.'

Florence flapped her hand. 'You'll be fine. Just remember to check your shoe for loo paper when you come out.'

'Thanks for reminding me.' It could've only happened to her, she thought trying not to think about all the eyes lined up by the bar as she made a beeline for the Ladies. She'd managed to trail toilet paper across the floor of Starry Nights club a few years back and had never lived it down. Nor had she been back to the nightclub since.

A few minutes later with the shoe check done as well as a surreptitious swipe around the back of her skirt to ensure it wasn't caught up in her knickers, she exited the chilly restroom.

She stopped at the bar, the group of lads having moved away, and bought her and Florence another drink each. She returned to the table without incident and as she placed the ale down, Florence grinned up at her.

'Definite interest there. He watched you all the way to the lav. Never took his eyes off you.'

'Really?'

'Really.'

'Where are they now?' Sabrina sat down and looked furtively about.

'You're not doing a good impersonation of someone who's not interested.' Florence flapped her hand in the direction of the jukebox and Sabrina turned, pretending to be interested in the illuminated music machine. They were sat around a table laughing at something or other, a cloud of smoke rising over their heads.

It was at that moment the music began to pulse louder. 'Oh, I love this, come on,' Sabrina said, forgetting all about Tim and his good-looking mate. She loved to dance and *Hot Blooded* by Foreigner always got her feet itching to move.

The two girls abandoned their bevvies and joined the handful of others who'd already begun shaking up the floor.

They were enjoying themselves dancing away the week at work when Florence started doing something shifty with her eyes. If Sabrina hadn't known her almost as well as she knew herself she'd have thought she had a tic going on.

She followed the direction of her side-eye and saw a group of girls on a hen night. They'd surrounded the table where Tim and his mates were sitting. There was an arrangement of helmets on the table next to them which no one dared move so as they could sit down. The hen party, including the inebriated bride-to-be, were hauling the lads up as they mock protested.

Florence and Sabrina watched laughing as they pulled them on to the dance floor.

'Look like we're having fun,' Florence leaned in and yelled above the music. 'Fellas love that. And I think my stars were right, he's dancing. It's the music connection again.'

'I *am* having fun!' Sabrina had tossed off her inhibitions. The only problem was the strapless bra she'd worn under her off the shoulder blouse was beginning to slip down. 'But I hate strapless bras!'

Florence laughed, forgetting all about Tim momentarily. That was why when the song drew to a close and Bob Seger took over she nearly tripped over herself finding him and his other two mates, one of whom was the fella with the skin-tight jeans, the hens had hauled up to dance, alongside her and Sabrina.

The hen party had staggered off and Sabrina glanced over her shoulder to see them collecting their coats and bags presumably off to another pub.

'Great song,' the lad whom she'd been checking out said.

'I love Bob Segar.' She did and she thought she could quite possibly love this fella too given the opportunity. Up close she could see the slight shadow along his jawline and he smelled lovely.

'Me too.' His grin seemed to convey he was pleased they'd found a common denominator even if it was an American musician.

'I'm Adam.'

'Sabrina.'

They threw themselves into the song and his awkward self-conscious dancing helped her relax.

She was aware of Florence breaking out all her best moves and beaming as though she'd been told she'd won the gold ticket as Tim and Mr Tight Trousers grooved away alongside her. This was turning out to be a very good evening indeed, even if her bra was now inching its way down toward her middle and she was very, very glad she'd hadn't been tempted by the salmon steak.

Chapter Three

Sabrina ladled the creamy oats into bowls, her mind straying to Adam as it had done at every opportunity since she'd floated home on Saturday night.

He'd grabbed her phone number, having left, much to her and Flo's mutual disappointment, with Tim and the rest of their crew three songs after Bob Segar. They were expected at Tim's cousin's twenty-first across town he'd explained. They'd heard the bikes roaring into life over the sound of the music.

He hadn't rung and it was now Wednesday and Sabrina had tied herself in knots replaying her time spent dancing opposite him. Had she read too much into it? Had she imagined the interested glimmer in those eyes?

It was something she'd hashed over with Florence each evening since on the telephone, twirling the curly phone cord around her fingers and ignoring Aunt Evie's tapping of her watch, a reminder she was clocking up the minutes on the phone bill. As for Flo, she was dejected that Tim hadn't asked for her number.

Sabrina had heard her dad yell at her to 'get off the flamin' phone!' but Flo had ignored him continuing to listen to Sabrina's will-he won't-he call me conversation.

It was a conundrum because Sabrina didn't want to be tying up the line mulling Saturday night over with Flo in case

Adam called her. The times when she wasn't talking to her friend though, the cream coloured telephone taunted her.

The evenings had stretched long and she'd been twitchy, only half watching the flickering television screen.

Now she put the pot in the sink and carried hers and Aunt Evie's porridge over to the table before picking up the steaming third bowl she'd been careful not to overfill.

'I'm off to see Fred, Aunt Evie. Your breakfast is on the table.' She glanced over at the electric heater in front of the old coal fire and saw the orange glow of its three bars. She'd started flicking it on since the start of September, the official advent of autumn. It took the chill that had been creeping into the mornings off the room. She got up half an hour earlier than her aunt to ensure the room was toasty for her when she ventured in for her breakfast.

Double-checking she'd turned the element on the cooker off she re-checked once more for good measure.

'I hope you've had a decent helping yourself, Sabrina. You're too thin. A strong wind would snap you in half and I don't know why you bother with that old drunk,' a plummy voice called back from the bedroom.

Sabrina knew her aunt had no time for men who were slaves to the bottle. She'd told her once her father had been a mean man and an even meaner one when he drank which was his favourite pastime.

The young Evelyn had known what it was to go to bed with an empty belly for most of her childhood, listening to the sounds of her siblings crying, her mam too weary from the sheer grind of it all to offer any comfort.

As such, the moment she'd been old enough, she'd left to make her own way in the world having made a solemn vow to herself she'd never be beholden to a man to put a roof over her head or food on her table like her mam had been. And she hadn't been either.

'He can't help himself, Aunt Evie.' Sabrina's voice startled Evelyn back to the present.

She made a tsking sound. 'Act soft and I'll buy you a coal yard, Sabrina!'

Sabrina rolled her eyes, well used to Aunt Evie and her forgotten sayings. She was hardly thin either. Anybody who didn't resemble Bessie Bunting was ailing in her aunt's opinion. 'Stop going on and come and have your tea and oats while they're still hot.'

'I'm getting up now.'

The creaking of bedsprings proved evidence of this and, satisfied, Sabrina made her way to the door. She had her morning ritual and opening it she flicked the light in the stairwell on. It was an act she repeated three times as was her custom before setting off down the stairs. It reassured her that all was as it should be.

The floorboards squeaked beneath her boots as shifting the bowl to one hand, she reached the bottom and opened the door to the workroom before padding through the shop to the entrance with practised ease.

Her body tensed inside her jacket as she opened the door and stepped outside into the crisp early morning air.

She was rather smitten with her new jacket; this season's latest bomber style with a faux fur trim around the cuffs and collar which she'd zipped up to ward off the chill.

The jacket had been a treat for herself from Lewis's. It was what Flo called a stactical jacket. Stylish and practical.

She closed the door to the boutique behind her and cast a glance either side of the street.

Brides of Bold Street was on the even-numbered side and next door to her left was pompous Mr Barlow's tailor's shop, Barlow & Co. He was a daintily built man with soft hands who'd a reputation for quality workmanship in the world of suits.

She'd no idea who the 'Co' was in the sign over the door because it was only Mr Barlow who worked there.

She liked to keep an eye on the comings and goings next door. Not because she had any interest in menswear but because upstairs was home to an entertainment agency and she was always hopeful of catching a glimpse of someone she recognised from *Top of the Pops* paying a visit.

The building had three storeys and the top floor was given over to an accounting firm which was nowhere near as exciting.

To her right was a woman's fashion shop called Esmeralda's Emporium. Esmerelda, as you'd expect with a name like that, minced about in colourful caftans and always had a colour co-ordinated turban on her head. She smoked her Silk Cut cigarettes through a long black holder and there was a permanent bluish-grey haze over the counter from where she presided.

Sabrina liked Esmerelda's shop despite the fact she wasn't a flamboyant sort of girl. It didn't mean she couldn't rifle through the racks on occasion and imagine herself with gold dangly earrings like the ones on the stand and wearing a zebra-striped jumpsuit. Esmerelda, too, was forever trying to get Sabrina to take a walk on the wild side but so far she'd yet to try anything on.

Aunt Evie said Esmerelda wouldn't be there long. Her type, the arty-farty sort who liked to burn incense (there was always muttering as to how it was a miracle she didn't burn the place down with all those joss sticks) came and went, she'd say.

She'd been saying it for the last five years.

For all her mutterings though, she never complained when Esmerelda popped her head in their door at closing time of a Wednesday night. It brightened the middle of the week for the pair of them. Esmerelda would be toting the bottle of gin she liked to slosh into one of Aunt Evie's teacups while the two women nattered over the day that had been.

The two storeys above the emporium were taken up by a printing firm and, wedged in between the staid suits and exotic emporium, as narrow as it was deep was Brides of Bold Street. The boutique took up the ground floor and the flat above it was where Sabrina had grown up.

Jack Frost had been busy overnight. There was a smattering of ice on the pavement and she set off carefully. It wouldn't be a good start to her day to go arse over with a bowl of porridge in her hands.

Fred was where he always was. His skinny frame hunched over, looking like a bundle of rags had been dumped in the doorway of the shop with the 'For Sale' sign jutting out. To the right of the sign was the blue canopy above the door that led upstairs to where Mystic Lou dealt in tarot cards and crystal balls if you crossed her palm with silver that was.

Unsurprisingly, Aunt Evie didn't believe in that sort of thing but Sabrina was curious and not just because she'd never actually seen Mystic Lou but because who knew? She might be able to see into the future. She'd call up there and see what that crystal ball of hers had in store for her one of these days.

The empty shop doorway Fred had called home for the last few months had been a Christian book store before it closed down. Aunt Evie had been heard to tut, 'I always said religion doesn't pay.'

'Ahright there, Fred, luv, I've bought your breakfast,' Sabrina said waiting for the rags to move and reassure her the old man was still alive. The glass pane in the window of the shop was smeared by the weather and the empty space inside looked forlorn.

A head emerged turtle-like from the coats and rugs piled on top of him and the face under the green woollen hat pulled down low on his forehead was wizened and weathered but the blue eyes were lively.

'Ah, Sabrina, my girl, and how are you this fine, autumnal morning?'

His breath as he spoke gave off white puffs and she knew it would reek of the cheap whisky stashed under his blankets. She'd never been able to pinpoint his accent. It wasn't Scouse that was for sure. It veered towards posh, from the south perhaps, but when she'd asked Fred had given her a vague, 'I'm from here, there and everywhere, my girl,' as a reply.

'Cold if you really want to know, Fred,' she said, stamping her feet to ward it off. He asked her the same thing every morning and her reply was always the same.

He held his hands out, protected from the chill by a pair of holey mittens. She handed him the bowl.

'You're an angel sent to me from the heavens so you are,' he wheezed before erupting into a coughing fit that had her frowning.

'Why won't you go to the shelter, Fred. It's too cold for you to be sleeping out.'

'They'd take my whisky off me,' he said once his coughing had subsided. 'And I love my whisky more than life itself.'

She sighed and watched for a moment as he tucked into his oats with gusto. A hot breakfast wasn't much but at least it was something.

He'd demolished the bowl's contents in the blink of an eye and she took the empty dish from him. 'You have a good day now, Fred.'

'And you, Sabrina, girl.'

She turned and made her way back down a street that was beginning to wake up.

She loved Bold Street she thought, getting a waft of spice and curry from the Indian restaurant that was still a novelty further up the street. She loved the sights, sounds and smells of this part of the city. The buildings were characterful and attracted all manner of interesting businesses. The bombed-out church was a nod to the hardship the city had endured during the war and a familiar landmark.

This was her part of Liverpool she thought as she reached the familiar blue door with its brass letter slot and handle. It was where she belonged.

———◦———

'SABRINA, YOU'RE AWAY with the fairies! Would you watch what you're doing?' There were grumblings of her being a liability and whatnot following Evelyn's remark as she took her foot off the treadle.

It was Tuesday and as such Evelyn was wearing her cheery canary yellow shop coat covered in a daisy pattern.

Evelyn was a big fan of the shop coat. She swore by them and was forever trying to convince Sabrina to wear one.

'You wouldn't always be asking me where the tape measure is if you had a coat like this on,' she'd say. 'Because you'd know.' She'd pat her pocket to demonstrate her point. 'And, Sabrina, you could keep a packet of those Opal Fruits you're so fond of munching on in there too instead of forever looking for where you left them.'

Sabrina would mouth, 'Because, they'd be in your shop coat pocket.' In well-timed unison with Evelyn, having heard it all before.

As for the Opal Fruits, she found it funny to offer her aunt one now and again just to hear her say, 'They'd be the ruin of my dentures they would, as well you know.'

Now, she blinked and looked down at the sheer bolt of organza she'd been in the process of cutting. It was a lightweight, woven silk material which required concentration when cutting.

Concentration was something she'd been lacking since Saturday night. Instead of thinking about how the fabric would hold its shape for Lilian Cookson's winter extravaganza wedding, she'd been thinking about the pair of sooty eyes she'd lost herself in on the dance floor.

Sabrina apologised. 'Sorry, I was miles away.' She glanced at her aunt who was eyeing her over the top of her spectacles, her lips pursed. The skirt of the busy, floral print bridesmaid's dress she'd been in the process of stitching a sleeve on was draped across her lap and puddling on the floor.

A frisson of sympathy for the unfortunate bridesmaid who'd been coerced into accepting the hideous material shot through Sabrina as she told herself to focus on the organza and stay on task.

She had to set the image of Adam with his blue-black hair firmly aside before she wound up butchering the expensive fabric.

Evelyn shook her head in exasperation. Although truth be known, she was secretly enjoying seeing Sabrina infatuated.

Oh, Sabrina hadn't said a word. She was a private girl by nature and kept a tight lid on her emotions but ever since she'd rolled out of bed on Sunday morning with a bleary-eyed Florence, who'd topped and tailed for the night, trailing behind her, she'd been absentminded.

She'd deduced there were fellas involved when, over breakfast she'd asked Florence, having given up on Sabrina, to pass the marmalade while Sabrina had continued to stare off into space her toast untouched on her plate.

Florence had blinked blankly and then seeing Evelyn pointing to the jam had slid it toward her with a sheepish smile.

She'd even taken Fred's toast down to him on her way to church, worried Sabrina would forget all about him. Not that she'd admit to that of course.

Evelyn was wary when it came to men. There'd been her early experiences with an alcoholic, bully of man she was loathe to call her father. When she'd finally allowed herself to trust, her heart had been broken.

She wasn't cynical about love despite this. She was a church-going woman and liked to think He had handed her her lot in life for a reason. Just as He'd seen fit to guide her into her bridal shop with all the twists and turns that had entailed and bring little Sabrina into her life.

She'd done her best to thank Him by taking her along to the service each Sunday but she'd grown up and reached an age where the choice as to whether she attended was now hers.

Sabrina had decided a lie-in was a more enticing option than sitting on a cold pew, in a draughty church, singing songs of praise. And that was all right because Evelyn knew, He knew, she had the kindest heart and the gentlest of souls.

So far as love went, Evelyn was certain she'd sewn a dress to fit every sort.

She'd seen grand-passion love. The kind that insists on a flashy dress and burns bright only to fizzle to ashes a few years in.

She'd seen the settling sort of love that suited a simple dress in which to tread along the path of a comfortable life.

She'd also seen true love deserving of detailed design and intricate lacework.

Evelyn had seen enough happy endings in her line of work over the years to know not everybody was dealt a bad hand in romance. So, while she'd given up on the idea of love for herself she wanted Sabrina to be happy. This was why, despite her protestations, it gave her a lift to see her mooning about the place.

Evelyn drew the line at hacking an expensive length of organza though and she was on the fence about the lengthy phone calls each evening with Florence.

In an effort to steer her mind away from Adam, Sabrina put the scissors down and asked. 'What would you like for your birthday dinner, Aunt Evie?'

It was Evelyn's birthday on Friday. She'd be seventy-one. Most of her friends were on the pension but not Evelyn. She was adamant she'd keel over in the bridal shop. When asked about her retirement plans Evelyn would retort, 'The fastest way to get old is to sit around acting old.'

'I do enjoy your fish pie, Sabrina. It's nice and soft on my dentures. I nearly lost them in that steak you bought cheap at the meat auction at St John's market.'

'It's not *my* fish pie, it's Delia Smith's and that steak was melt in the mouth,' Sabrina corrected.

'Humph. Melt in the mouth! I'd need the super glue to keep my teeth in tackling that. She's got some very modern ideas that Delia. I'm more of a Fanny Craddock fan myself but Delia does do a lovely fish pie. I'll give her that.'

Sabrina rolled her eyes. 'I'm sure Delia would be chuffed to know you approve of her pie, Aunt Evie.'

'I hope you're not being sarcastic, Sabrina.'

'Me? Never, Aunt Evie.'

Chapter Four

It never ceased to amaze Sabrina how you could turn a corner in Liverpool and find yourself somewhere completely different. She was walking up cobbled Wood Street and was almost bow-legged thanks to the grocery bags she was carting. In comparison to her beloved Bold Street, Wood Street which ran behind their shop was dull.

The low-lying warehouse-style buildings didn't beckon you to enter them for nothing more than curiosity as to what you mind find inside like its neighbouring street did.

The only point of interest was the pub and as she gazed ahead to the blue and gold lettering of the Swan, she saw several motorbikes lined up alongside the old blue tiles that hinted of Victorian times under the window. Her thoughts immediately swung to Adam.

It was now Friday and there'd been no phone call.

She might as well forget about him and if by not phoning her he was trying to play it cool then he'd overplayed his hand because she wasn't into game playing.

Reaching the back door of the shop she dumped the bags on the ground before rummaging through her pockets for the key. She stole one more glance at the pub but there was no sign of life and turning the key in the lock gave the door that extra nudge it always needed to open.

Perhaps cooking a birthday tea for Aunt Evie would fill the silence and retrieving the bags, she locked the door behind her, checking it three times before stating the obvious to her aunt's back which was bent over the Singer, 'I'm back.'

She waited a beat.

'I'm just going to finish the hem on Lucy Baker's dress and then I'll be up,' came back at her.

Sabrina smiled and shook her head. It would never cross Aunt Evie's mind to finish early or, heaven forbid, take a day off from the shop, not even on her birthday. She lugged the bags up the stairs, dumping them on the linoleum kitchen floor that had seen better days.

A little music while she cooked would be nice she decided, flicking the radio sitting on the windowsill above the sink on.

It would be flamin' Bob Segar wouldn't it, she thought, instantly being transported back to a sweaty Saturday night dance floor. Singing along to the tune she unpacked the bags placing the plump haddock, gherkins, capers—which had been a sod to find—fresh parsley and block of butter for the pastry topping on the worktop. She'd hardboiled eggs that morning and would peel them in a jiffy.

First things first though she needed her trusty Delia cookbook.

She retrieved it from their overflowing bookshelf noticing the shelves were in need of a dust. She cast a glance around the living room her eyes settling on the school photographs tracking her progress through infants to high school that Aunt Evelyn insisted on hanging on the wall. She grimaced. Had she really worn her hair like that? She moved on looking at the top of the television set and over to the sideboard. The whole place could do with a jolly good dust.

She put it on her mental to-do list. Then prising the pages of the much-thumbed book open to the recipe she was after she skimmed over the steps involved before turning her attention to the haddock.

By the time the pie was in the oven beginning to bubble around the edges, Evelyn had appeared. She'd a fat bunch of blue hydrangeas in her hand.

'Your favourites!' Sabrina exclaimed, knowing without asking who'd dropped them in for her. The local property developer who'd been sniffing around Aunt Evie these last few years never missed. Still, she asked, 'From Mr Taylor?'

Evelyn nodded. 'Fetch the vase from the cupboard for me, would you. They need a drink.'

Sabrina did so, filling it with water and, taking the flowers from Evelyn, she arranged them in the china vase. Where Ray Taylor, whom Aunt Evie referred to as a wide boy she knew from way back when he'd strutted around with the Lime Street Boys, managed to find hydrangeas this late in the season was always a mystery.

He was a local property developer who, like Aunt Evie, refused to retire. His wife had passed away several years ago and once a respectable amount of time had passed, he'd begun sniffing around Aunt Evie. She barely gave him the time of day.

'He's sweet on you, you know,' Sabrina said, carrying the vase over to the sideboard. There was more to Aunt Evie and Ray Taylor's history than she was letting on and one of these days she'd get to the bottom of it, she thought. Placing the vase down in pride of place next to the new willow pattern china teacup and saucer she'd presented her aunt with that morning she admired the pretty display for a moment.

Evelyn made a disparaging noise and disappeared off to her bedroom to hang today's lilac shop coat up. She returned a few seconds later and sank down in her chair. There were some that might refer to the comfortable old furniture that decorated this, Evelyn and Sabrina's home as being antwacky but it served its purpose.

'I don't need a man in my life, thank you very much. I've managed perfectly well on my own.' The chair was angled so as she could see the television and keep an eye on what was happening in the kitchen and the seat was indented from where she sat each evening. No amount of plumping could change it.

Evelyn slipped her shoes off and slid her feet into her slippers which were always there waiting by the legs of her chair of an evening.

'Our tea won't be long but there's time for a birthday sherry,' Sabrina said.

'Lovely.' Evelyn didn't imbibe as a rule but she was partial to a small dry sherry from time to time or a Babycham if she found herself on a very rare occasion in a public house.

Sabrina poured out two tots, handing a glass to her aunt before sitting down on the sofa. There was a spring digging into her leg and she shifted trying to find a comfortable spot before raising her glass.

'Happy birthday, Aunt Evie.' She recited the toast she'd been taught by Flo's dad.

'May neighbours respect you, trouble neglect you, the angels protect you and heaven accept you. Cheers.'

Evelyn raised her own glass, smiling at the sentiment before taking a tentative sip of the sweet liquid. She considered Sabrina for a moment, wondering what her seventy-first birthday would have been like had she not come into her life. She'd a sneaking suspicion it would have been a little less full without Sabrina brightening it and that where she could have grown hard-hearted through the circumstances of her youth in her later years, Sabrina's bright inner glow had softened her.

The warmth from the alcohol flooded Sabrina's system. They'd celebrated her birthday on the thirty-first of August. She'd turned twenty-one on the one just been.

'I'm meeting Ida at the bingo hall for eight o'clock.'

'I thought you would.' Aunt Evie wouldn't miss her weekly bingo for anything and especially not for her birthday.

Sabrina swallowed what was left of the umber liquid and stood up. 'That pie smells about ready to me.'

Evelyn put a hand to her cheek. 'I'm glowing. I'm ready for my tea alright, Sabrina. I didn't have a biscuit with my cup of tea this afternoon because I wanted to do your fish pie justice. I shouldn't drink on an empty stomach.'

'It was only a tiny tot of sherry, Aunt Evie, and it's Delia's fish pie.' Sabrina grinned, donning the oven mitts before opening the cooker's door to be hit by a wall of steam. There in the middle of the tray was the golden-crusted pie. It was ready to be taken out. Her mouth watered at the aroma, she was hungry too!

Evelyn settled herself at the table which Sabrina had set earlier and made the appropriate noises as the pie was placed in front of her.

'There's enough left for lunch tomorrow,' Sabrina said, sitting down to join her. Her stomach grumbled as Aunt Evie said a short grace, as keen as Sabrina to tuck in.

They made short work of their meal and then, managing to find room on the chaos of the kitchen worktop, Sabrina deposited their empty plates before retrieving the Sayers Bakery box.

She undid the string tied around it and carefully placed Evelyn's favourite princess sponge on a plate. She'd bought the cake because she could do many things but baking was not one of them. Her attempts over the years would have served a discus thrower well! Not even Delia could help her when it came to the art of cake baking.

But, she loved all things sweet and a visit to Sayers or Thorntons chocolate shop was akin to a trip to Disneyland for a small child so far as Sabrina was concerned. She'd a sweet tooth and she was looking forward to tucking into the cream cake she was presently pushing the candle into.

She struck a match and lit the skinny wax candle and then with the flame flickering carried it over to the table launching into the Happy Birthday song.

Evelyn sat back regally in her chair with her hands clasped around her middle declaring herself full as the cake was presented to her.

'You'll find room, you always do when it comes to cake. Blow the candle out, Aunt Evie, and make a wish.'

Evelyn did so and as a wisp of smoke curled up she watched Sabrina cut into the pink iced sponge with its decoration of coconut around the sides. The mock cream filling squished enticingly out the sides. 'Just a sliver for me, Sabrina.'

Sabrina ignored her request, cutting a generous wedge and no complaint was forthcoming as she slid it on a side plate and put it in front of Evelyn.

There was no sound for the next minute or two, other than the scraping of the forks across the plates. Both women were determined to ensure not a crumb was forgotten and when they were satisfied they'd done the cake justice they put their forks down and wiped the cream and coconut from their mouths.

'I'll wrap a piece of sponge for Ida to enjoy later,' Evelyn said.

'Good idea, Esmerelda's partial to a princess sponge as well and I'll take Fred a wedge down in the morning.' Sabrina planned on a quiet night in front of the television once she'd tackled the dishes. She wasn't a tidy cook she thought with a rueful glance at the bomb site on the worktop. Anyone would think she'd cooked a meal for ten, not two.

She and Florence had arranged to go to the flicks the following afternoon and then they'd no doubt while away the evening at the Swan. She wouldn't think about whether or not a certain fella would be there and if he was what she'd do if he spoke to her.

Evelyn went to apply a sweep of peach lipstick to her lips. She returned with her hat on and her coat buttoned up to her chin. She took the piece of sponge cake Sabrina had wrapped, stashing it in her handbag before announcing she'd be off.

'Wish me luck, Sabrina.' Evelyn knew there was no point telling her not to wait up. Not that she'd be late, she'd be home shortly after ten but Sabrina would not go to bed until she knew she was home, safe and sound. She was a girl who needed routine and certainty was Sabrina.

'Good luck and say hello to Ida.' Sabrina smiled, the empty cake plates in her hand.

Evelyn had a love, hate relationship with her friend Ida. They'd known each since they were girls and there was a competitiveness between the pair which was why Sabrina was not surprised to hear Evelyn making noises about how she was sure Ida had the bingo hall rigged. Two weeks in a row she'd won the big prize. Two weeks!

Sabrina was still smiling at her aunt's insinuation as the door banged shut downstairs signalling she'd gone.

She'd finished putting away the last of the dishes when the phone ringing made her jump. Her heart instantly ramped up its beats and she took a steadying breath before answering it with a tentative hello which came out more of a squeak than the huskily sexy voice she'd aimed for.

'Relax, queen, it's me.'

'Oh, hi, Flo.' Her heart sank.

'Ta very much.'

'Sorry, it's just I hoped, well you know.'

'I do know but listen that's why I'm calling.'

Sabrina was all ears.

'I know why Adam hasn't telephoned. He couldn't he's in the ozzy. He had an accident on Saturday night.'

Chapter Five

S abrina's eyes felt as though salt had been thrown in them. She'd barely slept after Florence's phone call the night before, tossing and turning in a tangle of sheets.

This morning she was stood at the stove stirring the porridge beginning to bubble in the pan in an attempt to stop it sticking to the bottom. Their conversation ran through her head for the umpteenth time.

The breaking news that Adam had been in a motorcycle accident had found its way to Flo through Carol, the typist at her work. It had transpired Carol's new fella was none other than Tim Burns' cousin, who'd of course been at the party the lads were supposed to have been going to.

This familial connection was something Flo explained meant, as annoying as Carol could be with that awful humming noise she made when she ate her lunchtime sandwiches, she'd now have to be extra nice to her.

As such, she'd decided to offer her services taking over the typing of the indecipherable scrawl of their pompous manager, Mr Steel, a job that normally fell to Carol given she was last on board. Florence wasn't doing this out of the kindness of heart but rather in the hope of a good word about her being dropped in Tim's cousin's ear.

The accident hadn't been Adam's fault, Flo had gushed down the phone like a television newsreader who'd just been handed their bulletin hot off the press. He'd been hit by a right-turning car that wasn't indicating as he tried to overtake it.

It could have been worse by all accounts, far worse. As it was he'd had surgery for a ruptured spleen and was now back on the ward recuperating. He'd be there for a few days yet.

Sabrina and Florence had batted back and forth as to what Sabrina should do now she had this information. Should she be bold and visit him? Flo had said she should borrow Aunt Evie's Liverpool scarf if she did. Fella's liked girls who liked the footie and she'd do well to let him know she was a Liverpool supporter like him and not Everton.

She had a point Sabrina thought. To cheer for the opposing team was the kiss of the death for any burgeoning romance.

Then they'd mused as to whether she should arrange flowers to be delivered. What was the correct protocol in situations like this?

Neither of them had any prior experience with someone they fancied being in the hospital and so it was unresolved by the time they said goodnight and hung up. Sabrina fancied she could hear Mr Teesdale's cheer all the way from their house on Reeves Ave over in Bootle.

It was a good job Aunt Evie was out, Sabrina thought, hauling herself up from where she'd been lying on the floor, legs resting up against the wall. The length of their call would have had her going on about how it was the size of their telephone bill keeping the entire British Telecom workforce in paid employment!

As it happened, Sabrina barely had time to stuff down her second slice of sponge cake for the evening before Aunt

Evie arrived home. She was jubilantly waving a leg of pork she'd won as though she were batting for England and was full of the joys of the bingo hall. The joint of meat was the perfect end to her birthday, she'd declared.

Not even the thought of roast pork with apple sauce and crackling had been able to help Sabrina shake off the thought of the dishy fella she'd met at the Swan on Saturday night lying injured in a hospital bed. In her mind's eye, he lay there lonely and just waiting for a friendly face, hers of course.

Nor could she shake it now, and pouring the porridge into the bowls she remembered to wrap a slice of cake for Fred. Then, with Evelyn calling out from the bedroom she was too soft for her own good, she performed her usual light-flicking ritual before stepping outside to face a new day.

She gave Fred a gentle nudge with her foot. 'Good morning. Rise and shine! It's going to be a cracker day,' she announced cheerily.

It was important to be cheery Sabrina always thought because hers might be the only friendly voice he heard all day.

The mound of blankets stirred and a phlegmy cough erupted beneath them.

Sabrina put the porridge down and alarmed at the ferocity of the hacking was about to run home for a glass of water when it stopped as abruptly as it started. Fred's grizzled head emerged from beneath the holey bedding.

'Ah, here she is my morning angel.'

'You sounded like an old docker, Fred, that cough's nasty. And the weather's getting cooler too.' Sabrina frowned.

'Have you been to have it checked out? The doctor might be able to give you something to take the bark out of it.'

He chortled and, dragging himself up, showed her the near-empty bottle tucked under his coat like a hot water bottle.

'Sorts me out better than any quack could every time. Besides, it'll take more than a tickle in my throat to see me off, my girl.' He beamed up at her, displaying a black space where one of his front teeth used to live. Then, smacking his lips together, he picked up the spoon. 'Warms the cockles does this.'

'Here's a piece of princess sponge from Sayers for your morning tea. It was Aunt Evie's birthday yesterday.'

'A fine woman indeed your aunt Evelyn. Wish her many happy returns for yesterday from me. That'll go down a treat later.'

'Fred, can I ask you something?'

'Out with it.' He looked up at her from beneath rampantly scraggly brows, the spoon poised to dig back into his oats.

Sabrina hesitated but decided she'd nothing to lose.

'There's this lad I've only just met. He was supposed to call me only he's been in an accident and wound up in hospital. Should I go and see him do you think? Or should I get flowers delivered with a get well soon note? I want him to know I'm thinking of him but I don't want to seem too keen either.' She shrugged and then took a step backwards in fright as Fred roared.

'Flowers! Is he man or mouse?'

It was done with such theatrical flourish, Sabrina fancied he must have trodden the boards at some stage in his life.

'So then, I should visit him?' She sought clarification.

'The sight of your pretty face would be a tonic to him, my dear.' He shook his stringy silver hair. ''Tis a complicated thing, affairs of the heart when you're young.'

She tried to visualise Fred as a young man courting a lady but couldn't.

'There was something about him, Fred. He seemed different from the other fellas I've met.'

'There you are then. I think you had your answer already.'

He was right. She had.

'Eat your breakfast before it gets cold.'

He tucked into it as though he hadn't eaten in days.

Aside from the porridge, Sabrina thought, he probably hadn't. She couldn't fix him though and there was no point in trying. Fred didn't want to be fixed. All she could do was bring him a hot breakfast each morning before he shuffled off for the day.

By the time he'd polished off his oats, she'd resolved to go to the Royal Liverpool Hospital as soon as the shop closed for the afternoon.

'I'll see you then, Fred. Have a good day,' she called over her shoulder, the empty bowl in her hand.

'You be sure to go and see that young man of yours, Sabrina.'

Chapter Six

Sabrina enjoyed Saturdays and this morning had been no different. She liked the bustling vibe inside their shop and outside on the street as well. The time between opening and closing had flown by with all manner of excited brides-to-be, bridesmaids and mothers or, mothers of the bride bursting through the door.

She closed the door on their last customer, locking it behind her and now, she hot-footed it upstairs. She planned on taking a little extra care in getting herself ready for her Florence Nightingale visit this afternoon.

When she reappeared, Evelyn had her red hat pulled low and was searching for her coat, eager to be off to catch the bus to Anfield.

'It's where it always is, Aunt Evie.' She swept her own jacket off the hook on the door leading to the stairs and revealed her aunt's.

Shrugging into her jacket she decided to bite the bullet. 'Aunt Evie would you mind if I borrowed your scarf. Just this once. There's a nip in the air out there and I know you're off to Anfield but you've your coat and your hat's red. They'll all know whose side you're on.' She picked up her aunt's red and white Liverpool scarf and held her breath. She planned on taking Flo's advice, wanting to wear it to impress Adam.

Evelyn, eying Sabrina, had an inkling as to why she wanted her precious scarf. Taking note of the fluff of fur decorating the collar of her jacket she knew full well it wasn't to ward off the cold. This lad she'd set her sights on, whoever he was, must be a Liverpool supporter. As such, who was she to stand in the way of true love?

To Sabrina's surprise she received a nod and thanking her aunt she quickly draped the knit around her neck and was halfway down the stairs before she paused to call out, 'I'm off to Flo's, so don't wait up. I'll probably go straight from hers to the pub tonight. Enjoy your salmon!'

She pounded down the rest of the stairs eager for a head start on her aunt so she didn't see her face flushing and guess she'd embellished the truth.

She was going to Flo's and she *would* go to the pub but first, she was going to the hospital.

The care she'd taken with her hair and makeup saw her receive more than one admiring glance as she weaved her way along the street, busy with afternoon shoppers. She was oblivious to them though, eager to make a detour to Thorntons on the corner of Ranelagh and Bold Street.

Normally she'd while away a happy half hour in the chocolate shop deciding which flavour to put her hand in her pocket for. A charade really because she always settled on her favourite caramel centred ones. This afternoon however she'd somewhere to be and so with the selection box stashed in her bag she carried on in record time.

She didn't falter in her stride, not even when she received a long low, wolf whistle followed by an 'Ahright there, luv?' There was only one man on her mind and the weasely eyed whistler wasn't him!

It wasn't long before the soot-stained concrete walls of the hospital loomed in front of her and she hesitated as her bravado slipped, puddling at her feet.

'Oi watch where you're going, girl,' a harried woman dragging a small squalling child in a red mac grumbled, swishing past her.

An ambulance screaming towards the emergency department across the way galvanized her. She must look a proper weirdo standing there gawping across the road.

One foot in front of the other, Sabrina, she told herself, wishing as her stomach flip-flopped she'd asked Flo to come with her. There was strength to be found in numbers or in having your bezzie mate by your side.

Pushing inside the austere building she found the waiting room heaving with everything from suspected broken arms to bleeding noses. A nurse with a clipboard was calling someone's name and a baby was wailing. The pine scent of disinfectant mingling with cigarette smoke burnt her nostrils as she waited her turn in line to ask the receptionist where she'd find Adam Taylor.

Ten minutes later, she was armed with the necessary directions to the surgical ward. She also knew the ins and outs of the woman with the headscarf knotted over her rollers, son Geoff's ongoing tonsil issues. Asking her to pass on her best wishes to Geoff for a speedy recovery and lots of ice cream and jelly now he'd had them out, Sabrina headed down the corridor. An orderly with three studs lined up his ear lobe pushing an empty stretcher swerved around her as she made her way to the lifts.

She stood in silence next to a fella who followed her into the elevator hidden behind an enormous bunch of flowers. The pungent scent of chrysanthemums tickled her nostrils as she was sedately carried up to the floor she'd been told she'd find Adam on.

When she located the ward, she had to stand in the doorway for a moment, blinking as her eyes adjusted to the sanitised whiteness of it, before doing a quick sweep of the beds.

There he was! She hovered, suddenly certain she was doing the wrong thing. She was about to turn and beat a hasty retreat when Adam turned his head and settled his dark eyes on her.

His face registered surprise and then he raised the hand that wasn't hooked up to an IV line in greeting. There was nothing else for it. She couldn't very well turn heel and run now.

Sabrina moved across the ward coming to a halt at the end of his bed. 'How're you?' It was a stupid question which came out high and squeaky. She swiftly followed up with an anxious. 'I hope you don't mind me coming?'

'I can't believe you're here. I thought I'd blown it. How did you know I was here?'

They'd spoken over one another and realising this, exchanged a smile. It broke the tension and Sabrina's shoulders visibly relaxed.

'I'm glad you came,' Adam said.

He was pleased to see her! Remembering what she had in her bag, she opened it and pulled the Thorntons selection out. 'My friend Flo, she was at the Swan with me.'

He nodded that he remembered.

'She works with a girl who's going out with your mate Tim's cousin. That's how I heard about the accident. I erm, I brought you these.' She thrust the chocolates towards him and saw there was already an open box beside his bed.

Adam tracked her gaze. 'Me auld fella brought me those. You just missed him.' He smiled and despite his skin's waxy pallor, he didn't look like someone who'd recently undergone surgery. 'He also ate his way through me favourite caramel centred ones.'

'Ooh, I love the caramel ones too but I promise, I haven't touched them.' She smiled back at him feeling her nerves evaporating as she moved around the bed to put the box down next to the other one.

'I still can't believe you're here.'

He had long lashes for a fella she thought, watching them shadow his eyes. He had lovely eyes. She could lose herself in those eyes she thought, registering his quizzical eyebrow raise. A rush of doubt swarmed her. 'It's okay, isn't it? My being here. I mean I don't want to intrude.'

Perhaps he'd never intended to call and now here he was trapped in a hospital bed with her having appeared in a stalker-like fashion toting a chocolate-box softener.

'It's *more* than okay. I'm really pleased to see you.' He rubbed the stubble on his chin. 'I felt like an idiot not being able to telephone you but I'd put your number in my shirt pocket for safekeeping and,' he attempted a shrug. 'I think the shirt's been binned.'

Sabrina didn't want to think about why it would have been tossed out. It was hard enough seeing him lying there, let alone thinking about the blood and gore of his accident. She unzipped her jacket; it was warm on the ward but she wasn't going to take the scarf off.

'You're a Liverpool girl!' He grinned.

She gave Flo a mental high five.

'Who else would I support?' she said, sitting down in the chair feeling self-conscious. It was one thing dancing opposite someone to great music with a few jars of ale sloshing around. It was quite another visiting a virtual stranger, especially one you fancied, in hospital and attempting small talk.

'Does it hurt?' *What a stupid, stupid question, Sabrina.*

'It's not too bad. The drugs are taking the edge off.'

'I heard you had to have surgery.'

He nodded. 'I had an open splenectomy. I'll have an impressive scar,' he pointed to his abdomen, 'to show for it. But I was lucky I guess. Coulda been worse.'

Sabrina murmured agreement before casting about for something to say that wasn't too inane. All she came up with was, 'Do you know how long you'll be off work?'

He shook his head, his dark hair still giving off the blueish sheen despite looking lank. 'It's not a big deal. I work for me dad. We're in the property business.'

She was about to ask what it was he did exactly when a nurse appeared. She was the picture of efficiency as she checked the notes at the foot of his bed but her uniform was just a little on the short side and she was a tad too pretty for Sabrina's liking.

'And how's my favourite patient doing this afternoon?' She twinkled at him before moving around to check the bag the line running from the back of his hand was attached to.

She might as well have been invisible where the nurse with the name badge Tina was concerned, Sabrina thought, her nose out of joint.

Adam grinned up at Nurse Tina. 'I heard you say that to the lad next door.' He gestured to the bed across from him where an elderly gent's snowy head was resting back on the pillow, his mouth agape like one of those moving clown heads at a funfair you've to try and toss a ball in as he snored loudly.

She winked broadly before announcing, 'Everything looks good.' She moved on with her rounds.

Sabrina watched her go, thinking if she were the matron she'd be ordering Nurse Tina to let the hem of her uniform down. It couldn't be good for some of the older gentlemen's hearts her swanning about like that.

He returned his attention to Sabrina. 'So, what do you do for a crust?'

Sabrina who always held herself back where her history was concerned suddenly felt comfortable enough to talk. 'I'm a partner in a bridal shop with my aunt. We make dresses to order and sell gowns off the rack.'

'You're in the wedding business. Should I be worried?' His mouth twitched cheekily.

'Other people's weddings.' Sabrina shot back. 'My aunt opened the shop in nineteen twenty-eight.' The pride was evident in her voice. 'It wasn't easy. I always think of her as Liverpool's answer to Gloria Steinem in the nineteen twenties. She's a fighter and she's still there.'

'And where's there?'

'Brides of Bold Street.'

'Tell me about it.' The interest on his face encouraged her.

'We live above the shop, me and Aunt Evie. I grew up watching her sewing dresses and running the boutique. Asides from not knowing anything else, I couldn't imagine doing anything else.' She shrugged. 'I love it.'

'You live with your aunt then?'

Sabrina hesitated, crossing and uncrossing her legs. She never talked about how she'd come to live at Aunt Evie's for fear of people seeing her differently. She'd told Flo of course but no one else.

'I do. She's not my real aunt though.'

Adam frowned. 'What do you mean?'

Sabrina hesitated but there was something about Adam that told her he wouldn't judge her.

'I mean I was a foundling.'

'That sounds like something from one of those wordy Dickens fella novels me old English teacher was always banging on about. Do you mean you were lost?'

Sabrina nodded, 'Then my aunt found me. I was only three at the time. It's all a mystery. I don't want to bore you with it.' She fiddled with the zipper of her jacket.

Adam tried to sit up and winced at the movement. 'It's not boring. Lying in here all day is boring. I'd like to hear what happened. If you'll tell me.'

His smile was reassuring and so, for only the second time in her life, Sabrina began to tell the unusual tale of how she'd come to be brought up above Brides of Bold Street.

Chapter Seven

'Aunt Evie was walking past Cripps, a dressmaker's that used to be where Hudson's Bookshop is now down the bottom of Bold Street. Do you remember it?'

'Vaguely,' Adam replied, frowning as he tried to picture the business.

'They were the competition so far as Aunt Evie was concerned back in the day.' Sabrina smiled, well able to imagine her aunt sniffing around to see what was on display in their window. 'She said she felt someone tug her skirt and when she looked down, there I was. I asked her where my mam was apparently.'

She paused to gauge what he was thinking but he merely looked intrigued by what she was saying so, emboldened, she carried on. 'She said it was as if I'd come out of nowhere.'

Sabrina took a deep breath and plunged into the story she'd been told as to how on a hot day in late August, Evelyn Flooks the spinster, proprietor of Brides of Bold Street had taken the little girl by the hand and asked her what her name was. Sabrina had been the lisped reply.

Evelyn, brusque as always, had ducked her head in the door of Cripps to inquire as to whether her mam was in there but no, there'd been no sign of her. She'd then spent an age stopping passers-by on the street asking if they'd seen a woman looking for her daughter. It was to no avail and she and little Sabrina were beginning to melt under the hot sun.

She'd debated taking her back inside the cool interior of Cripps to wait for her mam but there was something about the plaintive look on the child's face that stopped her from doing so.

So it was, Evelyn, who'd no prior experience with children, other than the brothers and sisters who were all a distant memory, found herself saying, 'We'll find your mam for you poppet but first we'll go to my shop. How does a cool drink and a biscuit, sound? You're all hot and bothered.'

Sabrina had perked up at the mention of this and so they'd set off, arriving back at Bolds of Bride Street to find an irate customer stamping her foot and pointing to the sign in the window. Evelyn had scrawled on it that she'd be back in twenty minutes. She'd been gone well over an hour. The heat wasn't being kind to anybody.

She'd opened up and appeased the woman by ushering her inside where she'd set a fan running knowing the day was forecast to be a scorcher. Sitting her down, she and Sabrina had taken to the stairs to fetch refreshments.

She set Sabrina up in the workroom with her Ribena and sugary Nice biscuit before taking the same out to her customer whose temper had begun to cool under the fan's breeze.

She'd intended to close for the afternoon and comb the street for Sabrina's mam as soon as her mother of the bride left but she'd forgotten about the appointment she'd made for a bride-to-be and her entourage.

She'd checked on Sabrina and given her a bowl of empty cotton reels to play with as the door burst open and the giggling, excited group of girls piled into the shop.

The time had whittled away in a flurry of flicking through pattern books, stroking of fabrics and finally in the taking of measurements.

Evelyn fully expected a distressed woman to burst through the shop door at any moment that afternoon seeking her poor, lost child because surely she'd be knocking on doors up and down the street looking for her?

But she wasn't.

The working day drew to a close and Evelyn decided perhaps the child had wandered further than she'd thought. She'd take her to the police station, she decided. There was nothing else for it.

She'd walked to the station with little Sabrina's warm hand clasping hers, pausing by Joe Berry's stand to scan the evening papers. There'd been no news of a missing child, the headlines all screaming about the Cuban Missile Crisis in America.

Evelyn had good intentions of handing Sabrina over to the care of the boys in blue but something stopped her when she got there.

When she thought about it later she realised it was the business-as-normal atmosphere in the station. There'd been no hint of the urgency a search for a missing child would invoke. It had spooked her. It was most odd.

Evelyn had heard the whisperings as to what happened to children whose parents put them into care or those who were orphaned and the like. There'd even been some unfortunates who'd been placed into temporary care by their mam or dad while they tried to find work and a roof over their head, but when their parent had gone to collect them they were gone. There was talk the poor luvs were put on ships and promised a life of oranges and sunshine never to be heard of again.

It would all come out in the wash one of these days, Evelyn thought, as she hung back from approaching the young PC on the front desk. What if Sabrina's mother came back? What if she'd been in an accident and was in hospital. She could have lost her memory. No, she couldn't risk this little one being shipped off to Australia. How could she live with herself?

'Can I help you with something, luv?' the young constable had called over and she'd made her mind up.

'No, thank you. It's all sorted now.'

It would be best for Sabrina if she stayed with her until her mam came looking for her. Surely it would only be for a few days and she was a far better option than foster care.

A few days had turned to weeks with no word in the papers or on the street of a missing child. Evelyn had stopped asking around as the weeks rolled into months. Nobody ever knocked on her door and asked how she'd come to be the carer of the little girl and she and Sabrina had settled into an agreeable routine. Eventually, people forgot there'd been a time when Sabrina didn't live with her aunt Evelyn above Brides of Bold Street.

———※———

SABRINA FINISHED TALKING as a trolley rattled past in the corridor outside the ward.

'That's some story,' Adam said, locking eyes with her.

She shrugged. 'I don't know any different. I don't remember any of it. It's not public knowledge.'

'I won't say a word.'

She believed him.

Nurse Tina reappeared at that moment tapping at the watch hanging from her breast pocket. 'Visiting hours are finishing now. This young man needs his rest.'

Adam looked as though he were going to protest but the nurse fixed him with a mock stern look.

Sabrina got to her feet, she was worn out from so much talking and slinging her bag over her shoulder, she said, 'I'll be off then.'

The nurse moved on down the ward towards where an older woman was sitting holding the hand of her husband, presumably to give her short shrift too.

'I'm stuck here for another week at least. I don't suppose you'd come and see me again would you?'

'I'd like that.'

A tenuous promise of things to come hung in the air and they smiled at one another.

'Ta-rah then,' Sabrina said.

She left the hospital with a veritable spring in her stride.

Chapter Eight

Esmerelda, in an acid yellow ensemble so bright it hurt Sabrina's eyes, poked her head around the door just as she was about to turn the sign in the window to closed.

'Yoo-hoo, anyone home,' she trilled

She said the same thing every Wednesday and Sabrina beckoned her in. 'Aunt Evie's in the workroom.'

The older woman wafted forth pausing to peruse Sabrina's cinnamon coloured blouse and plain black skirt. 'A fabulous leopard print dress arrived in today, Sabrina. I can see you in it.' She made a paw with her hand and purred.

Sabrina swallowed trying not to laugh but was distracted by the appearance of a familiar face behind the eccentric owner of next door's emporium.

'Sabs, you said you're going up to the ozzy to see Adam tomorrow night didn't you?'

Sabrina nodded and glanced over her shoulder hoping Aunt Evie hadn't overheard. She'd tell her about Adam when there was something to tell.

'Well, I've had a brilliant idea!' Florence was red in the face as though she'd run all the way from the docks.

'Just let me lock up and you can tell me all about it.' Sabrina turned the sign and bolted the door behind Florence.

Florence grinned a greeting at Esmerelda before calling out, 'Ahright there Aunt Evie?'

'Never better, Florence, thank you,' was called back. 'I'm nearly finished, Esmerelda, then I'll put the kettle on.'

Esmerelda was clutching her gin bottle and she made no move to join Evelyn as she waited to hear what the brilliant idea was.

'C'mon then, what's this idea of yours?' Sabrina asked. She'd tally the till up in a minute.

'We're off to see Mystic Lou. To find out what lies ahead with our two fellas.'

Evelyn appeared then, her flapping ears having caught the drift of conversation between Florence and Sabrina. 'What's this about going to see that charlatan a few doors down?'

'I thought it would be a bit of fun if Sabs and I paid a visit on Mystic Lou,' Florence dimpled, clearly pleased with herself.

Evelyn made a disparaging noise. 'Worra lorra rubbish!' Her inner Scouse showed itself as she shook her head at the two girls. 'More money than sense, the pair of you.'

'That colour's lovely on you, by the way, Aunt Evie,' Florence said brightly, trying to move her off the subject. Wednesday's shop coat was orange with psychedelic swirls harking back to sixties. She and Esmerelda would stop traffic in their outfits, she thought.

Evelyn however would not be bought. 'It takes more than a dollop of flattery to get me off a subject once I've sunk my teeth into it, Florence Teesdale. I'm like a dog with a bone me and I don't understand why you'd want to hand over your hard-earned money to her up there.' Evelyn pointed upwards in the vague direction of Mystic Lou's rooms.

'A dog with false teeth,' Sabrina corrected with a cheeky grin.

Evelyn clacked her teeth making both Sabrina and Florence wince.

Esmerelda, whose turban-covered head had been swivelling back and forth between Evelyn and the two girls never tore her gaze away from them as she raised her cigarette holder to her lips and produced a gold lighter.

'Not in here if you don't mind, Esmerelda,' Sabrina urged, not wanting their gowns to reek. 'It's a bit of fun, Aunt Evie. We want to find out what lies ahead for us in the romance department don't we, Flo?'

Florence bobbed her head in agreement.

'You don't need to pay Mystic worever her name is to tell you that,' Evelyn's tone dripped sarcasm as she added, 'I foresee a tall, dark, handsome stranger crossing your paths.'

'Well, I for one will be quite happy if that's the case,' Sabrina said, thinking of Adam with his thick, almost black hair.

'Her sort'll tell you what you want to hear.' Evelyn eyed both the girls and could see she wasn't going to change their minds. With a huffing sigh, she dipped her hand in her pocket and dug around. 'Here, make yourself useful, Florence, and fetch me ten Woodbine while Sabrina tallies up for the day.' She thrust a handful of coins at Florence. 'Come on, Esmerelda, I've saved a piece of princess sponge for you.'

Sabrina mumbled not really intending her aunt to overhear, 'I could say the same about you wasting your money on ciggies.'

'I heard that, Sabrina. And they're therapeutic. A woman's allowed a little pleasure in this life.'

Esmerelda raised her gin bottle in confirmation of this and Florence, well used to the banter between the two, called out she'd be back in a jiffy. She ventured out the door Sabrina had not long since locked as Esmerelda followed Evelyn up the stairs.

Sabrina began to empty the till, counting the coins into the palm of her hand and putting them in a plastic bag for the bank before thumbing through the pound notes. She had to add up the day's takings twice because her mind was on what Mystic Lou would have to say. She hoped it would be all about Adam.

———⊙———

'REMEMBER, DON'T GIVE her any prompts,' Florence bossed as she took the stairs leading up to Mystic Lou's rooms. 'Give me one of your Opal Fruits if you've any.'

'I won't,' Sabrina said, her curiosity growing the closer they got to the red door at the top of the landing. She delved into the breast pocket of her blouse to produce the packet she was never without. She flicked the top sweet off.

Florence didn't complain, peeling the paper off and popping it in her mouth before rapping sharply. She shoved the wrapper in her bag and then turned back to grin at Sabrina, her eyes dancing with excitement as she sucked the sweet.

A voice sang out in heavily accented English for them to come in and it was Florence who was first over the threshold.

The two girls took a moment to allow their eyes to adjust in the dimly lit room where the air was thick with an exotic essential oil burning above a flickering tea light. The curtains were drawn Sabrina noticed, despite it only being just after five and not quite dark outside. An overflowing bookshelf took up one side of the wall. On the other, a poster of a pair of hands clasped around a crystal ball alive with flickering lights like electrical currents drew the eye. In the middle of the small room was a round table covered in a red cloth, behind which sat Mystic Lou herself.

She looked, Sabrina thought, exactly like the Romany gypsy fortune teller illustrated between the pages of one of the stories in her beloved Girl Annuals. She'd long black hair with a scarf knotted about her head, oversized gold hoop earrings, and was dressed in a flowing robe held together at the neckline by a gemstone brooch. On the table in front of her was a crystal ball.

'I see only one of you at a time or ze messages they get confused,' she said with a wave of her hand.

'Oh,' the two friends looked at one another, nervous in the presence of the psychic.

'Zere ees a small waiting room through zere.' Mystic Lou gestured to a door they hadn't spotted next to the bookshelf.

'You go first, Sabs,' Florence said, making her friend the guinea pig as she made for the door.

Sabrina watched her friend disappear, catching a glimpse of an overstuffed sofa and a table with a stack of magazines before she shut the door behind her.

She turned back to the medium uncertainly. Aunt Evie was probably right, she reassured herself, she'd only tell her what she thought she wanted to hear.

'Have a seat,' Mystic Lou directed, and as Sabrina arranged herself on the chair on the opposite side of the table the psychic appraised her. The girl's aura was telling her she was lost. It was most peculiar she thought beginning to polish her crystal ball.

Mystic Lou, or Louise Doyle as she was otherwise known, might have known how to play the part of the Romany clairvoyant but the truth of the matter was the black wig she was wearing under the headscarf made her scalp itch and the hoop earrings irritated her ears.

Louise favoured cardigans and slacks when she wasn't working and she'd never been out of England — her true accent was pure Liverpudlian.

She'd learned the hard way though, it was no good being able to do the job if you didn't look and sound the part as well.

She'd also learned that people didn't like paying to hear things they didn't want to know so she'd grown economical with the truth over the years.

Yes, you'll be a grandmother soon (when in fact your daughter has no intention of doing away with her birth control pill for the foreseeable future).

Yes, your fella will pop the question before the year's out (when in fact he's happily having it away with your bezzie mate right at this very moment).

Yes, there's a surprise windfall heading your way (if you count the fifty pence you'll find rolling in the gutter on your way home).

Oh, yes, economical with the truth.

Sabrina had her hands clasped tightly in her lap and she bit her bottom lip watching as Mystic Lou finished wiping the crystal orb mounted on a stand before wafting her candle back and forth over it.

She then sat and stared intently into the orb for what felt like an age.

Flo would be chomping at the bit wondering what was going on Sabrina thought absently, unable to see anything other than a clear crystal. It was definitely all a show she decided. Aunt Evie was right; it was a waste of money. She wished the woman would hurry up and get on with it. She was beginning to think she'd gone to sleep with her eyes open.

She jumped when Mystic Lou broke her silence.

'I see a young man with dark eyes and hair.' She looked up then and Sabrina swallowed the smile. It was what Aunt Evie had said she'd say more or less. She was still pleased though; there was something to be said for hearing exactly what you wanted to hear.

'You will fall in love with this man but first you are going on a journey and when you return you will be unsettled.' Louise frowned. She didn't understand what the crystal had shown her and there was something about this girl's aura...

Sabrina wasn't so sure she liked the sound of this. She was all for a settled, routine life.

Mystic Lou gazed into the ball intensely, once more seeking clarity but still it was murky. 'Watch for a girl whose name begins with 'J'. She needs your help and you need hers. There's another man too but I don't know where he fits. It's not clear. 'S', Simon or Samuel perhaps? I can't see properly.'

No, no, no, Mystic Lou had it all wrong his name began with 'A'. 'A' for Adam. Sabrina's nails dug into her palms. She couldn't believe she was paying to listen to this and could almost hear Aunt Evie's 'I told you so.' Fishing in her bag for her purse she withdrew one of the crumpled notes inside.

'There's something else.'

Mystic Lou had run her palms over the orb and with one final dive into its depths she'd now sat back in her chair and was studying Sabrina contemplatively.

Sabrina paused, note in hand, her head cocked to one side.

'There's a woman. She's from a different time and she's searching for you. Only it's the younger you.'

The hair on the back of Sabrina's neck stood on end. *She couldn't know about her mother.*

Louise studied her. This young woman wasn't the first to sit across from her who'd stumbled into one of the city's notorious timeslips which was what she suspected had happened. It was the only explanation for what the ball had shown her. 'Your paths will cross again soon. The crystal is showing you as a child not much more than a baby and I think you unwittingly entered a timeslip when you were small.'

Sabrina shook her head. 'No,' she opened her mouth to explain what had happened when she was three and had found herself all alone but thought better of it. What on earth was she on about, *timeslip*?

'They're all around us, dear. Bold Street is a hotspot.'

'I don't understand. What's a timeslip?'

'Exactly what it sounds like. A slip in time.'

Sabrina still didn't get it.

Louise pondered how best to explain something that made no sense at all. The paranormal rarely did which was why people refused to accept its existence. She decided to repeat the descriptions her bewildered clients seeking an understanding of what they'd experienced had told her.

'People say they're going about their business when they notice the light's changed. Where it was sunny it will be overcast, a half-light if you like, or the air will feel thick like an invisible fog has descended around them. Some say they feel as though they've walked into an oasis of calm. Then they'll notice things aren't as they were. The cars on the road are different, the people walking down the street are dressed in out-dated fashion and the shops have changed. Most people slip in and out of time before they can comprehend what happened.' She shook her head and her earrings bobbed back and forth. 'But, you dear, somehow you got stuck.'

Louise studied Sabrina's face and felt a flicker of sympathy for her. It was hard to accept the concept of time not being what you thought it was but then, she'd accepted the world was a strange place a long time ago. 'Time's beyond our control, dear, but it eventually catches up with itself and that's when everything will become clear.'

She'd let her accent drop but Sabrina, who'd begun chewing her nails—a habit she'd broken years ago —didn't notice. She handed her money over with a frown. She wanted to put distance between herself and Mystic Lou with her crystal ball.

The psychic's words had unsettled her and she didn't know why because what she'd said amounted to rubbish.

She knocked gently on the door to the room where Florence was flicking through a magazine. She looked up at Sabrina with a questioning expression. Sabrina pulled a face to tell her friend she was unimpressed as she said, 'Your turn.'

Chapter Nine

Sabrina and Florence wound their way around to the Swan. They were eager to chat over what Mystic Lou had revealed and had agreed not to discuss it until they were seated with a half-pint in front of each of them.

Florence's tight lips and frown as they'd taken the stairs back down to the street were a clue she hadn't been told Tim Bryant featured in her future, Sabrina had thought. She was eager for Flo to pooh-pooh what the psychic had revealed about timeslips and a woman looking for her. The thought of it all made her head swim.

Pushing open the door to the pub, they made their way to the bar. It was only early and a handful of punters filled the tables sharing an after-work bevvy.

'Ahright, sweethearts?' Mickey greeted them, pouring their ales without them having to ask.

Sabrina hadn't seen any motorbikes outside but Florence scanned the pub anyway while they waited for their drinks. She was hoping Tim wasn't here. She didn't want him seeing her in her drab workwear of striped navy blouse, in a nod to the nautical, and skirt.

The coast was clear and as they carried their glasses to a table far enough away from anyone else to ensure a private conversation she said, 'Makes you feel special doesn't it? Mick knowing what we're having without us having to say. Good customer service that is.'

'Either that, Flo, or we spend too much time in the pub.'
Sabrina laughed.

'There is that.'

They sat themselves down and each took a sip of their
brew before relaxing into their seats.

'You go first.' Florence repeated her earlier sentiment.

Sabrina eyed her friend. 'It was weird, wasn't it? The
whole going into a trance as she stared into the crystal, I
mean.'

Florence nodded her agreement, impatient to hear what
Sabrina had to say next.

'She said I'm going to meet someone with dark eyes and
hair.'

'Adam,' Florence said, banging her glass down so as the
contents sloshed over the rim.

'Shush, and look what you've done.' Sabrina wondered
if she should get a cloth from the bar but Flo was already
reaching into her bag for a hanky. She never left home
without one. It had been drummed into her during her spell
as a Brownie.

'Sorry. But it's so exciting, Sabs. At least she got it right
for one of us,' Flo said, mopping up the spilled beer.

'But she didn't.'

Florence's chin jutted up and Sabrina told her how she
was to look out for a man with dark hair and eyes but how
Mystic Lou had gone on to mention a man whose name
began with 'S'. '*And* she said I'm going on a journey which
will leave me unsettled. What did she tell you that's got you
looking like you're sucking a lemon sherbet instead of an
orange Opal Fruit?'

Florence sucked her cheeks in and then blew out a slow stream of air. 'She told me there's a man who will play an important part in my future and I've already met him.'

Sabrina was confused. 'Tim,' she stated, wondering why her pal wasn't bouncing off the walls with excitement.

'No, Sabs, that's where the lemon sherbet look comes into it. Not Tim.'

'Then who?'

'Don't you dare laugh.'

'Why would I laugh?'

'Because she said, look for a man in tight jeans. He holds the key to my heart.'

Sabrina spurted her beer as she began to laugh. 'She did not!'

'Sab's, you promised.' Flo handed her the sodden hanky for her to dab her mouth with.

Sabrina wrestled to get her giggles under control. 'Sorry, Flo, but it is funny.'

'Very bloody funny, but she can't always get it right. She didn't with you. Anyway, Tim's jeans don't exactly fall off him. He fills them out very nicely so she could have meant him and not his mate.'

'Oh yes, definitely.'

Florence shot her a look.

Sabrina remembered what else the clairvoyant had told her. 'Mystic Lou said some other odd stuff.'

'Oh yeah?'

'Yeah. She said a woman from another time's been looking for me and that our paths will cross soon. She went on about timeslips and how Bold Street's renowned for them but I've never heard of them.'

'Me neither. What are they?' Florence was as puzzled as Sabrina had been.

'It's mad.' Sabrina began giving her friend the same explanation as Mystic Lou had given her.

'And she thinks you got stuck back in time somehow?'

'Yes. I told you it was odd. What do you make of it?' Sabrina asked.

Florence eyed her friend for a moment and then shook her head. 'I say we should forget all about Mystic Lou's prophecies and have another drink.'

'My round,' Sabrina said, pleased Flo had brushed it all aside. Still, when she got to the bar she couldn't help herself.

'Mickey, you've worked here for a long time. Have you ever heard anything strange about people having stepped back in time?' She cringed as the sentence flowed from her mouth. It sounded even madder now than it had mentioning it to Flo.

She expected the barman to stare at her blankly or ask her if she'd forgotten to eat lunch and was drinking on an empty stomach but he didn't. He took the empty glasses from her and put them behind the bar and as he poured her a fresh ale, said, 'I have right enough, sweetheart.'

He was a man of few words, Mickey, and Sabrina knew she'd have to probe deeper if she wanted any more information from him.

'Erm, what sort of thing exactly?'

He looked at her speculatively and slid the glass towards her before pulling the tap for the next. 'Between you and me,

I've had more than one punter wander in here bewildered as to what the year is.'

Sabrina turned and beckoned Florence over, waiting until her friend reached her. 'Flo, listen to this. Have they told you what happened, Mickey?' Sensing Flo was about to butt in and ask what they were talking about, she held a finger to her lips.

Mickey finished pouring the second drink and, picking up a cloth, began to wipe down the bar top. His head was shinier than freshly polished shoes and his gold tooth glinted under the lights as he said, 'It was a few years ago now but there's a fella who sticks out in me mind ahright. He was in his early fifties I'd say, and trussed up in a fancy suit. Bowled in here all agitated like because he was supposed to have met his wife in a restaurant for lunch around the corner on Bold Street. Said he met her there every week and would walk from where he worked to this favourite steakhouse of theirs. Now, I can name most of the establishments on Bold Street and I've never heard of a steakhouse.'

'Me either,' Sabrina concurred softly. 'And I've lived on it all of my life.' *Most of my life* she corrected herself.

'When I said so far as I knew there was no steak place on Bold Street he looked at me like I was the one acting strangely and said the street's full of eating and drinking places so he wasn't surprised I didn't know it. I thought, 'full' was a bit of a stretch but I let him finish his story. He reckoned when he got to this so-called steakhouse of his he opened the door, stepped inside and didn't recognise where he was.'

The girls were all ears, their drinks untouched as they waited for Mickey to carry on.

'It was a bookshop he found himself in. He asked the staff about this Zorro, or Torro I think it was called but no one knew what he was on about and when he stepped back outside on to the street he said it was all different like. Everything was out of date, the cars, the clothes, and he didn't recognise the shops. He told me he'd been walking around trying to get his bearings and was relieved when he found this place where it's always been.' Mickey leaned over conspiratorially then.

'That's when he got out this strange contraption. I asked him what it was and he looked at me again like it was me behaving oddly. He said it was a phone.' Mickey demonstrated with his hands, 'It was about this big, a rectangle shape and flat with a glass screen. Not like any telephone you or I have ever seen. When he pushed a button, it lit up with the date and time.'

Sabrina was holding her breath.

'I don't remember the date but I do remember the year.'

'What did it say?' Florence asked, gripping the bar as though in need of steadying.

'Two thousand and eighteen.'

'No,' both girls breathed.

Mickey nodded confirmation. 'Like I said I've met others but I remember him because of that phone thing he had with him. Said he couldn't use it to ring anyone. Something about it not working.'

'But what happened to him?' Sabrina asked.

'When I told him he'd got it wrong it was nineteen seventy-nine he panicked and left in a rush. I went out after him because he left it behind.'

'The phone?' Sabrina asked.

Mickey nodded. 'Only he'd disappeared.'

'Do you still have it? The phone?' Sabrina was holding her breath once more.

'I do as it happens. It's out the back in me lost property box.' He glanced along the bar. It was too early for it to be busy and he said, 'I'll go and fetch it for you to have a look if you like?'

Both girls nodded, excitement mounting.

'What do you think?' Florence asked once Mickey had disappeared.

'I don't know. It's hard to swallow, isn't it? The idea of people from different eras blundering into the past.'

Mickey returned before they could debate things further. 'Here you go.'

Sabrina took it and held it in her hand. It was smooth and hardly weighed a thing, there were fingerprints on the glass. She turned it over and then gave it to Flo who pressed the buttons on the side.

'Try that one.' Sabrina said pointing to the one below the screen.

Flo held it down and again nothing happened. It was all very anticlimactic.

'It's not lighting up like you said it did.' Sabrina stated the obvious, disappointed.

Mickey shrugged. 'All's I know is what I saw and I'm not saying there's any truth to any of it either.'

Sabrina passed him the gadget back.

'What brought on this sudden interest of yours then, queen?' The bartender asked pocketing the phone.

'Oh, one of the girls who came in the shop today was relaying a tale she was told similar to the one you've just told us. I was curious if anyone else had heard anything about timeslips, that was all.' Her tone was blasé and she could feel Flo's eyes boring into her. She picked up her glass. 'Cheers, Mick.' She turned and walked back to their table.

Florence was in hot pursuit sitting down across from Sabrina.

'Why didn't you tell him about what Mystic Lou said?'

'Because I think it's spooky.' She rubbed at her arms for effect. 'And a load of rubbish.'

Florence stared at her for a moment before lifting her glass to her lips. She understood the clairvoyant's sentiments about a woman looking for her had unnerved her friend, hitting a little too close to home as they had. 'You're probably right, queen.'

Chapter Ten

'I wanted to bring you in some grapes but by the time I managed to find some, visiting hours would've been over.' Sabrina gave an apologetic shrug as she stood at the foot of Adam's bed, her hands resting on the bed rail. The ward smelled of the enormous bunch of get well flowers in a vase beside a gentleman nearer the windows and a meaty aroma she couldn't pinpoint hung in the air.

Adam pulled himself upright in the bed upon seeing her. The grimace as he did so didn't escape her. He ran a self-conscious hand through his hair which flopped back down into his eyes as soon as he dropped his hand. The waxy sheen to his skin had gone, she noticed. He'd the roses back in his cheeks again as Aunt Evie would say.

'It's a nice thought but I'd far rather see you than have a bunch of grapes. Besides, I've plenty to keep me going.' He waved his hand at the box of biscuits sitting on top of the chocolates she'd brought in. A well-thumbed copy of *The Hitchhiker's Guide to the Galaxy* lay open next to them. 'Would you like one? They're shortbread.'

'No, ta. I'm meeting my friend Flo for a fish 'n' chip supper at Clive's. I want to save my appetite.' It wasn't often Sabrina turned down a biscuit.

Adam moaned. 'Fish 'n' chips! What I'd give for a nice piece of Clive's battered haddock. It was roast beef and gravy for lunch here, or at least that's what I think it was. It could just have easily been cardboard.'

Sabrina giggled; that explained the dubious meat smell. She filled him on the previous Sunday night's roast pork debacle.

Aunt Evie had been administering to her hard-won joint since four o'clock that afternoon. Only she needn't have bothered with all the basting because the meat was tough as old boots and so dry no amount of apple sauce or gravy could redeem it.

So it was, she'd spent Sunday evening listening to Aunt Evie and Ida whom she'd invited around to partake in the pork, moaning the meat wasn't doing their dentures any good.

Aunt Evie had put her knife and fork down halfway through masticating her meal declaring she'd been had and would be lodging a complaint at the bingo hall. She was adamant her prize had been bought on the cheap from a stallholder offloading old cuts on St John's market.

'The powers that be at bingo would be hearing from Evelyn Flooks. They'd not get away with it!' she'd said, banging her fork down on the table.

Ida had cheered her on.

The evening hadn't improved after dinner when Ida and Evelyn had roped Sabrina into a game of rummy either. She'd decided to lose on purpose and leave them to battle it out.

Battle it out they had, declaring a tiebreaker at ten o'clock, shortly before Ida went home having declined a plate of the cold meat for her sandwiches the next day.

Sabrina finished talking, her mouth twitching at the memory even as she shook her head over it.

Adam laughed too and clutched his stomach as he did so.

'Sore?'

'Only when I laugh but then they say laughter's the best medicine right?' His eyes twinkled making her heart flutter.

'Who's this bonnie lass come to visit you, Adam?' The old man with the white hair across from Adam who'd been asleep on Saturday was looking very sprightly on it now.

'Oi, keep your eyes to yourself, Jock. This is Sabrina.' Adam winked at her to let her know he was kidding around.

Sabrina waved over. 'How are you getting on, Jock?'

'All the better for seeing a pretty lass like yourself.' His accent had a hint of Scottish burr about it and he chortled at his own cheekiness but it soon turned into a wheezing gasp.

Sabrina moved over to his bedside fetching him a cup of water from the jug on his bedside table. His hand shook as he took it from her gratefully. It eased the spasms.

'Och, you've got a good one there, Adam, don't be letting her get away on you.' He flashed Sabrina a grateful smile.

She turned back, pink-faced at the assumption she and Adam were an item. He looked a little flustered too as he asked her if she'd like to sit down. She unzipped her jacket and slipped it off, not wanting her carefully chosen blue and white striped sweater to go to waste. She hung it on the back of the chair and sat down by his bedside.

'Don't pay old Jock any mind, he's always chatting up the younger nurses. The coughing was probably a ploy to get you

over there,' Adam said. His hands were resting on top of the
sheet covering him and Sabrina studied them for a second.
They were strong hands, she decided.

'He's off home tomorrow.'

'Coughing aside, he looks well on it.' Sabrina smiled,
drawing her eyes to his face. She found herself wanting to tell
him about what Mystic Lou had said.

'Something weird happened yesterday.'

'What?'

Sabrina decided to leave out the part about her and Flo
being desperate to find out what the future had in store for
them where romance was concerned. She launched straight
into the psychic's talk of timeslips instead. She told him
what she'd said about Sabrina having walked into one as a
youngster and that a woman was looking for her.

'I figured she was a crank but I asked Mickey, you know
from the Swan, if he'd ever heard of anything strange like
people stepping out of their time and into another.'

'What did he say?' Adam took a sip of water, resting his
head back on the pillow and despite the fatigue on his face,
his eyes were keenly alert.

'He had.' She retold the story of the man who'd shown
the bartender what he called a phone but was like no phone
they'd ever seen and how it flashed the date as being twenty
eighteen. 'When Mickey told him, it was nineteen
eighty-one he freaked out and took off.'

Adam raised an eyebrow.

Sabrina wasn't sure what she'd expected from Adam.
She'd half hoped he'd declare it a good story but a load of
old bollocks and that Mickey was renowned for spinning

a good yarn. It was part and parcel of his job to entertain the punters. He didn't though and when he spoke he said, 'Something weird like that happened to me Uncle Eddie once. He was only about my age at the time but it's his favourite party piece. He always brings it up when he's had a couple of bevvies.'

Sabrina tilted her head to one side, her jaw tightening as he continued.

'He was walking down Bold Street. Swaggering more like it knowing my uncle Eddie. Now that I think of it, it wasn't far from Hudson's only it wouldn't have been Hudson's back then.'

'No, it would've been Cripps,' Sabrina said quietly. She'd that same prickling feeling she'd had sitting opposite Mystic Lou the night before.

As Adam talked, the scene played out before them.

Eddie felt a hand claw at his shirt sleeve and startled, he stopped in his tracks. Several people walking past glanced at the spectacle of the oddly dressed young woman who'd a hold of his arm curiously but they carried on their way.

'Could you tell me what street I'm on?'

Eddie took note of her eyes. They were wild. He shook his arm free but she offered no apology and he rubbed at the spot where her nails had dug in.

They were a scourge drugs, Eddie thought, thinking it a shame such a pretty lass as this one had succumbed.

'Bold Street, luv.' He made to move off, eager not to get caught up in her drama but seeing what he fancied was fear flash across her face he stayed put. 'Are you lost?' He wasn't up with the play where women's fashion was concerned but even he could see her clobber was proper weird.

'No. I thought it was Bold Street.' She rubbed her temples. 'Only it's different. I've been looking everywhere for her.'

Oh dear, he'd a right one here, he thought, but he was nothing if not a gentleman. 'Look, how about I buy you a cuppa? You can sit down and get your bearings like.'

Come down from whatever it was she was on was what he meant.

'What year is it?' she suddenly demanded, looking at the cars tootling down the street.

'It's nineteen sixty-three.' This was getting stranger by the second and on second thoughts, Eddie decided he might leave her to it.

'No,' she shook her head slowly. 'It can't be. It's nineteen eighty-three.'

God help him, Eddie sighed. 'It's nineteen sixty-three, luv.'

The young woman stared at him for a moment and then her mouth formed an 'O'.

'Go home and sleep it off, eh.'

'I've got to find her!' The girl's terrified eyes cast about, soaking in the scene around her before, without a backward glance at him, she took off at a run.

Two women in pastel summer frocks with their arms linked blocked his view for a split second but when it cleared, she was gone. It was as if she'd vanished into thin air.

Adam finished talking and Sabrina was silent. He stared at her as the implication of what he'd said soaked in. 'I should have made the connection when you came to see me on Saturday. It could have been your mam my uncle met.'

Sabrina's throat constricted at the thought of the panic and ultimate sorrow of the woman she couldn't remember. She swallowed hard and shook her head as she tried to rationalise Adam's uncle's story. 'No, it's too far-fetched. Your uncle said himself he thought the woman was high. That's far more likely than her having stepped back in time.'

'It is, but it's pretty cool. The idea of it I mean.' Adam's eyes lit up but he hastily added, 'Not the part about you and your mam getting separated obviously. That's terrible if that's what happened.' His words were softened even more when he reached over and rested his hand on top of hers. She liked the way it felt and was sorry when he moved it away and carried on. The subject clearly fascinated him.

'There was a report a man gave of a collision with a phantom tram and another in nineteen seventy-one where two people reported seeing an inventor testing out his weird contraption in the River Mersey. It's documented as having happened in eighteen twenty-one.'

He gestured to *The Hitchhikers Guide to the Galaxy*. 'That kind of thing interests me.'

'I bet you believe in UFOs too.' She tried to make light of the conversation.

He grinned. 'I don't know about that but I don't think we know everything. I mean how can we?'

'We can't but I think it's far more likely my mother had a breakdown of some sort and she didn't mean to leave me but she wasn't well.' Sabrina liked to think her mam had come back when she was well again and had seen that her daughter was happy and cared for and had decided to leave her where she was. It was the story she'd convinced herself as being what had happened that day Aunt Evie found her.

She wanted to get off the subject and so she decided to angle it toward something else she knew interested him. 'Has what happened put you off riding your motorbike?'

Adam shook his head and his face immediately became animated at the turn the conversation had taken. 'No way. My bike's in at the mechanics where my mate Tim works. I couldn't not ride. There's no chance of repairing my leather jacket though, it's shredded.'

Sabrina pulled a sympathetic face. 'Better the jacket than you. I've never been on a motorbike.'

'You don't know what you're missing. If you trust me, I'll take you for a ride when I'm back on my feet and you'll see why it's addictive.'

'I'd like that.' A thrill at the thought of sitting astride his—she realised she didn't know what sort of bike he rode.

'What make is it?'

'A nineteen seventy Triumph Bonneville, the best bike ever made.'

The pride was evident in his voice and it made her smile. Not that she'd a clue when it came to motorcycles.

'Do you know when you're going home yet?'

'Hopefully, the day after tomorrow. I'll be off work for a few weeks though.'

It dawned on Sabrina she didn't know where he lived or what he did and she was about to ask when a stern-faced nurse appeared in the doorway to the ward. She was the opposite of pretty Nurse Tina.

'You've got to be on your best behaviour with Nurse Ratched there,' Adam whispered. '*One Flew over the Cuckoo's Nest*. You know, Jack Nicholson in the mental institution with the evil nurse. Great film,' he explained, seeing Sabrina's blank expression.

Sabrina gave the nurse a tentative smile as she checked the equipment beside Adam's bed and doled out a couple of tablets, waiting until he'd swallowed them before telling Sabrina her patients needed their rest.

The withering look the nurse gave her would have seen the most hard faced of women doing what they were told and Sabrina got up, slipping her jacket on.

'It's time I went anyway.'

'The fish 'n' chips.'

She nodded not wanting to leave but knowing she had to.

'Would it be alright if I phone you when I get home from the ozzy?'

'Yes.' She smiled.

'I lost your number, remember?' Adam reached over, his eyes squinting at the jolt of pain as he tried to reach toward the pen and pad beside the bed.

'I'll get it,' Sabrina said, writing it down and being sure to make the number seven look like a seven and not a fancy one. She put the pen and pad back down from where she'd got it. 'Maybe we could have a fish 'n' chip supper when you're up to it?'

'I'd like that.' He grinned at her. 'And a ride on the Triumph.'

The sound of the nurse clearing her throat saw Sabrina pick up her bag pronto. 'Ta-rah then.'

'I'll call you.'

Chapter Eleven

'He's so easy to talk to, Flo,' Sabrina said with a dreamy expression on her face. 'And he's gorgeous. I've never seen eyes that shade of brown-black before.'

'I have,' Florence piped up. 'They're the colour of a Fry's Chocolate Cream bar.'

'Be serious! Although I do like dark chocolate, milk chocolate too.'

'And white chocolate, mmm.'

'All chocolate,' Sabrina finished wondering how they'd gone from talking about her visit with Adam earlier that evening to chocolate.

She was sitting across the table from Florence in Clive's Chippy. They each had a can of pop and a half-eaten newspaper parcel of fish 'n' chips in front of them. In the middle of the table was a basket with paper napkins, vinegar, ketchup and salt and pepper shakers. Behind the counter, Clive with his buzz-cut salt and pepper hair was deep-frying a storm.

The plastic tables and chairs dotted out the front part of the chippy were full because Clive's fish 'n' chips were legendary. The air was thick with a haze of smoke thanks to the cigarette chuffing patrons hovering over the tables and the smell of cooking fat provided a greasy welcome when you first walked in out of the cold.

'I don't want to wash my hand.' Sabrina eyed it, trying to conjure up the way Adam's hand had felt covering hers.

'Well, you're going to have to, girl, because it will smell like old chips otherwise.' Flo smiled.

Sabrina pulled a face. Her friend was right. She was aware she hadn't stopped twittering on about Adam but had yet to raise the topic of conversation burning at the forefront of her mind. She wasn't ready for Flo's gushing reaction to what he'd told her about his uncle's encounter all those years ago. It was something she wanted some time to mull over in her own mind.

Besides, she'd been talking too much. 'How did you get on at your meeting tonight?' she asked, deftly turning the conversation to her friend.

'I lost two pounds, three ounces,' Flo said, dipping a chip in a dollop of sauce. 'And by the time I finish this gorgeous lot, I shall have gained two pounds four ounces, no doubt.'

Sabrina grinned. 'Did Bossy Bev behave herself then?'

'You, queen, are looking at the poster girl for our branch. Bossy Bev made everyone give me a clap for having lost over two pounds this week and told them they could all take a leaf out of my book. Ha! If they could see me now!' She put two chips together and made a V holding them aloft as though doing a rude finger sign. 'Up yours WW.'

Sabrina laughed, picking up her fish and raising it. 'Here, here!'

Florence ate the two chips. 'I went for a run around the park on Sunday afternoon.'

Sabrina froze, the piece of crispy, battered fish she'd broken off halfway to her mouth. 'Running? But you hate running.' She stared at her friend incredulously.

'Well, running's a stretch I suppose. It was more of a walk, jog, rest, jog a little more, collapse on a bench and then stagger home.' Florence shrugged. 'I'm going to go tomorrow night after work too.'

'Well done, girl.' Sabrina patted her middle which was verging on uncomfortable squished inside her favourite jeans.

'What are you doing that for?' Flo's brown eyes rounded.

Sabrina snorted causing the man reading the paper as he waited for his order at the table in front of them to glance overtop of it.

'Miss Lowry always said you had a good imagination.' Sabrina referred to their high school English teacher. 'It would be the immaculate conception if I was.'

This time it was Flo who snorted.

'I might join you running. These,' she gestured to the denim trousers, 'are getting tight because I can't say no to anything sweet. Although I did tonight, did I tell you Adam offered me a shortbread biscuit when I visited him?'

'You did, twice.'

Sabrina grinned, her lips greasy from the fish. 'Sorry. I can't afford a new pair so I'll have to do something and jogging might just be it.' The Calvin Klein branded jeans had been a splurge on both girls' part.

Flo donned a sultry face or at least tried to.

'Do you want to know what comes between me and my Calvin's? Nothing.' Florence affected an American accent as she did her best impersonation of the new Brooke Shields advert.

'Nothing, except one scoop and one fish.' Sabrina giggled, covering her mouth. 'And don't make me laugh when I'm eating.'

SABRINA GAVE FLO A hug goodbye before seeing her on the red double-decker that rumbled into the stop where they'd been waiting. She waved at her until it had pulled away before setting off for home. She was glad of the walk, hoping it might stop her mind from buzzing.

The night air was chilly and damp as Sabrina strode along lost in thought through streets much quieter now than they'd been on her walk over. Despite her best efforts she couldn't stop thinking about her conversation with Adam.

She shivered inside her jacket even though she wasn't cold. It was the thought of a woman who might be her mam, frantic at her loss, that had chilled her. It was almost too much to bear. Aunt Evie had been as any good mam but still the hole of not knowing where she'd come from was always there. She missed her mam if it was even possible to miss someone you didn't know.

By the time she'd turned on to the street she called home, she'd made her mind up.

Fred had yet to take up his position for the evening and she carried on past his alcove and the shop. Her feet had taken on a life of their own. They carried her to Hudson's Bookshop and she stood outside the building and gazed up at its wrought-iron fretwork. It was just a building like all the others on Bold Street. She paced back and forth garnering a perturbed glance from a couple walking past hand in hand.

She'd no idea what she thought she was doing and with a sigh decided she was being ridiculous. She'd go home to where Aunt Evie would be arguing with the television and things would be just as they always were.

Drawing a deep breath, Sabrina cast one more glance at the bookshop which offered up no clues and turned to walk back to the bridal shop. She didn't know what she'd expected. She'd walked up and down this street most of her life and nothing remotely strange had ever happened.

It was then she realised it was no longer dark and she stood stock still because the bells of St Luke's Church were ringing. She knew, as did everyone from these parts that they hadn't rung since World War Two when they'd come crashing down in the tower the night the bomb dropped on it.

A cold trickle of fear dripped down her spine as her eye caught that of a woman in strange garb who was eyeing her like she'd landed from Mars. A parp-parp sounded and Sabrina swung toward the source. It was the sort of car you'd see at vintage rallies and the street was virtually deserted.

She shook her head. Her mind was playing tricks on her that was what was happening. She'd been so caught up in all the talk of timeslips she'd imagined herself in one.

'Go home, Sabrina. Everything will be alright when you get there,' she muttered to herself.

Only it wasn't.

Part Two

Chapter Twelve

Liverpool, 1928

There were some mornings like this one when Jane Evans would wake in the tiny, unadorned room and wonder where she was.

She'd been here at the widow Muldoon's residence on Liverpool's Allerton Road for three weeks now and it still felt as unfamiliar and cold as it had the day she arrived.

She'd navigated her way from the train station, aware of the busyness of the city over which the haunting sound of ships' horns could be heard. The clanging of trams, parping of motor car horns and clip-clopping of horses and carts had been overwhelming to her senses. The air too was different. It was sooty, grimy, and just a little salty.

As she'd stood outside the wrought-iron gates of the house where she was to live she'd gazed up the sweep of gravel driveway and felt very alone. The garden either side of the drive was overgrown and the brick house with its steep gables at the end, enormous. She lost count of how many chimney pots decorated the roof and saw the birds had had a field day leaving their deposits.

There was no going back. She was here now and, steeling herself for what lay ahead, she pushed the gates open. They creaked and groaned their complaint and closing them behind her, she'd felt a stab of panic at being enclosed.

Then, she'd put one foot in front of the other and walked towards the entrance shivering despite the warmth of the early summer's day as her suitcase banged against her leg.

Mrs Brown, the cook and acting housekeeper who'd been expecting her had opened the front door seconds after she'd raised the heavy knocker and whisked her away downstairs.

She knew only the bare essentials about the woman she'd come to work for and those had been handed out sparingly from Mrs Brown as the days had passed.

The house had been the lady of house, Magnolia Muldoon's parents and she and the late Mr Muldoon had moved in shortly after their deaths. They'd both fallen prey to the great flu epidemic.

Unfortunately, Magnolia's father, who'd been in the shipping industry, had left behind considerable debt and eventually the couple had had to let all but essential staff go. A great many of the rooms were kept shut up these days with dust covers draped over the furniture like shrouds.

Mrs Brown had informed Jane the doors were opened once a year and the covers swept off for a spring clean.

Magnolia was desperately attached to her childhood home and her memories of the grandeur of her youth. She refused to sell the property despite the cost of its upkeep and so the Muldoon's floundered on in the echoing spaces with only a cook and everchanging housemaid to tend to their needs and keep house. This, Jane had read between the lines of the story Mrs Brown told her.

The family were well respected in the world of antiques with a shop established at the turn of the century on Bold

Street by Mr Muldoon's father. It afforded them a good life but not the life to which Magnolia had been accustomed.

She'd been widowed five years now and had one son. It was to him the family business had passed. He was currently away on a buying trip for the shop which he oversaw with the help of a business partner.

Each morning as Jane's eyes fluttered open it still took her by surprise that her mam wasn't in their tiny kitchen sawing through yesterday's bread to hand her a slice as she set off to the mill for the day.

She craned her ears but the rooms above her were silent at this hour. The quiet was disconcerting for a girl who'd grown up with three to a bed in the family's stone cottage in Wigan.

It hadn't been much that cottage. She'd gone to bed hungry on more than one occasion after her dad's chest had worsened. This was thanks to the dust from the mine where he'd worked since he wasn't much more than a child. Still, the cottage was home and she hated being away from it.

Some would say she was lucky as a housemaid to have a room to herself. Indeed, she had the run of the place downstairs each evening when Mrs Brown hung up her apron and went home. She missed the companionship of her sisters though. Although, she didn't miss little Emma tugging on her hair in her sleep. She'd a habit of winding one of Jane's sunshine curls as she called them around her finger tightly before she nodded off of a night.

She missed working at the mill too. Not the place itself of course. It was noisy and dirty, the work repetitive. It could be dangerous too because young Dick Philpot lost two fingers crawling about cleaning the machinery. It had caused an uproar with the village folk but nothing had changed and they'd all carried on just as they had before.

She missed the laughter of the other girls as they linked arms and made their way to and from Trencherfield Mill. Their camaraderie had made the grind of their work bearable. Then there was the fact she got to go home of an evening. Yes, she hated being away.

Wigan was only an hour's journey from her new residence but it was too far for her to walk on her afternoon off and she didn't have the train fare so it might as well have been Timbuktu.

The war had a lot to answer for Jane thought, staring up at the ceiling and seeing the spidering cracks in the plaster. It might have finished ten years ago but the sadness was still there in her mam's eyes, the slump in her dad's shoulders.

She'd lost her two older brothers, John and Henry, barely more than children themselves when they'd gone off to fight for their country. The war's ongoing ramifications meant it continued to take from them. Dad was sick and her surviving brother Frank had had his hours cut at the mine. She'd been let go from the mill too with the drop off in the cotton industry. They'd been surviving but only just.

She heard a door bang shut in the distance and knew Mrs Brown had let herself in. She held her breath and counted to five, exhaling when at five there was a sharp rap on her door.

'Jane, those beds won't make themselves, girl, and the fires won't magically start neither, out of bed with you.'

Jane pulled herself up to a sitting position and poked her tongue out at the door. She felt as though her head had barely touched the pillow and now here she was about to get up and start all over again. She was like the big water wheel at the mill turning around and around.

For all Mrs Brown's bossiness, however, Jane was glad when she arrived each morning. It meant she was no longer alone beneath the stairs. If she hadn't been exhausted from her day's toil she'd have struggled to get to sleep each night.

There were two empty rooms either side of her where other servants had once slept but despite Mrs Muldoon's posh ways, the family fell firmly into the middle-class bracket these days. There was just Jane, Mrs Brown, talk of a kitchen maid but she'd yet to materialise, and Gertrude who called twice a week to take the washing away in her employ but Magnolia Muldoon persisted in the charade that all was as it had always been.

This was to the detriment of Jane who was expected to carry out the chores of at least five servants.

Her new life on Allerton Road might have been bearable if there was someone her own age to bounce off instead of it just being her and Mrs Brown for the best part of every day.

Oh, how she'd have liked to have giggled conspiratorially over the rules, typewritten and framed, hanging on the wall by the door to the stairs. They were a strategically placed reminder of the divide between upstairs and downstairs.

She could recite them by heart.

Never let your voice be heard by the ladies and gentlemen of the house.

Always give room if you meet one of your employers or betters on the stairs and avert your gaze.

Always stand still when being spoken to by a lady and look at the person speaking to you.

Never begin to talk to ladies and gentlemen.

Servants should never offer any opinion to their employers, nor even say goodnight.

Never talk to another servant in the presence of your mistress.

Never call from one room to another and always answer when you have received an order.

Always keep outer doors fastened. Only the butler may answer the bell.

No servant is to take any knives or forks or other article, nor on any account to remove any provisions, nor ale or beer out of the hall.

The female staff are forbidden from smoking.

Any maid found fraternising with a member of the opposite sex will be dismissed without a hearing.

Any breakages or damage to the house will be deducted from wages.

The paper underneath the glass was yellowed with age and Jane fancied it had been hanging there since the last century.

Now, she heard the cook cough in the distance and knowing how sharp her tongue could be early in the morning she pushed her blankets aside, her feet slapping down on the bare floor.

She didn't muck about getting washed and clambered into her stockings first so as to put something between her feet and the icy floor. Then she slid her morning uniform over her head knotting the apron around her waist.

Peering into the mirror on the wall above the basin, she frowned at the rogue ringlet that insisted on escaping from the bun she'd knotted her hair into. There was no time for faffing about trying to find a hairpin though, and she shook her head at the mystery as to how she was forever losing them.

She'd still her bed to make and Mrs Brown's eagle eyes would be on the clock. It hung on the wall so it could be seen clearly when she was sat at the table eating in the kitchen. A reminder not to dilly-dally and it had the loudest tick she'd ever heard. Or perhaps it was that Jane had never eaten a meal in silence before.

She pulled the blankets up and smoothed them to ensure Mrs Brown couldn't accuse her of being slovenly and, satisfied all was as it should be, she tucked the ringlet bobbing about behind her ear and opened her door. Inhaling deeply, she stepped out into the corridor leading to the kitchen.

She was as ready as she'd ever be to face the ensuing fifteen hours of ensuring the mistress of the house's day ran smoothly.

Chapter Thirteen

Mrs Brown's cream skirt as she bent over in the larder was all that was visible when Jane appeared in the gloomy kitchen. It reminded her of a plump, round mushroom cap. She wrinkled her nose as the smell of the fish her upstairs had had for her supper last night assailed her.

The coke boiler had yet to flare and take the icy edge off the room and beneath the cotton uniform, her slender frame shivered.

She'd put on a little weight since her mam had told her to answer the advertisement for a Lady's Help, regular meals had seen to that. There was no doubt Mrs Brown fed her well.

She'd not had it in her to tell her mam in her letters home that lady's help had in fact meant single servant and not the glamorous role of lady's maid she'd envisaged. There'd be no travel with the family or cosy chats with the mistress at the Muldoon residence.

The pittance she earned scrubbing, polishing and whatever else needed doing ensured her younger sisters got a hot meal once a day. She hoped her mam had scraped enough together for new stockings too. The sight of her as she'd walked Jane to the station, the fare having been sent by Mrs Muldoon as an advance on her wages, with her lisle stockings pooling around her ankles and downtrodden shoes, had spurred Jane on. Her dear old mam deserved better. They all deserved better.

It was her duty to help her family and she'd no right to make a fuss about having to go away to do so.

'Good morning, Mrs Brown,' she said, causing the older woman to startle and bump her head on the shelf overhead. Turning, she held a hand to her head.

'What have I told you about sneaking about the place, Jane.' Her tea coloured eyes were almost lost in the fleshiness of her face.

'Sorry, Mrs Brown,' Jane said, trying her hardest not to stare at the whiskers on the cook's chin.

She swallowed her protestations of it not being fair; all they'd achieve was a lecture on answering back and knowing her place in the world. She was supposed to be neither seen nor heard upstairs and now she was being accused of stealth downstairs.

'Well now you're up, you could get that boiler going properly. You've the magic touch. Where's she got to?'

Jane wondered who she was talking about but didn't enquire as she did as she was told, crouching down to tease and coax the stubborn fuel into lighting. When she had it sputtering she stood up and took a moment to feel the warmth of the flames.

Her chin tilted toward the door she had just come through as it opened.

A girl who looked a few years older than Jane's eighteen had appeared and was dressed in a uniform similar to hers only in a pale blue. She stood uncertainly in the doorway.

'Ah, there you are Sabrina. All settled in I hope. Jane this is our new kitchen maid, Sabrina. She's going to be in the room next to yours on the left.' Mrs Brown left out how she'd found the girl hunched over, sobbing in St Luke's Church having ducked in to say a prayer for her dear departed Tobias when she'd gone into town on Saturday. Her day off.

She'd taken pity on her and put a comforting arm around her. Once she'd finished jabbering on about being lost and not having anywhere to go, she'd decided to do the Christian thing. She'd handed her a handkerchief and offered her the position of kitchen maid here at the Muldoon residence on Allerton Road.

The fact that it saved her advertising the position and interviewing all the hopeful applicants, was neither here nor there. Although she'd admit to being a little swayed by the girl's resemblance to her late daughter, Margaret.

She'd brought the girl who'd sniffled her name was Sabrina home, telling her if she knew what was best for her she'd stop going on about how she didn't belong here and make the best of where she was.

The poppycock the lass had spouted about time had gone over the top of her head. She didn't need to know the ins and outs of why she'd found herself homeless in a city that could be mean and hard for those with nowhere to go.

She'd dug out one of her Margaret's old dresses for Sabrina to wear, eager to discard the get-up she had on. Positively indecent it was. Trousers! And on a woman—not to mention they were worn so tight they were indecent. Then there was that peculiar coat.

She'd decided to let Sabrina rest on Sunday. She could see the girl was exhausted. She could start fresh on Monday.

Now, Jane sized the stranger up with a flutter of excitement. She was to have company in the servants' quarters and help with her chores!

Sabrina, she saw on inspection, had a sweet, pretty face with unusual eyes the colour of the brandy in the decanter in the drawing room. She'd a full mouth and the hair she could see peeking out from under her mop cap was the opposite of her unruly curls. She liked the smattering of freckles running across her upturned nose. They gave her a mischievous look.

'Hello, Sabrina, how do you do?' She hoped they'd be firm friends.

'Hello, Jane.' Her smile was tentative but as Jane was drawn to those unusual eyes once more, she saw sadness lurking in them.

She'd get to the bottom of that later, she decided. She'd an hour before her up there, as she thought of her employer, stirred and so taking the back stairs she emerged into the unfurling dawn to begin her rounds.

She lit the fires even in summer as the rooms Magnolia Muldoon chose to inhabit during the day were chilly first thing in the morning not catching any sun until the afternoon. She'd learned the hard way not to blow too hard on the coal. Its propensity to spit when it flared had singed her hair more than once.

By the time she'd finished polishing the front doorknob and sweeping the steps, she knew breakfast would be ready. She breathed in the scent of the smoky yew tree lined street lying beyond the gates knowing it would be her last sniff of the outdoors. It clung to her as she made her way back inside through the side servants' entrance and down the stairs to the kitchen.

A box of fresh vegetables had magically appeared in her absence along with a prime rib roast that could have fed her family for a fortnight.

'Don't be standing there gawping, Jane, get on with your breakfast. We've a busy day ahead of us.'

'Yes, Mrs Brown.' Every day was busy, she thought, sitting down at the table opposite Sabrina who was pale and clearly overwhelmed.

While Mrs Brown dished up eggs she leaned across the table causing it to wobble and in a whisper said, 'Don't worry, you'll get the hang of it all in a day or two.'

'What are you whispering about?' Mrs Brown asked plonking a plate down in front of Sabrina. 'There we are, me girl. That'll see you right.'

Jane, careful not to lean back because the chairs were old and had no backs in them waited impatiently for hers. She'd done an hour and a half's work this morning already and she was famished.

Mrs Brown carried their food over and sat down heavily next to Sabrina and the table shook as she settled herself to the business of saying grace.

'Thank you, Mrs Brown,' Sabrina murmured when she'd finished before diving in.

'Nobody's going to take it off you, young lady,' Mrs Brown clucked watching her. Jane flicked her an apologetic glance forcing herself to slow down.

Old habits died hard. It was having known hunger made her shovel her food in so.

They ate in silence until a knock on the door caused the trio to down their forks. It could only be one person, Jane thought, but in the weeks she'd worked here she'd never deigned to venture downstairs.

'Come in,' Mrs Brown called, scraping her chair back, nudging Sabrina to do the same and shooting Jane a look that had her following suit.

The door opened and the mistress of the house swept into the room in a cloud of Chanel No. 5.

Magnolia Muldoon cut a commanding figure in a drop-waist navy dress with her customary strands of pearls creamy against the austere silk fabric of her day dress. Jane suspected she chose to wear darker colours because she fancied they made her look slimmer. They didn't and she'd look a lot slimmer if she didn't insist on a dessert with her lunch and supper each day. Her slate coloured hair was curled in marcel waves that did nothing to soften the hard set to her discontented features. She'd been a beauty in her day Mrs Brown said but Jane found it hard to imagine.

Her gaze was impervious as she ignored the two younger women and spoke directly to the cook.

'Good morning, Mrs Brown.'

'Good morning, me lady.'

'As I told you last week Sidney is returning this afternoon.'

'You did, me lady, and very exciting it is too. I've sorely missed his hearty appetite.'

Magnolia's lip quivered into a smile. 'Yes, it will be wonderful to have him home. I've missed him dearly. Which brings me to why I'm here. I'd like you to tell me what the menu planned for this evening's celebratory dinner is. There will be seven of us dining.' Her eyes skated over the fresh produce on the work table in the middle of the room.

'Of course, me lady.' Mrs Brown bustled off to the bureau where she kept her household accounts and produced a notebook. Opening it she pulled the spectacles from her apron pocket and putting them on peered down at the page to read.

Jane was processing what Mrs Brown and the lady of the house had just discussed. Sidney, she deduced was Mrs Muldoon's son. Her only child and he was coming home but from where she didn't know.

It was the latter part of the exchange that had prickly beads of panic forming on her forehead. *Seven at the table for dinner!* Mrs Brown surely could have mentioned this so she could have prepared herself. Then again perhaps she'd spared her so as she didn't stew herself into a state.

Magnolia toyed with her pearls, her head tilted to one side, as she listened to what Mrs Brown had planned.

Jane caught words like pastry pigs, Waldorf salad, prime rib and cucumber gin, mint sorbet and thought she might be listening to a foreign language. Her mind boggled as the cook finished reading off her list. She snapped her notebook shut and looked at the lady of the house for her approval.

'Very good, Mrs Brown.' Magnolia gave a regal dip of her head, her eyes momentarily flitting over Jane. 'I trust you'll do a good job serving this evening.' It wasn't a question, rather a statement, but her stare commanded an answer, nonetheless.

'Yes, me lady.' Jane's silvery-blue eyes briefly met Magnolia's before she dipped her head in deference. Her heart was pounding because surely she wasn't expected to serve dinner for seven on her own!

'And you are?'

'Erm, Sabrina Flooks, my lady, the new kitchen maid. I arrived this morning.'

'And what good timing with tonight's dinner, me lady. Sabrina's from good stock in Cheshire,' Mrs Brown interjected. 'You're a hard worker aren't you, Sabrina?'

Sabrina nodded, marvelling at the smoothness of the fib that had tripped off the cook's tongue. Mind, she could hardly have repeated what Sabrina had been trying to tell her about being from the future. She was grateful to the cook for taking her in because she'd had a taste of how Fred lived and hadn't liked it at all. There'd been no hot breakfast brought out to her either as she'd hunched into herself in that doorway.

Magnolia eyed her just long enough to make Sabrina fidget. 'I should hope so. Thank you, Mrs Brown.' She turned on her heel and swept out of the room, the door closing with a click behind her. There was no sound except for the ticking of the clock and Magnolia's heavy tread on the stairs. Once it had faded into the distance, Mrs Brown rounded on Jane.

'And you can close your mouth, me girl, it's all hands to the deck today. I expect you to get your duties finished early this morning because I'm going to need your help if there's to be any sort of meal served at all.' She rubbed her hands together. 'Oh, it's just like old times.'

She had an agitated excitement about her as she rolled her sleeves up a moment later. 'The parties Mrs Muldoon and her parents used to hold were wonderful. Of course, back then we had a full staff but we'll manage won't we, girls? We'll do Mister Sidney proud.' It wasn't a question rather a statement.

'But, Mrs Brown,' Jane was about to protest she'd no experience serving at a dinner party and how was she, one girl supposed to manage, but she was cut off.

'There'll be no fussing, Jane. Sabrina will help you. We won't be letting the mistress or sir down. Chop, chop get your breakfast down you.' She clapped loudly and the noise startled Jane into doing just that.

In between mouthfuls, she looked to Sabrina seeking reassurance and receiving a watery smile by return. She'd a feeling this dinner party was going to be a trial by fire for both of them. Jane finished what was on her plate and the clock's ticking reminded her there was a bed waiting to be made and a bathroom in need of cleaning. She scraped her chair back because it was time she cracked on.

———————⊙———————

JANE HAD LONG SINCE changed into her afternoon uniform of a black dress, decorative white apron and cap. She'd just finished setting the enormous mahogany table for seven with the silver she'd spent the best part of an hour polishing.

Mrs Brown was to check she'd laid the table correctly once she was satisfied her mousse was the right consistency and as for Sabrina, she'd been up to her eyes in vegetable peelings when she'd last ventured downstairs. Mrs Brown had wasted no time in throwing her in the deep end.

Mrs Muldoon was oblivious to the mayhem her plans for the evening's meal had caused downstairs. Nor would she have cared had she known. She'd nodded off with the warmth of the unseasonal fire in the sitting room, a cold cup of tea next to her.

Jane had smiled to herself as she'd tiptoed into the room to stoke the fire noting her mouth was agape and hearing her snore in a most unladylike manner.

Now she closed the dining room behind her and her hand flew to her mouth, her heart pounding because a man was standing with one foot on the top of the stairs and one on the landing. His hand rested casually on the polished bannister.

Catching sight of her white face, he held his other hand up and urged, 'Don't scream. I'm sorry I didn't mean to frighten you. I'm Sidney Muldoon.' He took his hat off and smiled at her.

Jane tried to regain her composure and remembered her station. 'Mr Muldoon, sir, welcome home.'

'And you are?'

'Jane Evans, sir, the housemaid.'

'Call me Sidney, please Miss Evans.'

She'd do no such thing! But his smile was warm and quite unlike his mother's which looked as if it had been dragged into place when she deigned to bestow it.

Jane basked in that warmth, grateful for any kindness that came her way. She tried not to notice how blue his eyes were. If her friend Molly was here she'd say something flowery like they were the colour of a robin's egg. She was guessing he was only a few years older than herself.

He smoothed his hair, slicked back and shiny with tonic. 'Have you happened to come across my mother on your rounds?'

'Yes, sir, she's in the sitting room but you might want to knock first.'

He ignored the sir, raising an eyebrow. It was darker than his hair, which was sable in colour and he'd strong features which made him interesting. Jane would have liked to have taken a second, lingering look but didn't dare.

'Fast asleep no doubt.' He pulled a face whereby his mouth was hanging open and his head lolling to the side just as his mother's had indeed been.

Jane couldn't help but grin and she choked back a giggle.

He grinned back at her and she felt strangely complicit. There was a fluttering in her belly and she resisted the urge to wipe her clammy hands on her uniform as she stood pinned under his appraising gaze. She was unsure whether she imagined the current of something she didn't recognise running between them.

'Excuse me, sir.' She bobbed her head and pried her eyes away from his stare feeling his gaze follow her down the hall to the back stairwell.

How on earth was she going to keep a steady hand serving dinner with those blue eyes watching her throughout the meal?

Chapter Fourteen

Jane's hands trembled, aware of the seven sets of eyes on her. The weight of the roast platter she was placing down on the table in front of Sidney Muldoon as Mrs Brown had instructed her to do earlier wasn't helping her tremors either. As the man of the house, he would carve it and then she would serve it the cook informed Jane, shaking her cap-covered head at her naivety while beating up a creamy storm at the work table.

Mrs Brown's cheeks were showcased with two bright pink spots and her face was shiny from the elbow grease she was putting into her work, her mood noticeably terse due to the stress of the expectations on her shoulders for the evening's meal.

Jane had deduced, in between Mrs Brown's barked instructions, she was fond of young Mister Sidney even though by all accounts he'd been somewhat of a handful when he'd been running about the place in short pants.

Jane was grateful for the sympathetic smile she'd received from Sabrina at the vexed tone in Mrs Brown's voice and, pleased to have an ally here at Allerton Road, she'd gone back to whisking the batter for the Yorkshire puddings.

There were appreciative murmurings around the table at the sight of the main course and so there should be Jane mused silently having been part of the backbreaking work that had gone on for the best part of the day downstairs.

The Yorkshire puddings would have made her mam proud she thought, wistfully admiring their robustness. The key was in letting the batter rest and then giving it a second whisk, that and using a good fat.

Magnolia sat regally at the opposite end of the table to her son playing the dowager duchess to the hilt as she basked in the praise bouncing back and forth between her and Sidney's guests.

It was as though it were her who'd slaved for hours to prepare this celebratory feast, Jane thought mutinously, watching the older woman's soft, veined hands that had never known a day's work in their life bat away the compliments.

'Thank you, Miss Evans,' Sidney said. 'Be sure to tell Mrs Brown, I said she's excelled herself. It looks and,' he inhaled the platter, 'smells wonderful.'

'I will, sir.' Jane refused to meet his gaze knowing doing so would do nothing to quell her nerves which had not abated throughout the drawing room hors d'oeuvres, the entree served here in the dining room or this, the main course. His easy manner with her wrong-footed her and she was sure the guests disapproved.

She'd been aware of Sidney's watchful gaze all evening as she waited on their guests and wondered what he thought he was doing. Was he teasing her? Did he think it amusing to see her blush under his obvious attention? Was he waiting for her to show herself up as the simple village girl? It was easier to be angry than to try and understand the heat that stole through her when she looked at his lips, full and shapely.

His attentions hadn't gone unnoticed either, she thought, straightening and catching sight of the thin, arched eyebrow of the young woman, a Miss Claudia Monroe, seated next to him on his right. She'd a modern Louise Brooks cut. A severe style which not everyone who chose to wear their hair such a way could carry off. Her sculpted jawline and sharp cheekbones suited it well though which was something she was clearly aware of. Around her head was a sequinned and feathered black headband.

You could tell a lot about a person by their eyes, Jane always thought and this woman's, who looked only to be a year or two older than herself, jade eyes were beautiful but there was a flinty fleck reflected in them that gave her a brittleness where softness would have been a more flattering fit.

Jane merged silently back to stand against the wall next to the sideboard with Sabrina. She could sense the new girl's apprehension as to the situation she found herself in. The poor thing had had an afternoon of barked instructions from Mrs Brown and hadn't a clue how to work her way around the kitchen. She wondered as to how Mrs Brown had come to give her the position in the first place.

She wished she dared make eye contact with her to reassure her she was doing well though. She'd weathered the afternoon and was playing her part here in the dining room. They both deserved a pat on the back given they'd been thrown in the deep end.

She had to wait now until the meat had been carved and she could offer it around the table. This was her chance to allow her mind and eyes to wander over the guests.

She wondered what it would be like to wear soft silks and drape heirloom jewellery around her neck. To have the hours and money to spend on fashionable haircuts.

She wondered too what it would be like to be self-assured of your place in the world. To casually lean in to chat with a man as though it were the most normal thing in the world and to laugh with a tinkly laugh not dissimilar to the bell Magnolia Muldoon used to summon Jane when the whim took her.

She caught drifts of sparkly conversation as Claudia Monroe enquired as to the treasures Sidney had found on his journeys.

Sidney, for his part, regaled her with a story about a cantankerous gentleman who'd initially refused to let him over his threshold but he'd won him around and left with a vase well worth his charm offensive.

Jane had decided as she'd passed the hors d'oeuvres around earlier, the only way she'd survive dinner service this evening was to pretend she was back home. She'd have to put aside the fact she was in a room full of gilt-framed Muldoon ancestors all peering down at her disapprovingly from the papered walls.

Instead, she'd imagine they were versions of the photograph of her mam, dad, brothers and herself, taken on the cottage doorstep before her sisters were born. Her mam was so proud of it and now it was all she had left of Henry and John.

She'd imagine it was her dad's rumbling laugh that would always turn into a rasping cough she could hear and not the braying haw-haw-hawing of the well-heeled guests.

She would not allow the cloying floral perfumes of the women seated around the dining table to make her sneeze and she would ignore the lusty gaze of the fat fellow with the thick moustache; Claudia's father she presumed. He was drinking far more than he was eating.

All of this she'd vowed as the pigs in blankets which had turned out to be bite-sized sausage wrapped in pastry, were snaffled by the Muldoons' dinner guests.

———◦———

JANE'S FEET FELT LIKE needles were prodding their undersides when the last motor car rumbled off shortly after eleven pm. She ached with the urge for sleep but the dining table would have to be cleared along with the pre-dinner detritus left behind in the drawing room first.

Through the open door of the dining room, she caught sight of Mrs Muldoon with her arm linked through her son's as they made their way up the stairs having locked the front door behind them.

'I'm worn out from all the excitement of having you home, Sidney,' she declared, sounding anything but.

Jane watched a moment longer to see him smile down at his mother with an indulgent expression.

'I enjoyed my welcome home dinner, Mother, thank you. It was thoughtful of you to organise it.'

'And did you enjoy the company of Miss Monroe?' Magnolia Muldoon asked with a sly tone. 'She's very fetching, Sidney, and it was so kind of her to entertain us on the piano after dinner. She played charmingly I thought, and I do so enjoy the company of her mother, Iris.'

'She did, Mother.'

Jane didn't wait to hear whether he'd enjoyed Miss Monroe's company. Instead, she moved out of sight and gathered up the dessert bowls, stacking them with more force than was good for them. Sabrina, placing wine glasses in the dumbwaiter, glanced over curiously.

'Did you see what Miss Monroe was wearing? She was very glamorous wasn't she?' Jane asked, not really seeking an answer.

'I thought she was rather brittle,' Sabrina said, and Jane liked her all the more.

Both girls were keen to finish the tasks at hand so they could retire for what was left of the night. Tomorrow, tackling the never-ending pile of dishes, was sure to be as long a day as this one had been.

Sabrina took herself off down the servants' staircase. She'd unload the dumbwaiter and send it back up for another few runs, then Jane could douse the fires and crawl into bed.

Jane went through to the drawing room and was collecting the side plates when the sound of a throat clearing in the entrance nearly saw her stumble with them.

'You must be exhausted, Miss Evans,' Sidney said, stepping into the light. He flashed a smile at her and pulled a cigar from his pocket.

'Do you mind?' He gestured to the chair closest to the fire.

Jane could hardly complain that the lady of the house's son wanted to sit fireside and enjoy a cigar so she shook her head and continued with her work, aware the tremor in her hands had returned.

Sidney collapsed into the chair and loosened the collar of his shirt.

'Thank God that's over,' he said, before lighting the cigar and drawing in short puffs until he had it smoking satisfactorily.

Jane's lips tightened. She'd worked like a Trojan as had Sabrina and Mrs Brown and he had the gall to complain. The thought of all the food they'd be scraping from the plates in the morning almost brought her to tears. She knew back home that evening her mam would have eked out the stew foregoing a serving of meat in favour of her husband, son and daughters. She kept these thoughts to herself.

Sidney must have noticed the tensing in her shoulders as she clattered the plates together.

'Oh, don't get me wrong. The food was wonderful. Every last bite of it but I don't agree with it you know.'

She didn't understand and even though it was breaking the rules the question tripped unbidden from her tongue. 'With what, sir?'

'Please, it's Sidney. With Mother's ridiculous insistence on pomp and ceremony. Times have changed and for the better. It's nineteen twenty-eight for God sake.'

In Jane's opinion, he'd seemed to enjoy his evening perfectly well and besides, she'd overheard him not five minutes ago telling his mother so. She turned her face away so he wouldn't see the doubt in her eyes. His habit of pinioning her under those blue eyes made her feel all elbows and knees.

'My father fought in World War One alongside men who worked the mines or in the factories and he came back changed. He believed we're all the same and that there was no place for the class system in modern Britain. My mother clings to the past though, as you saw this evening.' His sigh was hearty. 'The thing is she lives in a fantasy world, always has done. We can ill afford dinner parties the likes of which were held tonight but there's no stopping her.' He rubbed his chin. 'They were an odd match my mother and father when I think of it now, but so long as the repugnant subject of money never came up Mother was happy enough and so was Father.'

Jane's face was flaming at the personal nature of the information he was sharing and he hadn't finished.

'I learned when I was small if I want an easy life I needed to play along with it. She can be extremely headstrong my mother. Besides, I'm only home a month or two and then I'm heading north on another buying trip.' He exhaled a plume of grey-blue smoke.

'The war changed my family too.' Jane surprised herself by speaking up.

He nodded and the expression of interest he wore spurred her on.

'I lost my two older brothers in the war, John and Henry.' It was ten years ago now and she'd only been a girl when her handsome brothers had left to fight. Tears pricked nonetheless and she put it down to tiredness and the perpetual homesickness.

She couldn't wallow in sentimentality though and she made to carry the dishes through to the dining room.

'Excuse me, sir, I spoke out of turn.'

He reached up and his hand brushed her arm.

The electricity that vaulted through her nearly made her drop what she had in her hands and she moved away from his touch as though she'd been scalded.

He didn't seem to notice her reaction. 'Not at all and please, I mean it, it's Sidney. Where are you from, Miss Evans?' There was no arrogance in his question just curiosity.

She stopped, half turning as she wished he'd leave her alone, but even as the thought raced across her mind she knew on some level she was enjoying the attention.

'Wigan.' Oh, what she would give to be tucked up in her bed now with her sisters.

'Is this your first live-in position?'

She dipped her head to say it was and his quizzical look saw her explain herself. 'I worked in Trencherfield Mill but I was let go.'

'Ah yes, our cotton industry is taking a battering. And so you came here away from your family. That must be hard.'

'It is, sir.'

'Sidney.' Amusement flickered across his face.

He could repeat it as often as he liked, she'd not address him on a first-name basis.

'Do you come from a large family?'

Jane wasn't used to so many questions being directed at her nor was she one for talking about herself but this was neutral territory and at the thought of her family, her eyes lit up. She informed Sidney she'd a mam, dad, two younger sisters and an older brother.

'What sort of house did you live in?'

'A cottage, sir, it's not much. We were always all on top of one another but it's warm in winter and it was filled with love.' She didn't add it was also filled with anguish over how food was to be put on the table, how hard it was to explain to a small child there was no more when she held out her bowl, how they'd afford shoes for Mary to walk to school in come winter and how they'd pay for the medicine her dad needed for his cough.

She risked a glance from under her lashes and to her surprise saw he wore a wistful expression as he flicked the ash of his cigar.

'It sounds nice.'

Hard was what it was, hard interspersed with brief moments of shining joy and happiness but she didn't say this.

'You must miss your family.'

She nodded. 'My dad has a cough from the coal dust, he's not well. I don't know how long he'll last.' Her voice trailed off. She was unwilling to say she was terrified when she finally managed the trek home he might no longer be with them.

Despite the tumult of heat at his presence and uncertainty that she wasn't in danger of getting a dressing down from Mrs Muldoon were she to suddenly reappear, there was something about the young Mr Muldoon that put her at ease and she lingered.

'You've had time off to see them?'

'I've a half-day on Sundays but when I finish my duties after church it's too late for the train.' It was not his business that she'd no money for the fare even if she'd time to make the journey there and back. Nor would she until she'd paid back the advance Mrs Muldoon had sent to bring her here and for her uniform, even then she wasn't certain the little extra wouldn't be better off going straight to her mam.

Sidney sat up straight in the chair then and clapped his free hand down on his thigh. 'I could take you.'

The door opened and Sabrina appeared. 'Oh excuse, me.' She'd clearly interrupted something.

Jane left his offer hanging on the air and cursed herself for blushing as she replied. 'Mr Muldoon was just asking me to pass on to Mrs Brown how much he enjoyed his meal.' She hurried through to the dining room and loaded what was left in the dumbwaiter feeling Sabrina's curious stare follow her.

Chapter Fifteen

Jane sat at the foot of Sabrina's bed with her knees tucked under her nightdress and her hands clasped around them. She was filling Sabrina in on where she'd come from and how she'd wound up here at Allerton Road. The glow from the lamp she'd carried in with her flickered on the bedside table, bathing them in a warm glow, and the faint scent of the roast chook cooked for upstairs dinner mingled with the musty scent of a room unused to inhabitation.

Their day had been long with the clean-up from the dinner party to attend to along with their normal chores. There'd been no time until now since Sabrina had arrived to get to know one another without Mrs Brown's ears flapping but Jane for one felt instinctively the two of them would become good friends.

It was her who'd tapped on Sabrina's door asking if she could sit and talk with her awhile. The light had been out but Sabrina had called out that yes, she was awake and Jane tentatively pushed the door open. Once she'd been invited to sit down at the foot of the bed and had begun to talk she'd realised how much she'd missed the proximity of others to chat to of an evening. It was something she'd taken for granted when she was living at home, at times even complained about where her younger sisters were concerned.

Only now that she had company did she realise how terribly lonely she'd been.

Sabrina was mirroring Jane in her position and had her back resting against the iron bedhead as she soaked in what the housemaid had told her about her life before Allerton Road.

The nightdress felt tight around her neck, unused as she was to such restrictive clothes and tugging at it the bed squeaked its protest at the sudden movement. She eyed the grey blanket tucked in atop the well-worn sheets. She wouldn't think about how many others had lain under that blanket over the years. At least the sheets smelled clean, that was something, and after having spent a fearful night on the street she was grateful for having a bed and blanket at all.

Jane was looking at her quizzically, expecting her to reciprocate but she wasn't sure what to say. The truth was too fantastical and she didn't want the younger girl to think she was taking the mickey out of her.

She'd tried over and over to get Mrs Brown to listen but in the end, the cook had begun to get annoyed at her insistence she was from another time. Given she was the only person who'd been kind to her since she'd blundered into what she now knew was nineteen twenty-eight, she'd let it drop for fear of finding herself out on the street alone, once more.

The terror, when it finally dawned on her she was in another decade had been overwhelming and something she'd struggled to put voice to.

As such, she tried to divert the conversation back to Jane. 'You must have been frightened arriving at a strange house with no inkling of what the job entailed.' She herself had never worked so hard as she'd done yesterday and today in her life. Her hands were red and chaffed.

'No more than you I expect.'

If only she knew, Sabrina thought.

'But it helps to know my earnings are putting food on the table at home. I won't pretend I wasn't pleased by your arrival to help lift the load though, Sabrina, and of course for the company.' Her smile was shy.

Sabrina put her tumbling thoughts aside and smiled back. She was glad of the company too. It would be awful to be alone here of a night in the cavernous servants' quarters and she felt sorry for Jane having slept here alone since her arrival.

The lamp cast shadows about the room which made her shiver. Just a few days before she'd have ridiculed the idea of ghosts but now, after what she'd been through she no longer knew what she believed.

'And where do your people come from, Sabrina?'

Sabrina hit the crossroads. She didn't want to lie but also didn't want to alienate one of the only friendly faces she'd encountered since she'd stepped back to this time. There was another part of her that was desperate for a confidante though. Her mind played tug of war for a few seconds until the side that wanted to blurt out everything pulled the hardest and she decided to test the waters.

'Jane, this is going to sound mad. I thought it did when I first heard about it but now, well I know better.' She met the younger girl's gaze holding it for a beat. 'Do you think you could keep an open mind if I tell you how I came to be here?'

Jane's eyes held hers steadily. 'You can tell me, Sabrina. My mam raised me not to sit in judgment of others.'

Sabrina exhaled, unsure where to begin and she twisted the blanket for a moment.

'Start at the beginning. It's usually the best place,' Jane coaxed.

And so Sabrina did. She told her how as a child she'd been found by Evelyn Flooks in nineteen sixty-three and had thought she was abandoned until now. Because now she'd good reason to believe her mam hadn't left her at all. They'd been separated by a timeslip.

Jane didn't say a word while Sabrina talked on telling her everything. It was only when she paused and came up for air that she asked, 'What about the bridal shop on Bold Street? Why didn't you go straight home when you found yourself disorientated?'

'I did and I saw my Aunt Evie only she was a much younger version.' It had been so peculiar to see her aunt who'd always seemed comfortably middle-aged, erring toward her golden years as a girl around her own age.

'I was a stranger to her, Jane. She thought I was delusional.' It had brought tears of hurt and frustration to her eyes to not be recognised but she'd understood too.

From her aunt's perspective, a random person in bizarre clothing had barrelled into her shop wild-eyed and ranting about having gone back in time. She'd offered her tea to calm her but Sabrina had been too het up and when she'd grabbed her aunt's hands to plead with her to listen it had pushed Evelyn's kind-heartedness too far. She'd pushed her from the shop and back out onto the street.

'What did you do then?' Jane's gaze was a mix of sympathy and curiosity.

'I walked back to where it happened outside Hudson's or, rather Cripps and paced about for an age but nothing happened and eventually, the strange looks I was getting from people got too much. I was frightened someone might report me to the police and I'd wind up in a cell with no chance of stepping back to my time and I was so tired. I ducked down an alleyway I didn't recognise to get away from the foot traffic and hunkered down in the doorway of an empty building.'

Jane shuddered. 'All night?'

Sabrina nodded. It had been the most frightening night of her life. She'd barely slept from being cold and hungry. She'd nothing to eat save for two Opal Fruits left in the packet she'd found in her pocket. The sounds of a night-time city had her jumping but it was the scratching that had been the worst of it. She'd been unable to shake the skin-crawling sensation of knowing rats were prowling nearby and had been terrified of closing her eyes.

'At first light, when the street was virtually deserted, I paced about again outside Cripps but I didn't want to be there when the business began opening for the day so I took myself off to St Luke's.'

It had made her breath catch, stepping inside the church as it had been until the Germans' efforts to flatten Liverpool had left it a hollowed shell. The rainbow of light slanted in through the stained glass at the altar end and there was a warmth in the ornate timber panelling she was surrounded by. She sat down on a wooden pew and did something she hadn't done in years. She prayed.

It was then Mrs Brown had sat down alongside her.

Jane struggled with the notion of the no-nonsense Mrs Brown being an angel sent to look after Sabrina but then the good Lord moved in mysterious ways which weren't hers to question.

'You must be susceptible to whatever this phenomenon with time is, Sabrina. For it to happen twice, once as a small child and again now.'

Sabrina held her chin up. 'You believe me then?'

Jane nodded. 'I do.'

She received a grateful smile.

'Sabrina, why do you touch the wall in the corridor the way you do before you walk down it?'

'Do I?'

'Yes, three times. Every time.' Jane had noticed this habit and was curious.

Sabrina shrugged. 'I don't even know I'm doing it. I have this thing about threes. At home, it's the light switches. Each time I turn them on of a morning or evening I have to flick them on and off three times. There's other things but the lights are important.'

'But why?' Jane persisted.

'It makes me feel safe. I suppose it's something I can control. I've always done it.'

'And here it's the wall?'

Sabrina nodded and paled as a thought came to her. 'Jane, when I was three I stayed in that time. I never got back to my mam.' A small sob escaped. 'I can't stay here, I can't.

There's Aunt Evie, my friend Flo.' Her voice was a hoarse whisper as she added, 'Adam.' A hard lump had formed in her throat at the thought of all the people she cared about not knowing what had become of her.

'I'll help you, Sabrina.'

'How?' A tear rolled down her cheek and Jane unfolded herself to give her new friend a hug.

Jane didn't answer because she didn't know.

Chapter Sixteen

Jane, Sabrina, and Mrs Brown filed in the door, down the steps and into the kitchen. Mrs Brown was humming All Things Bright and Beautiful, a little off-key if the truth be told, Jane thought. The cook always seemed to be in competition to sing louder than those around her, which would be fine if she could hold a tune.

Father Thomas had done them proud this morning with the service. He'd chosen a particularly rousing selection of songs of praise.

Jane always enjoyed the hymns even with Mrs Brown's caterwauling. Although, this morning she'd lost her way halfway through Mine Eyes Have Seen the Glory because she'd been watching Sidney, or at least the back of his head. He was standing nearer the front next to his mother who was bedecked like a peacock in all her finery.

She willed him to turn and see her but, of course, he didn't. She'd concentrated on her prayers after that, praying extra hard for Sabrina to find her way home even though the thought of losing her only friend in Liverpool was hard to bear.

'Go and get changed, girls, we've a lunch to get ready.' Mrs Brown stopped humming as she rolled her sleeves up and glanced around the kitchen back in her domain once more.

Sabrina and Jane did as they were told.

Jane was looking forward to her afternoon off, although it would be easily two thirty, more likely closer to three o'clock, by the time the last of the lunch dishes were cleared away. As she slipped her uniform over her head she felt an uncharacteristic stab of resentment at the thought of all those dishes. It was a waste of energy though and with a sigh, she smoothed her apron before going to see what task Mrs Brown planned on setting her.

She was presented with a pot of hardboiled eggs in need of peeling for the salad. There'd be more dishes than usual to wash up today too because Mrs Muldoon had invited Miss Monroe and her mother to join her and Mister Sidney for lunch. This news saw her crack the egg she'd picked up from the pot unnecessarily hard against the stone worktop.

She didn't know what had her more irritated she thought, accidentally gouging the white as she picked off the shattered shell. Magnolia Muldoon's blatant matchmaking, the thought of Miss Monroe with her oh-so-fashionable hairstyle and clothes, that bell-like laugh as she flirted with Mister Sidney or, the mound of washing up she and Sabrina would be left to tackle. Only then when the kitchen was clear of the lunchtime debris would she be free to forget about the Muldoon family's wants and needs for a few precious hours.

Resentment curdled as the shelled eggs piled up in the bowl and she reminded herself there were some who had it worse with a glance at Sabrina's back bent over the table next to Mrs Brown's.

It had been three days since the dinner party and her curious conversation with Sidney Muldoon.

It was a conversation that would've had her reprimanded by Mrs Brown if she'd caught wind of it. It broke every rule on the framed list over the door and she'd replayed it word for word to Sabrina who'd told her in return all about the young man she was smitten on.

Jane didn't know whether she was disappointed or not that her path hadn't crossed with his as she'd silently gone about her duties in the ensuing days. The first glimpse she'd had of him had been this morning during church. She did know, along with Sabrina, he'd brought a splash of colour to her dreary world, even if it was only in the form of a distraction in her thoughts.

She was still feeling the after-effects of the dinner party and was eager to kick off her shoes and stretch out on her bed in order to write an overdue letter home. She'd tell her mam all about the grand dinner party and what the guests had been wearing. She'd enjoy reading about that.

She would not tell her about Mr Monroe and his slippery hands. Nor would she repeat what Sabrina had told her. It wouldn't help and her mam would insist she come home if she thought she were living in close quarters with someone unhinged which was how Sabrina's story would sound written down on paper.

She might go for a walk later. It would have been nice if she and Sabrina shared their hours off but it didn't work that way and if she were to venture out it would have to be on her own.

Still, the stiff breeze that was letting it be known autumn was upon them would blow away the cobwebs of her week's work. Yes, she decided a stroll would freshen her up to face another day and remind her there was a world beyond the gates of the house on Allerton Road. A world which she now knew was far more mysterious than she'd ever imagined.

Sabrina, she knew, had spent her afternoon off the day before wandering up and down Bold Street once more to no avail. She'd not returned until their curfew at ten and her mood, despite Jane's best efforts had been despondent.

The unexpected knock at the door saw all their shoulders tense in mutual dread that it might be Magnolia Muldoon come to announce plans were afoot for another dinner party.

It wasn't Mrs Muldoon who opened the door after Mrs Brown had trilled come in however, it was Sidney.

'Good afternoon, ladies.' He smiled, looking a curious mix of boyish and dapper in his suit.

'Sir, what a lovely surprise!' Mrs Brown gushed, two bright pink spots of pleasure burning on her cheeks at the sight of him. 'Have you come to check on lunch?'

'No, not at all, Mrs Brown. Whatever you whip up is sure to be as delicious as always.'

The giggle Mrs Brown emitted was positively girlish and Jane and Sabrina glanced at her startled. It wasn't like her at all.

Jane's nerves skittered as she waited for him to tell them what he wanted. She pushed the rogue ringlet away and then remembering herself stood to attention as the other two were doing, Sabrina having received the sharp end of Mrs Brown's elbow.

'It's Miss Evans I've come to see. I wondered if you could spare her for a moment so as I could have a word, Mrs Brown?'

If she hadn't been blushing beetroot at having been singled out, Jane might have laughed at the incredulous look on Mrs Brown's chubby features. Sabrina gave her an encouraging smile.

The amused spark in Sidney's eyes at Mrs Brown's reaction to his request didn't escape Jane either and again she had the feeling he was toying with her. Annoyance flared but he was also the lady of the house's son and if she wanted to keep her job she couldn't very well tell him she was busy and whatever it was would have to wait.

She surreptitiously wiped her hands on her apron aware of the eggy smell. What did he want with her when he had the glamorous Miss Monroe arriving in an hour? Curiosity overrode her annoyance however and she looked expectantly to Mrs Brown.

The clock ticked audibly and Sidney cleared his throat. 'Mrs Brown?'

The cook gathered herself. 'Yes, yes of course. Jane, what are you standing there for? Off you go.'

She ventured out the door Sidney was holding open for her.

'I'll only keep her a moment,' he promised before closing it behind them.

Jane, her face still burning, was very much aware of the impropriety of her being alone with him. He was taking liberties! She also fancied Mrs Brown would have moved over to the door so as to eavesdrop and whether he'd had the same thought or not, Sidney gestured toward the smaller room off the corridor which had once been the domain of a long since departed housekeeper.

He got straight to point as they stepped inside the now empty space, save for a desk with a dried inkwell on it. 'It's your half-day today isn't it, Miss Evans?'

Jane nodded not trusting herself to speak.

'That being the case, I'd very much like you to permit me to drive you home to see your family.'

She must have misheard she thought, blinking up at him uncomprehendingly.

'You mentioned you haven't seen them since you came to work here and I could tell by your face when you spoke of them how much you miss them.'

'I do miss them.' Her heart tugged with this promise that she might see them.

'Well then. The motor could do with a run. That's sorted.' He smiled, pleased with the arrangement. 'I shall fetch you at half past two sharp after lunch. Does that give you enough time?'

Jane searched his face seeing the faint shadowing around his jawline but there was no guile there and she remembered herself. 'Yes. Thank you.' Her smile was tremulous, not quite believing the kindness of his offer. 'It's very kind of you, sir.'

'Sidney. I insist. And not at all. It's the least I can do given how hard you work. It will be my pleasure.' He dipped his head and a lock of hair rebelled and fell into his eyes. He pushed it away impatiently before standing aside so as she could pass.

Jane hesitated, aware of his proximity as she inhaled a scent that was reminiscent of the cinnamon Mrs Brown sprinkled on her puddings mixed with the cigars he smoked as she thanked him one more time.

She nearly tripped over the cook as she pushed the door open to the kitchen, hugging herself with the thought of seeing her family in a few short hours.

Jane, spying Sabrina's questioning look, would have loved to have told her what had just transpired but didn't fancy being accused of skiving further. She went back to work aware of Mrs Brown's snooping stare boring into her back. It was too much for the cook who demanded. 'And what, young lady, was that all about?' She'd positioned herself strategically, or at least Jane fancied it was deliberate underneath the rules.

Sabrina's hand hovered over the rolled-out pastry she'd been about to press the cutter into, she was eager to hear what Jane had to say.

'Mister Sidney has offered to drive me home to Wigan to see my family this afternoon. I haven't seen them since I came to work here and I miss them dreadfully. It's really very kind of him.'

Mrs Brown's face stained puce. 'Well, I'm not sure, what does Mrs Muldoon have to say? It's not the done thing.' She couldn't formulate her sentences properly as she processed this titbit of information.

'He offered, Mrs Brown, and I thought it would be rude to turn down such a kind and generous offer.'

'It's a lovely thing for him to suggest, Jane.' Sabrina gave her friend a pleased smile.

'And who asked your opinion, young lady?'

She ducked her gaze and Mrs Brown, looking like she'd plenty more to say on the subject, gave a harumphing sigh and got on instead with arranging her sliced meat on the platter.

The thing was, Jane thought smugly and with a dollop of satisfaction, she could protest all she liked. It had been Mister Sidney's idea not hers and so Mrs Brown was in no position to cast aspersions on Jane's behaviour and nor would she dare criticize him.

She hugged the knowledge she'd be wrapped in her mam's embrace later that day and hear the chatter of her sisters that had driven her around the bend at times but which she missed with all her heart now. She felt a pang for Sabrina so far from her own loved ones but her mind swiftly turned to sitting all alone in a motorcar for an hour or so with the handsome Sidney Muldoon.

———◉———

JANE STRUGGLED TO STAY on task as she served the lunch. She was too excited about her afternoon's adventure and it was only when she caught Sidney's laughing glance as she very nearly dolloped a spoonful of egg salad on Claudia Monroe's magenta coloured lap, that she took hold of herself.

Miss Monroe breathed out her annoyance and to Jane's mortification she heard her trill as she moved on to serve her mother, 'It's so hard to find good staff these days don't you agree, Sidney?' It was followed by her tinkling laugh.

She didn't hear Sidney's reply and was grateful Magnolia Muldoon who was engaged in conversation with Miss Monroe's dour-faced mother hadn't overheard.

She bit her lip so as not to smile at the thought that popped into her mind. She recalled her father telling her brothers that when it came to finding a suitable wife a man would do well to look to the mother to see what lay in store for him.

Sidney would do well to pay attention to Mrs Monroe with her bloodhound jowls then she thought, feeling justified at her pettiness.

She listened to Miss Monroe regaling Sidney with the 'cracking' game of tennis she'd played the other day as she finished serving the meat before blending back into the wall. As she stood to attention, she overheard Mrs Muldoon exclaim, 'What a perfectly lovely idea, Iris. What do you say, Sidney?' She toyed with her pearls waiting for his answer an expectant expression on her heavily powdered face.

Claudia removed the arm she'd rested companionably on Sidney's as she chatted to him. It was a gesture which did not escape his wily mother or Mrs Monroe. Both women were pleased by how well the duo seemed to be getting on.

'Iris suggested as it's such a beautiful day we should take a stroll around Calderstones Park after lunch. We should make the most of the glorious autumn weather.'

Jane's heart was racing. She felt sick as to what he was about to say. She'd be crushed if her hopes of seeing her family were whipped out from under her.

'A splendid idea, Mother,' Claudia said dabbing at her rosebud mouth delicately.

'A wonderful idea indeed, Iris, although you might be wise to wear your coats. That wind would cut you in half. I'm afraid, however, I can't join you. I'm otherwise engaged,' Sidney replied.

Right then Jane could have hugged him and she stood a little straighter.

'Surely nothing that can't be postponed.' Magnolia's tone was decidedly pointed, her rouge standing out in two vermilion dots on her cheek.

'No, I'm sorry, Iris, Claudia,' his eyes swept from one to the other, 'I really can't change my plans at this late hour. It would be terribly rude of me to do so.'

'Oh no, Sidney, of course, you can't,' Claudia simpered, the picture of understanding as she fluttered her eyelashes at him.

Jane observed his mother battling. She imagined she was trying to stop herself demanding to know what it was her son couldn't possibly cancel. She could only imagine what she'd have to say if she knew.

On Magnolia's part, she knew her son well enough to know he could be obstinate and if he didn't want to share his plans he'd have no qualms in telling her it wasn't her business. She did not want to be left even more red-faced in front of her guests. She'd not push the matter, she decided, winning the war within herself.

'Oh, Sidney darling, it is a shame but perhaps next time?' she said sweetly, waving the white flag.

'Perhaps.' He was non-committal yet he managed to charm the two Monroe women with his smile. He changed the subject deftly with the story of how he'd stumbled across a Chippendale table in a ramshackle farmhouse in Sussex which was now for sale in their antique store.

Chapter Seventeen

To Jane's utter amazement, Mrs Brown allowed her to finish earlier that afternoon so as she could freshen up and get changed out of her uniform.

'We don't want to be keeping sir waiting now, Jane, do we?' She shooed her out the door with a flap of her tea towel, 'Sabrina and I can manage, off you go.'

Sabrina murmured her agreement.

Jane returned a little while later wearing the dress she'd arrived in and her best and only coat. It was moss green with brass buttons and she'd a matching cloche hat on her head.

The hat and the coat had been passed on to her by Mrs Winstanley who ran the corner shop. She was fond of Jane for reasons Jane was unsure of. Her daughter, she'd explained had a perfectly good red coat, therefore, she'd no longer need of it.

Jane thought every girl could make use of two coats and she recognised charity when she saw it. She wasn't too proud to accept it though and she'd done so gratefully.

'You'd best take this with you,' Mrs Brown said gruffly, handing her a cloth-covered basket.

Sabrina dimpled knowing what it contained and she watched as Jane risked a peek under the cloth, her eyes widening.

'It's for your mam. I know she's a lot of mouths to feed and we can't have Mister Sidney going hungry at tea time,' the cook added gruffly.

There were slices of the cold meat left over from the luncheon. A loaf of bread, a generous wedge of cheese, a bowl of the creamy egg salad, and thick slices of her rich fruit cake.

'Thank you, Mrs Brown.' Jane blinked furiously, taken aback by her thoughtfulness. It had crossed her mind that once her mam got over her surprise at seeing her daughter she'd be embarrassed at not having much in the way of refreshments to offer their guest.

The cook brushed her gratitude aside. 'Now don't be getting all sentimental on me. It was only going to waste.'

Sidney knocked on the door on the dot of two thirty. He'd changed into a tweed suit and had a matching cap which he doffed at Mrs Brown and Sabrina in greeting.

Jane, with the basket over her arm, bade them a good afternoon and followed Sidney's lead up the stairs that led to the house's side exit. They emerged onto the sweep of driveway into an afternoon the wind had whipped clear and her feet crunched over the loose gravel to what once had served as the stables. A shiny royal blue motor car was parked in there.

'Miss Evans, meet Harold.' Sidney gestured toward the motor, clearly proud of it.

'Erm hello, Harold.' Jane giggled. She was almost giddy. It was happening. It was really happening! She would see her mam, dad, brother and sisters in just over an hour!

Sidney took the basket from her and placed it on the backseat before holding open the passenger door for Jane. She clambered in, arranging herself with her handbag on her lap. She was awash with adrenalin and excitement at the journey ahead and her eyes flitted over the fabric interior.

She'd never ridden in a motor car and she couldn't wait to see the look on her brother and sisters' faces when she pulled up outside their cottage in this gleaming saloon. They wouldn't believe their eyes!

Sidney clambered in and looked at her grinning. It was clear he was happy behind the wheel.

'All set?'

'All set,' she affirmed, resisting the urge to grab hold of the dashboard as he turned the key and the car grumbled into life. He reversed it out of the garage and they tootled down the driveway, the greenery either side of them a jungle-like tangle threatening to encroach on the driveway if a gardener wasn't brought in to cut it back for the winter months ahead.

Sidney left the engine running to open the gates and closed them behind them. Then, they were off!

Two young lads wandering up the yew tree lined street gave the Morris Minor an envious glance and for a moment, sitting there in her coat and hat, her uniform hanging in the wardrobe of her room, Jane forgot she was Jane Evans the maid.

Sidney parped the horn and she couldn't help but giggle behind her hand seeing a prim woman, a nanny perhaps, pushing a perambulator startle before shooting them daggers.

If Jane had been worried as to what she could possibly find to talk about on the journey she needn't have been. Sidney's manner was relaxed as he chatted about the family's antique business and his love of treasure hunting around the country. He much preferred that side of the antique trade to being stuck in the shop so, the arrangement he had with his late father's business partner, a Mr Ned Thompson, worked well on the whole.

Although, he added somewhat flatly, he'd be back on Bold Street as of next week for the foreseeable future as Ned was unwell and it had fallen to Sidney to man the fort while he convalesced at home.

Jane urged the butterflies dancing in her stomach at the proximity of Sidney to settle but every now and then her eyes disobeyed her and flitted across to the solidness of his thigh resting dangerously close to hers in the front seat.

As they left the smokiness of the city behind he turned the conversation to her, asking her questions about her life before she'd come to Allerton Road.

Jane opened up, telling him about her friends at the mill. He'd put her at ease and she found she wasn't embarrassed to mention the hard times that had fallen on the Evans family since her father's illness had seen him laid off from the mine. There was a compassion in Sidney that was lacking in his spoiled mother.

She wanted to know more about him. She'd lots of questions but wasn't bold enough to ask them and besides, by the time she was beginning to feel brave enough they were pulling up outside her family's cottage.

Sidney tooted the horn several times. Smoke spiralled out of the cottage's stone chimney and it was a sight for sore eyes, Jane thought, hugging herself with excitement at being home.

The front door swung open and there was her mam, unchanged with her apron over her skirt. The longer Jane soaked in the sight of her she saw there'd been subtle changes. She was thinner and looked a little wearier than she had. Her hair was pulled back into a silvered bun from which curls just like her daughter's insisted on escaping. She stared at the car, puzzled as to who would have pulled up outside their house.

The penny dropped and her hand went to her chest before she spun around to the open door and hollered, 'George, George, quick, come and see who's here.' She made her way to the front gate unlatching it and flinging it open.

Jane didn't wait for Sidney to open the door for her as she swung it open and scrambled out to run into her mam's open arms.

By the time she was released, her father was there, pasty and withered, a hanky pressed to his mouth.

'Dad, it's good to see you.'

'And you, our Jane.' He hugged her to him and she pretended she couldn't feel his ribs pressing into her or the sharp blades in his back.

Her sisters too had appeared to see what all the fuss was about as had her brother. They all looked from Jane to the car and Sidney as though it were a mirage.

Jane remembered her manners and she went over to fetch Sidney who'd retrieved the basket from the back seat and was waiting to be introduced. She brought him over introducing him to them all one by one.

She was aware of the nosy gazes from behind the windows of the neighbouring cottages and having no wish to have to introduce Sidney to the whole street, she was relieved when her mam ushered them inside.

'I believe this is for you, Mrs Evans.' Sidney held up the basket.

'Thank you.' Jane's mam, Elsie took it.

'It's from the cook, Mrs Brown,' Jane said, urging her to take the cloth off and see what was in it for herself.

Elsie's eyes burned and her throat tightened as she lifted the cloth. She was overwhelmed by the surprise of seeing her daughter whom she missed terribly and worried over as to whether she was managing in her new role. The kind gesture of the food from the cook threatened to tip her over the edge and she blinked the tears away furiously. It was a happy afternoon, there'd be no tears, she determined.

Little Emma as they all called her squealed at the sight of the cake and Elsie shushed her, not wanting them to show Jane up in front of her handsome friend.

Sidney was ushered to a seat at the table and he sat down smiling his thanks at the work-worn woman.

'Come and sit down, our Jane, tell us all about your new life,' her father said, his words morphing into a deep cough. Jane winced at the sound of it and as her mam set about boiling the pot for tea, she helped him sit down at the table.

When his fit had subsided, she began to fill in the blanks for her family. Mary and little Emma had sat themselves on the floor at her feet and her brother was next to Sidney.

Jane decided there was nothing to be gained by telling the truth of her posting to her mam and dad and so she made light of her duties. She caught Sidney's quizzical glance and was grateful he didn't correct what she was saying.

It was a festive afternoon at the Evans' cottage especially when the table was laid with the supper. Sidney seemed perfectly at home and got on particularly well with her brother. Little Emma had taken a shine to him too and hadn't taken her enormous eyes off him.

The hours passed quickly and all too soon it was time for them to climb back into Harold and head back to Liverpool. She hugged her mother goodbye especially tightly, drinking in her scent, and was reluctant to let her sisters go. She felt the salty prickle of threatened tears as she kissed her dad goodbye and told her brother, Frank to look after them all for her.

Sidney thanked them all for a perfectly lovely afternoon and Jane saw her mother's eyes shine. She fancied it was hope that the future might look different for her eldest daughter than it did for the rest of them.

As they drove away, Jane's heart was heavy even though there was no way she could know she'd never see her mam and dad again.

Chapter Eighteen

'Thank you, Sidney. I had a wonderful afternoon.' His name tripped off Jane's tongue much more easily than *Mister* Muldoon or sir and over the course of the time they'd spent at her family home she'd grownn used to addressing him informally.

There was so much more she wanted to say to him. She wanted to thank him for his courteous manner with her mam and his easy-going conversation with her dad and brother.

She wanted to say how sweet he'd been, making her little sisters laugh, and how he'd put them all at ease by making out the simple meal of leftovers Mrs Brown had pressed upon Jane was the best he'd ever eaten.

'So did I, Miss Evans. I thoroughly enjoyed your company and meeting your family.'

The moon came out from behind a cloud then and Jane's breath snagged seeing the softening in his expression as he gazed down at her.

Instinct told her he intended to kiss her and she stepped back, suddenly frightened of having come across as forward in accepting his invitation today. She knew too she wanted him to kiss her more than she'd ever wanted anything.

He wasn't for her though and she looked down at the worn leather of her shoes. 'It's Jane. Please call me Jane. Goodnight then.' Without looking back at him she turned and walked swiftly to the servants' entrance, letting herself in.

She heard him call after her softly.

'Goodnight, Jane.'

She closed the heavy old door and rested her back against the thick slab of timber for a moment, trying to compose herself. She fancied she heard Sidney's crunching footsteps as he made his way around to the front of the house. Her heart was all over the place and her cheeks hot and flushed despite the coolness of the night air outside.

The kitchen was lit by the moonlight filtering in and she picked her way across the slab floor to the corridor leading to her room which lay in darkness.

She'd no prior experience when it came to men, nor boys for that matter. She couldn't count Robbie Jones who'd thrust a fistful of daisies at her when they were both ten. He'd told her he was going to marry her one day as if she didn't get a say in the matter. He'd proved fickle in his affections because the last she'd heard he'd been courting Anne Brady. Anne walked around with her nose so far in the air she was in danger of tripping over, simply because her dad was the foreman at the mine.

She hugged the memory of the unusual light she'd glimpsed in Sidney's eyes as he'd drunk her in to herself. It had made her feel special and her insides had melted with yearning.

Jane's hand flew to her chest as a spectral figure appeared ahead of her. 'Sabrina, you startled me!'

'Sorry, I didn't mean to but I've been waiting for you. I want to hear all about it.' Sabrina leaned against the frame of her door her lamp casting long flickering, shadows.

Jane wanted to slip under her bed covers and mull over every look and sentence she'd exchanged with Sidney but she also wanted to share her glorious afternoon. She moved closer to the light.

'It was lovely to see my mam and dad, they've not changed nor has my brother but my sisters have grown a whole head taller. I could hardly believe it was them.'

It was true, they were like bean poles the pair of them. Her mam had assured her on the quiet though that the money she was sending home was a big help. It had made her feel good to hear that.

'I'm glad you got to see them. And what about Mister Muldoon? Did you and he find plenty to talk about?' The glow from the lamp made Sabrina's eyes seem like hollows.

'We did. Sidney's just like you and me.'

Sabrina laughed. 'Sidney now is it?'

Jane flushed and Sabrina reached out and patted her arm. 'Sorry, I didn't mean to tease you but he is only human, Jane. The us and them doesn't exist anything like it does now in the eighties.'

'Truly?' The younger girl's eyes widened.

'Oh, don't get me wrong, there's still the landed gentry and those that think they're superior because of their name or heritage but it doesn't seem to matter as much as it does now.'

'I can't imagine it.' Jane shook her head in wonder at their ever coming a time when it wasn't scandalous for a housemaid to go on an outing with the master of the house.

'You got on well then?'

'He's very easy company and it was ever so kind of him to take me.' Jane yawned, the day catching up with her.

'I don't think it was all down to kindness.' Sabrina twinkled.

'There was this moment just now outside.' Jane's voice lowered to a whisper. 'I thought he might kiss me.'

'Did you want him to?'

Jane dipped her head in a nod and then looked about as though the wall might have ears as she said, 'But I broke the spell. It wouldn't be right, Sabrina.'

'Jane, you deserve more than this.' Sabrina waved her hand about.

'You don't understand the way things are.' Before that evening, Jane would have given anything to rewind to a simpler if not easier time where she still lived under her mam and dad's roof and walked to her work at the mill each day.

She'd assumed she'd marry someone from the village who worked in the mine like her mam had her dad. She'd never considered a different sort of life. She'd never considered she deserved more.

Her feelings had changed over the course of the hours she'd spent in Sidney's company today, however, because if she wasn't here then she wouldn't get to see him and she wanted to see him tomorrow and the day after that and so on, very, very much. She was growing fond of Sabrina too and it would be a wrench to leave her, knowing how alone she was.

'Promise me you won't fob him off next time if it's what you want.'

Jane shifted uncomfortably. She was too honest to promise something she wasn't sure she could keep.

When she didn't respond, Sabrina sighed. 'We'd best get off to bed. Mrs Brown will be knocking on our doors before we know it.'

Jane nodded her agreement, grateful to escape because she had a lot she wanted to think over.

'Goodnight, Sabrina.'

'Night-night.'

Jane undressed in her darkened room and, clambering under her bedding, she lay on her side staring into the inkiness.

Sidney had said the world had changed too but Jane had yet to see any sign of it. Sabrina said the future was very different to the here and now too. Was it possible then? Could she rise above her pre-prescribed lot in life? The way Sidney had looked at her gave her cause to dream she decided.

Chapter Nineteen

It was the fifth morning since Jane had been to visit her family and life at Allerton Road was not as it had been.

Not for Jane at any rate. With Sidney going to work at the antique shop on Bold Street he was taking his breakfast earlier. His mother rarely opened her eyes much before nine and on the first morning after their outing to Wigan, Jane had been on tenterhooks. She'd placed his soft boiled egg and toast down on the table that seemed enormous for one person, wondering how he'd be around her.

Would he be formal, regretting the over-familiarity of the day before, coolly polite?

Or would he show her glimpses of the friendship she'd felt unfurling between them?

She should have trusted in him because he was the latter.

'Good morning, Jane. Did you sleep well?'

'Good morning...'

'Sidney.' He'd looked exasperated.

'Sidney,' her smile was shy. 'I did, thank you and you?'

'Very well.' He'd stood up then and pulling the chair out next to him asked her to join him.

Jane had hesitated. There were only so many hours in a day and not enough as it was for her to finish her list of tasks. She'd feel like an interloper too. She could only imagine Mrs Muldoon's reaction were she to appear and find her sitting there. A cuckoo in the nest, she'd be turfed out and reminded her of place.

'There's nobody here, Jane, if that's what you're worried about. Even if there were would it matter? I asked you to join me. I hate eating alone. Come on, please sit down. I won't enjoy my egg at all if you're standing over there keeping watch.'

Sidney had been insistent and she couldn't very well refuse him so, against her better judgment, Jane had perched on the edge of the seat all the while keeping an ear out for Mrs Muldoon.

He'd poured her a cup of tea and had acted as though it were the most natural thing in the world for the housemaid to sit alongside him at the breakfast table.

Jane had sipped her tea in a heightened state of anxiety initially but as he'd chattered on about their outing and his day ahead the tension had gone out of her shoulders.

To her amazement, he asked her about how her day would unfold. She reeled off what was expected of her and he'd shaken his head and she'd thought she caught the words, 'slave labour is what it is'.

She'd not protested quite so much the next day when he'd asked her to join him or the day after and by Friday morning she'd sat down without a word. This morning ritual had become the highlight of her day and she'd kept Sabrina abreast of this new and exciting arrangement.

The time between breakfast and dinner dragged with the knowledge there'd be no chance of rounding the corner and bumping into Sidney. Those long in-between hours left her feeling flat as she played over their morning chat, analysing every word and gesture, while she scrubbed and dubbed.

The evening meal which had been a previous source of dread because her feet would ache by that time of day had become a much-anticipated event.

This particular morning Sidney had left for the shop and Magnolia's breakfast had been laid out for her by the time Jane sat down in the kitchen opposite Sabrina. She glanced over to where Mrs Brown was busy in the larder taking note of what staples were getting low.

Deciding the coast was clear, she half whispered, half giggled, 'You should have seen the look on Mrs Muldoon's face when I put the vegetables on the table last night and Sidney asked me how my day had been. It should have been bottled, like the plums Mrs Brown's so fond of, for posterity'

Sabrina's mouth twitched at the picture that sprang to mind and a voice from the larder echoed out, 'I heard that, Jane Evans. You'd do well to remember your station, young lady. It's Mister Muldoon to you. No good ever became of anyone who tried to rise above it. Think on.'

Mrs Brown had hearing that defied belief for a woman of her age, Jane thought, and she'd have reddened at the ticking off if Sabrina hadn't pulled a funny face in the direction of the larder. Even so, she ate the rest of her breakfast in silence, feeling chastened. Perhaps she was getting a little big for her boots and if she was indeed getting ideas above her station did that mean she was headed for a fall?

SIDNEY, JANE LEARNED, still rose early on a Saturday. It was business as usual on Bold Street although the shop would close an hour earlier. Despite the marginally shorter day, his mood was terse when Jane sat down alongside him having checked the coast was clear.

She looked at him quizzically as he stirred her tea a little too robustly.

'Sorry,' he muttered as the brown liquid sloshed into the saucer. He attempted to mop it up with a napkin but Jane told him it was fine and took it from him.

'Is something the matter?'

'*Mother* is the matter. She's gone and accepted a dinner invitation on my behalf as well as her own at the Monroes' tonight.'

Disappointment that she wouldn't see him again after breakfast and envy at the thought of pampered Miss Monroe fawning all over him saw her dig her nails into her palms. She hoped it didn't show on her face but Sidney seemed oblivious.

He turned to look at her, putting his thickly buttered toast down on the plate. 'There is something that would make tonight bearable.'

Jane said nothing, clueless as to what he'd say next. She waited curiously.

'Would you come out with me tomorrow night?'

'Where to?' She told herself off for sounding ungracious but he'd taken her by surprise.

'Have you listened to jazz music being played live before?'

'No.' She shook her head. Oh, she'd heard of the bright young things of course. Who hadn't? Their penchant for kicking up their heels to the Charleston and sipping champagne without a care in the world was legendary.

'Well then, would you do me the honour of joining me at the Grafton ballroom tomorrow evening?'

The Grafton. Jane rolled it over in her mind. A feeling of excitement stole over her. She'd never been inside a ballroom. She kept her eyes downcast so he couldn't read them as she mulled his offer over.

There were so many reasons why she should decline his invitation.

She was no flapper and was sure to make a fool of herself should Sidney ask her to dance. She'd only ever kicked her heels up with her friends as they practised the Charleston and dreamed about what it would be like to wear shimmery, fringed dresses and drink champagne.

What would she wear? She'd only the two dresses hanging in her room, one for church and the other she'd worn on their outing the other weekend. Neither was suitable to wear dancing.

She knew too that a line would be crossed were she to go. It was a line from which there'd be no going back.

Despite the protestations of her mind, her mouth took on a life of its own. 'I'd like that very much.'

Sidney picked up his toast. 'Good.' He grinned, his previous mood now forgotten. 'That's settled then. I'll call for you at nine tomorrow evening.'

THE DAY AND EVENING had been yawningly long. Jane would never have thought she'd resent the Muldoons venturing out for dinner and effectively giving her a night off but resent it she did.

She'd rattled around downstairs, plagued by thoughts as to what on earth she'd wear the following evening. Her mam had always said she was too headstrong for her own good. She should never have accepted Sidney's invitation. A sick sensation had settled in the pit of her stomach.

It was Sabrina's afternoon off and her friend was once more pacing Bold Street looking for whatever portal she'd stepped into. The thought of Sabrina not returning rattled her too. What if she found her way back to her time? She'd be left here all alone again. Her selfishness at not wanting her friend to leave made her feel even worse.

She'd decided there was nothing for it but to cancel her arrangement with Sidney when, to her relief, Sabrina arrived back, her wandering having again proved fruitless.

Jane was pleased to see her, being in as desperate need of distraction as Sabrina for whom the frustration of being trapped and unable to reach those she loved was bubbling inside her. The only thing she could think of to take her mind off it all was a game of cards. She'd found an old playing deck down the back of her drawers.

When she suggested a game of gin rummy to Jane, she jumped at, it even though she'd no clue how to play the card game.

'I can teach you,' Sabrina said, disappearing off to her room to fetch the cards.

Jane waited at the kitchen table under the flickering yellow lights for her to return.

Sabrina came back and sat down across from her to shuffle the deck before dealing them. She was a few minutes into her instructions as to the rules when she gave up. 'You're not paying attention, Jane.'

Jane looked up from the cards she was holding. 'I know. I'm sorry. I've things on my mind. I thought a game of cards would be a good distraction but I can't concentrate.'

'Sidney things?' Sabrina surmised.

'He's invited me to go dancing at the Grafton tomorrow evening.'

Sabrina put her fanned cards face down on the table. 'The Grafton?' She knew it of course. She and Flo had danced a few nights away under its ballroom lights.

Jane nodded. 'But of course, I shan't be going.'

Sabrina shook her head. 'But you can't possibly not go.'

'How can I go, Sabrina. I'd be late in for one thing and if Mrs Muldoon were to find out, I'd be dismissed. I can't afford for that to happen and I haven't anything suitable to wear. I'll not show Sidney up.'

Sabrina's expression grew pensive and the only sound was the tick, tick, ticking of the clock on the wall. Finally, she spoke up. 'I've an idea.'

Jane looked across the table at her. 'Oh yes?' She couldn't see Sabrina coming up with anything that would change her decision to back out of the invitation but there was no harm in listening.

'They're out at dinner for the evening, yes?' Sabrina raised her eyes heavenward.

'Yes. But what's that got to do with anything?'

'Wait here.' Sabrina said, pushing her chair back. There was a keyed-up air about her as she opened the door and without so much as a backward glance disappeared up the stairs before Jane could gather her wits and stop her.

Tick, tick, tick went the clock as Jane stared up at the ceiling wondering what on earth Sabrina was doing up there. There was no tell-tale creak of the floorboards overhead to give her a clue as to where she was and it seemed to take an age for her footfall to sound on the stairs.

As she appeared back in the kitchen Jane exhaled, 'What on earth were you... her sentence petered to a halt seeing the dress Sabrina had slung over her arm.

'Where did you get that?' Although she wasn't entirely sure she wanted to hear the answer to her question.

Sabrina held the dress up, examining it under the light. The swathe of silver silk fabric shimmered under the yellow illumination.

'It's a little dated and, of course, it will be too big and far too long for dancing but I do believe if I took the hem up and nipped it in under the arms and down the back seam no one would ever know it hadn't been made for you. I'm a dressmaker by trade, Jane. I can work wonders. There's a mending kit in Mrs Brown's bureau that will do the trick nicely.'

'But where did you get it?'

'When you went home the other Sunday, Mrs Muldoon went out for afternoon tea with a friend and I took the opportunity to explore the closed-off rooms upstairs. This was hanging in the wardrobe of one of the unused guestrooms. There're dozens of them from when Mrs Muldoon was younger. They've been hung in there and forgotten about.'

'That doesn't mean we can just take it.'

'Jane, you work like a skivvy for a pittance. The dress is nowhere near your due. Let me do this for you because I want you to go out and have fun with Sidney tomorrow night.'

Jane's conscience was torn and a little voice inside her whispered, You'll look well in that colour, as well as Claudia Monroe at any rate.

The thought of Claudia Monroe in her evening finery, flirting with Sidney, swayed her as the unfairness of the box she'd been born into had crashed down around her ears. Sabrina was right she did work hard for very little in the way of either payment or thanks.

She took the dress from Sabrina and held it against herself. Cinderella would go to the ball.

Chapter Twenty

Jane put her hand in Sidney's as he helped her out of Harold. He'd veered in to park at the end of a row of motorcars lined up down the gas lamplit street. The drive from Allerton Road had been slow as he navigated the smoggy streets which had taken on an entirely different feel for Jane, unused as she was to venturing out after dark.

The smog was even thicker as she alighted onto the pavement and took in her surrounds. Shadowy shapes of the buildings either side of the street reared up and puddles of light from the lamps broke through billows of smog.

A lively beat along with the disembodied laughter and shouts of night-time revellers spliced through the night softening the spooky atmosphere. Jane's breath caught in her throat.

She barely recognised this girl about to go dancing with her employer's son. She pushed aside the thought of what her mam would have to say about her frequenting a dance hall where flappers liked to congregate. She'd overstepped the mark of approval where she was concerned the moment she'd taken the dress from Sabrina the night before.

She'd slipped the cool silk material over her head once Mrs Brown had left for the day and had felt a transformation beginning. She was like a butterfly emerging from its chrysalis and tonight she'd stretch her wings for the very first time.

Sabrina had indeed been a wonder with the needle and thread and by the time she'd finished with it, the dress could have been made to measure for Jane.

She felt a shiver of excitement at the thought of what Sidney would think when she took her coat off and he saw her in it for the first time. She'd fretted it was too short but Sabrina had been adamant it was the fashion she'd seen in the shops on her walks around the city.

They'd stayed up until the wee hours the night before as Sabrina had worked her magic on the dress and they should have both been yawning by the time the meal was cleared away that evening but they were running on adrenalin at the thought of what lay ahead.

As Sabrina had helped coil her hair, fixing it so it curled under before pinning it so that it looked, if not a la Louise Brooks, at least modern, she'd made Jane swear she'd imprint every detail of the evening ahead to share with her when she got home.

Jane had promised she would; it was the least she could do.

Sabrina whipped a lipstick from her pocket telling her it was Rimmel which was as a foreign a word as the feel of makeup on her mouth. When she'd looked in the mirror at the end result, Jane Evans the mill girl from Wigan had vanished.

She waited on the street for Sidney to see to Harold and then, as he held his arm out for her to take, she linked hers through his, glad of her coat, and they made their way down the pavement, being pulled towards the music, laughter and bright lights of the Grafton Rooms.

———◦———

JANE SAT AT THE TABLE with its white cloth feeling the bubbles of the unfamiliar golden drink playing on her tongue.

The appreciative gaze that Sidney had given her as she checked her coat hadn't alleviated her feelings of gaucheness when they'd first walked into the heaving ballroom. She'd been certain her naivety at where she found herself would be stamped on her face and had walked self-consciously over to the table they'd been ushered to by a bohemian looking waitress with a long white plume protruding from her headband.

Sidney had held the chair out for her looking every inch the gentlemen in his suit with his jacket's high lapels giving a glimpse of the shirt and tie beneath. She'd sat down and her eyes swung toward the dance floor eager to soak in the scene. The exuberance of the dancers was palpable and the energy frenetic.

The women were so carefree as they threw themselves wholeheartedly into the scandalous moves. Jane couldn't imagine herself in the midst of them even if she did look every inch the flapper thanks to Sabrina.

Now though, with the effects of the unaccustomed champagne the waitress had brought to their table warming her, she was ready to take on the world or at the very least take to the dance floor.

She'd never been anywhere quite so magnificent as the ballroom in which she found herself in all her life; the sumptuous gold gilt and deep rose panelled walls, the red velvet drapes framing the stage where the band had the crowd hopping and the glimpses of the waxed wooden floor between the myriad of T-bar heels stepping forward, backwards and kicking wildly. The air smelled of bodies, booze, cigarettes and something dangerously sensual that Jane couldn't put a name to.

She swung the foot of her crossed leg to the beat. The band—a drummer, a trumpeter, saxophonist and pianist—wore black suits, white shirts and black dicky bow ties. They showed no sign of puff as they smoothly launched into another set.

Sidney watched her foot for a moment and then grinding his cigarette out, he stood and undid his jacket hanging it on the back of the chair before rolling the sleeves of his shirt up. When he'd finished, he took her hand.

'Shall we dance?'

She couldn't hear his request over the ragtime beat but she read his lips and smiling her acquiescence stood.

Sidney steered her around the tables, where other couples and huddled groups were drinking and laughing in the seated mezzanine area, to the stairs which led down to the dance floor. She let him pull her down into the melee.

They came together as though to waltz and Sidney trapped her in his gaze as they swung their arms down holding hands as they shimmied apart before kicking their heels out to the side then to the front and back. Jane let go of his left hand and pushed her arm out fanning her hand back and forth.

The music coursed through her and her limbs took on a life of their own as she fell into the fast footwork she'd practised over and over with her friends.

Sidney was a superb partner and she couldn't stop smiling at the sheer joy of being one with the rhythm and in tune with him. He spun her around and kept pace as they came back together.

It was fun, pure, unadulterated fun, she thought, laughing up at Sidney who was grinning broadly down at her as the tune came to a finish.

Couples shuffled off the dance floor to seek refreshment and through a gap in the crowd, Jane caught sight of someone who was staring at her and Sidney with undisguised horror. Her heart stopped beating.

It was Claudia Monroe.

* * *

JANE KNEW SHE'D BEEN a fool for agreeing to come out. A fool for encouraging Sidney and an even bigger fool for allowing herself to believe something special was blossoming between them.

The sparkle had gone out of her evening when she locked eyes with Claudia on that crowded dance floor. The look on the other woman's face made her shudder. It had been an expression that meant trouble. Of that she was certain.

She put her hand to his ear as he led her from the dance floor and told him she felt bilious. She did feel queasy and a sense of panic was rising in her. She was desperate to get away.

'I'd like to go home, Sidney,' she shouted as they joined the throng of thirsty dancers edging back to their tables. Instead of sitting back down however she made for the foyer pushing past a couple who glanced back at her with raised brows wondering what her urgency was.

Sidney hurried after her perturbed, and once they'd retrieved their coats she followed him out into the cold night air the ragtime beat still ringing in her ears as he took her arm once more. Hers felt like a lead weight entangled in his.

The earlier joviality between them was gone.

He halted under a gas lamp to inspect her face and Jane knew she'd paled even though there was nothing physically the matter with her.

'That came on rather suddenly. Are you alright?' he asked, still catching his breath over their sudden exit.

'I think it must have been the champagne and the dancing,' Jane replied, trying to inject a note of apology into her tone for spoiling his evening by bringing it to an early close.

She made to walk on. 'If you don't mind I'm really not feeling very well.'

Sidney didn't say anything.

The drive home was a silent one and Jane blinked back the tears that were close to the edge. Her throat was tight. She wished he'd talk because she could sense his annoyance with her but there was nothing she could do about that.

It seemed an interminable age before Harold crunched over the gravel and nosed into the outbuilding.

She waited until the motor had stilled and, not waiting for Sidney to open the door, clambered out. She needed to put distance between herself and him and the whole horrible turn the evening had taken.

Her skin burned under the dress she'd no right to be wearing and she was desperate to take it off, climb into her nightgown and pull her bedcovers over her head. There was little chance of her being left to wallow though, she thought, trudging across the driveway to where she knew the side door had been left unlocked, not with Sabrina waiting up for her.

She heard Sidney's footsteps quicken as he strode to catch her up.

'Jane!' he called softly. 'I'm sorry you had an awful time. Please let me make it up to you.'

She stopped shivering despite her coat and turned to face him. She could make out the contours of his face but couldn't read his expression. There was no moon to illuminate them this evening.

'I didn't have an awful time, Sidney.' A sob caught in her throat.

'I'm not sure what I did but I've upset you and for that I'm sorry.'

Jane couldn't bear it. 'It wasn't you. Don't you see I had a marvellous time but I don't belong in that world. Your world. And I don't see the point in trying to pretend otherwise.'

His hands were suddenly on her waist as he pulled her close to him. She breathed in his cinnamon, smoky scent and felt the heat from his chest pressed against hers. As he dipped his head, his mouth seeking hers, she was aware of an urgency to his actions and then as her lips parted to meet his she was aware of nothing else.

Later, Jane would wonder how she'd known instinctively how to respond and how completely right that kiss had felt.

In that moment though, as the intensity of his mouth covering hers gathered and her legs felt in danger of giving way, she knew she was in danger of losing all her senses.

An owl's twit-twoo ripped through the silent night and they broke apart, panting and flushed at what had transpired.

Jane didn't know what to do with the tumult of emotions coursing through her. 'That shouldn't have happened, Sidney. It's wrong.' With a half sob, she turned and ran into the house.

Chapter Twenty-one

Jane burst through the door locking it behind her and resting her head against the solid timber. She took slow, steadying breaths grateful to find the kitchen in darkness.

Sabrina's voice broke through the shadows as she called out from her room, 'Jane?'

Jane padded across the floor and down the corridor; she could see a glow emanating from Sabrina's room. 'Yes, it's me.' She caught her breath.

There was the creaking of bedsprings. 'You're back early?' Sabrina appeared in the doorway holding her lamp up. She held the lamp higher to inspect Jane's face and Jane blinked at the light burning her retinas.

'You're very pink and your chin is red.' Sabrina smiled at the tell-tale signs she'd giggled over with Flo in the past.

Jane's hand went unbidden to her chin. It was tender where the shadow that decorated his jawline had rubbed it. A reminder of what had transpired minutes earlier.

'What was it like, then the Grafton? Was it full of beautiful people, you know bright, young things?'

'I suppose it was.' Jane moved towards her room. She wanted to go to bed. To pull the covers over her head and try to sleep so she could forget all about the evening. She should never have agreed to go but she owed Sabrina an account of what had happened.

'Help me get ready for bed and I'll tell you about it.'

Sabrina followed Jane into her room, setting her lamp down on the bedside table and under the flickering light she unpinned Jane's hair for her. It tumbled freely down her back.

Normally, Jane would brush her curls out and then twist her hair into a plait before getting into bed but she'd no energy for that.

Instead, she began to undress as she said, 'The ballroom was very grand as you'd expect.' The cotton of her nightgown was cool against her skin and it was a relief to fold the dress, hiding it away under her meagre belongings in her drawer. She waxed lyrically about the décor and the fashions of the other women while she did so then quickly washed before sitting down on the bed next to Sabrina.

'You danced of course?' Sabrina asked.

Jane nodded. She didn't want to mention why she'd brought the evening to a crashing halt because that meant thinking about Claudia Monroe. The way her pretty cut-glass eyes had narrowed once she'd recovered from the shock of seeing the Muldoons' housemaid with Sidney made shiver.

Something was wrong, Sabrina thought, inspecting her friend's face. 'Did you not want Sidney to kiss you?' she probed.

'I did. And it was wonderful and that's the problem.' Jane blurted out the awful moment she'd locked eyes with Claudia. 'I know what you've said but this is now, Sabrina, and me and Sidney, we're not supposed to be together. It'd never work.'

'You're only saying that because seeing Claudia Monroe wrong-footed you. Don't let her spoil your evening. She's jealous that's all. You're every inch her equal. Better in fact because you know how to do a hard day's graft and you've a kind heart, Jane Evans, don't you forget it. You're not to let her make you feel small or ruin your evening.'

'I'm worried she'll make trouble.' Jane's chin trembled.

'Listen to me. I suspect there are Claudia Monroes all through time. Put her out of your mind and concentrate on the lovely evening you had dancing and the goodnight kiss.'

Jane's hand fluttered to her lips. 'It was wonderful. But I mean it, Sabrina, I won't be encouraging his attentions any more. It's a fool's game and it's me who'll come off the fool.'

Sabrina was filled by a wistful longing for Adam. She'd never had the chance to know what it would be like to be kissed by him but she didn't want her sadness to temper Jane's mood further.

'You might be surprised, Jane. Night, night. Sweet dreams. I'll see you in the morning.'

Jane doused her light and clambered into bed, her fingers once more resting on her mouth. She knew sleep wouldn't come easily not when she could still feel Sidney's lips on hers.

———⬥———

'WHAT'S THE MATTER WITH you this morning, Jane?'

'Sorry, Mrs Brown.'

'I'm not a parrot. I shouldn't have to repeat myself.'

'No, Mrs Brown.'

'Well then, take the breakfast tray upstairs before the toast gets cold.'

Jane's stomach churned. She'd no choice but to face Sidney.

She had thought, when she'd prised her eyes open at Mrs Brown's sharp rat-tat on the door, about feigning illness. Pretending to be ill would only delay the inevitable though. She'd have to face him sometime. Better to get it over and done with she'd told herself.

Her own breakfast was barely touched and she flashed the picked at eggs a guilty glance. What her sisters would give to have that placed in front of them each morning. She'd have given anything to somehow magically put it in front of them.

Now, she trudged upstairs.

The landing, when she emerged from the servants' staircase was empty and the house quiet. She carried the tray through to the dining room but there was no sign of Sidney.

Her breath expelled with a gush. So much for might as well get it over with. She'd gladly be spared she thought, setting out the breakfast things.

She was set to beat a hasty retreat when, spinning around, she nearly collided with him.

'Oh, excuse me, sir!' She reverted to his formal title.

'Jane,' he didn't bother to correct her as he blocked her way. 'I'm sorry if I offended you last night. I didn't mean to overstep the mark. It's just—'

Jane didn't give him the opportunity to finish what he was going to say. 'I think, sir, it's for the best if we pretend last night never happened.'

She refused to meet his gaze and after a moment he stepped to the side and allowed her to pass.

Chapter Twenty-two

The week after Jane's ill-fated night dancing was the longest of her life.

The breakfast and dinner service each day was excruciating. She'd become an expert at avoiding all eye contact with Sidney.

He would always greet her with enthusiasm as though pleased to see her each morning and evening. It was as if he was determined to break down her precarious defences.

She wondered that Mrs Muldoon didn't ask her son why the atmosphere was thick with the sense of things unsaid as she served their evening meal.

Breakfast was the worst. Being alone with him for those few moments each morning was torturous. She hated herself for the way she ached for his hand to brush hers as she placed his plate down.

He persisted in asking her to join him and she persisted in saying no, she had chores to be getting on with. She missed sitting talking to him and the way it had buoyed her to face the rest of the day.

If she were honest with herself a part of her was terrified he'd get fed up with asking her and move on. She'd got what she'd wanted though. She'd told him whatever it was that had nearly taken root between them was wrong and it shouldn't happen again. It was her who'd pushed him away and if he did tire of cajoling her into joining him while he breakfasted then it was all her own doing.

The fact she considered she'd had a lucky escape insomuch as she had spent an evening with him without ramifications from his mother did not make her feel better. That evening where for a few short hours she was someone else, now seemed like a dream. This, she thought, as she sprinkled the damp tea leaves on the floor to prevent the dust rising as she swept the drawing room until her arm ached, was who she was. A skivvy, a servant.

She carted her broom and bucket down the stairs, her mood low. Mrs Brown looked up from where she was basting a ham at the work table as she appeared in the kitchen.

'Ah, there you are, Jane, look likely, lass. There's snails move faster than you do.'

Given her arm was knotted from the repetitive sweeping it was all she could do to keep quiet although she did make a rebellious clattering as she tidied her cleaning things away.

She closed the cupboard door and turning around caught sight of Sabrina giving her a cheery smile as she looked over her shoulder from where she was up to her elbows in water. She was washing the last of the lunch dishes and then she'd be tasked with the preparation of the evening meal's vegetables.

Jane tried her best to reciprocate. She didn't have it so bad, she told herself and if Sabrina could muster a smile like that given her circumstances she needed to try harder to be grateful for what she did have.

'The Monroes are dining with Mister Sidney and Mrs Muldoon this evening,' Mrs Brown announced painting the ham in a syrupy liquid with as much loving care as though she were Constable himself painting a landscape.

Jane's mood plummeted back down at this news. She caught a whiff of rum from the jug Mrs Brown was dipping her brush into and wondered what else was in the syrup.

'You can make a start on the stuffed mushrooms.' The cook gestured to the box of vegetables on the work table that must have been delivered while Jane was upstairs.

She dutifully retrieved the mushrooms, inhaling their earthy scent as she began to wipe them with a damp cloth as Mrs Brown had shown her how to do previously. The cook twittered on happy in her basting.

'Mark my words, you two. There'll be an announcement soon. It's only a matter of time before Mister Sidney and Miss Monroe become engaged. Won't they make a handsome couple?'

She was in her apple-cheeked element as she beamed delightedly across the wooden table at Jane and then twisted towards Sabrina. 'More elbow grease, Sabrina, that's what's needed. Those dishes won't wash themselves, now will they?'

'No, Mrs Brown.' Sabrina's heart was going out to poor Jane, having to listen to the cook going on about Sidney and the awful Miss Monroe.

Jane felt bile rise in her throat. Both at Mrs Brown's prediction and the thought of seeing Claudia Monroe this evening. She was certain Claudia had recognised her. Would she say something at dinner, following her barbed little comment up with that tinkly laugh?

It wasn't as if Sidney would be the one who'd bear the consequences of stepping out with the housemaid. Oh, his mother would not be happy especially given the time and effort she and Mrs Monroe were putting into trying to pair their offspring. But it wouldn't be Sidney she'd take her displeasure out on. No, it would be her who'd be out on her ear.

Jane's face went hot at the thought of having to go home to tell them all she'd left in disgrace.

'Jane, you're not scouring the mushrooms. Wipe them gently, girl, or there'll be nothing left of them to stuff.'

———⊙———

MRS BROWN PLACED THE laden tray of decorative mushrooms in Jane's hands. 'Off you go and take that sour puss expression off your face. You'll frighten the guests.'

Jane arranged her features into neutral and headed for the stairs. She felt as though she were going to face the guillotine.

She heard the animated chatter and chinking glasses as she exited the stairs and made her way the short distance to the drawing room.

'Ah, the hors d'oeuvres.' Mrs Muldoon smiled around the room which was heady with the scent of competing perfumes and cigar smoke. 'And what delight has Mrs Brown prepared for us this evening?'

'Crab stuffed mushrooms, my lady.' Jane curtsied and her voice came out thin and reedy. The tray shook in her hands earning her a frown from Mrs Muldoon. She was in her element as the gracious hostess and a nervy servant simply would not do.

'Crab? How delicious!' Iris Monroe exclaimed. 'Where on earth did your cook find that? She is indeed a wonder, Magnolia.' There was envy in the woman's tone.

'Oh yes, she's a miracle worker our Mrs Brown. We're so fortunate to have her.' Magnolia Muldoon smiled enigmatically, pleased to have invoked the green-eyed monster in her old friend. Iris could be insufferable at times with her insistence on one-upmanship. Round one to me, she thought.

Jane felt certain Claudia Monroe's eyes were branding her from where she sat in the armchair surveying her from under long lashes with her legs crossed elegantly at the ankles.

Sidney was standing by the fireplace, in conversation with Mr Monroe, he of the wandering eyes and hands. Mercifully both hands were visible to the ladies of the room which meant as Jane approached to offer the platter to the two gentlemen she wasn't in danger of a sly pat or squeeze of the leg.

Sidney, nursing a glass of amber liquid, declined the mushrooms with a shake of his head. She sensed he was annoyed over something. It was in the tenseness of his stance. She averted her eyes, giving a small smile as Mr Monroe declared the hors d'oeuvre quite delicious before his pudgy hand helped himself to another. She couldn't help a small shudder passing through her as she saw the blob of crabmeat clinging to the bristles of his moustache.

Jane moved away to proffer the platter to Mrs Monroe and Mrs Muldoon who were perched precariously on the two-seater sofa eagerly awaiting their turn to sample the delicacies.

There was much chatter as to how divine the mushrooms looked. They popped them in their mouths and as Jane traversed the short distance to where Miss Monroe was watching her like a cat tracking a mouse, a conversation as to the sweetness of the meat ensued.

Miss Monroe, holding a glass of something sparkly in her right hand, raised a neat eyebrow as Jane attempted a smile presenting her with the bite-sized morsels.

She looked particularly lovely in a green, fringed dress that was the exact shade of her eyes; her headband and feather matched but the hard set of her lipsticked mouth detracted from her beauty.

She stretched upward cobra-like and in a voice pitched for Jane's ears only hissed, 'You're a maid, girl. A plaything and no more.'

Jane's face flamed and she recoiled as though slapped. She managed to retain her footing and desperately wanted to turn and run but her feet had taken root. She was hypnotised by the other woman's poisonous gaze.

She thought that surely the others must have noticed what was happening but the background chatter was carrying on as it had before.

'He'll sow his wild oats and then when I click my fingers, he'll come running.'

Claudia licked her lips then, her tiny pointed pink tongue snaking out in anticipation as she took a mushroom from the tray. Holding it daintily between thumb and forefinger she glanced over at her mother and Mrs Muldoon declaring it to be a work of art.

Jane escaped to the wall, swallowing frantically so as not to be sick. Her stomach was roiling. She glanced at Sidney to see him searching her face, concern reflected in his eyes. It made her eyes burn and she blinked furiously. She could not cry or show weakness. She studied her shoes as she regulated her breathing.

The worst was over, she told herself. Claudia Monroe had had her say. She'd let it lie now. There was only the dinner to get through and then this evening's ordeal would be over.

This time, as she worked the room with the hors d'oeuvres Claudia waved her away.

'Oh, I couldn't possibly.' She tittered before downing what was left in her glass.

———◉———

THE CONVERSATION OVER the dinner table was stilted, much to Magnolia Muldoon's disappointment. If she could have stretched her leg far enough she'd have liked to have nudged Sidney with her foot, hard, in a signal for him to snap out of it.

He was being positively taciturn and he'd been like it all week. She'd not seen him behave like this since he was a child in a sulk over something or other he felt wronged by. Perhaps, she mused, as the girl Jane fussed around serving a thick slice of ham to Iris, it was being stuck in the shop and not on the road as was his preference that had him in such foul form. It was no excuse for his behaviour though.

She watched Claudia valiantly trying to engage her moody son in conversation only to receive short almost monosyllabic replies. She'd have words with him later. He was being rude and it would not do.

Iris's awful husband was making short work of his claret. She wasn't silly; she'd seen the girl jump as she passed by him. Iris needed to reign the old lech in she thought.

She couldn't understand Sidney's reticence where Claudia was concerned. The dear girl was gorgeous and that green was divine on her. Her conversation was sparkling and she was accomplished on the piano. It was high time he stopped playing the field and settled down. She needed grandchildren to continue the Muldoon legacy and what more could he want in a wife?

Magnolia sipped her wine but it didn't quell the niggle of annoyance at things not going to plan and she sipped a little faster. It would not do because Magnolia Muldoon was a woman who was used to getting her own way.

Jane continued around the table, offering Miss Monroe a slice of the ham with the sticky glaze. She could feel Sidney watching her and a flush crept up her neck.

She had to stop the shudder that threatened at the sickly-sweet smile offered up to her as she opened the tongs and placed the ham on the young woman's plate.

It all happened very quickly after that. As she moved past Claudia her foot caught on something and the unexpectedness of it saw her overbalance with the weight of the heavy platter. She found herself falling forward, the platter airborne and before she'd even had time to register what was happening she'd landed in an undignified heap.

In shock, Jane stayed like that for a moment before Sidney pushed his chair back and offered her his hand to help her up. Her scorched face whispered apologies to him, Mrs Muldoon and their guests as she fought hard against the brimming tears. All the while Claudia Monroe's mouth twitched with a barely suppressed smirk.

She'd tripped her deliberately Jane realised, anger flaring through her mortification but it was futile.

'Are you alright, Jane?' Sidney searched her face as his mother watched from the other end of the table. *Jane?* The penny dropped. Magnolia knew exactly why Sidney was paying no heed to Claudia. He was smitten with the servant girl. It was written all over his face. And that would not do.

Chapter Twenty-three

Days had passed since the evening of Jane's humiliation at the hands of Claudia Monroe but it was still fresh and raw in her mind. The remainder of the evening after the debacle with the ham had been stilted and the family had not been back to visit since.

Jane had fully expected to be given her marching orders by Mrs Muldoon that very night but it hadn't been forthcoming. She'd sensed the older woman watching her ever since though and had vowed not to give her cause for any complaint.

Thank God for Sabrina who'd let her cry on her shoulder and insisted it wasn't the end of the world and that girls like Claudia Monroe always revealed their true colours in the end. She'd get her comeuppance. Jane had taken comfort in that but it hadn't helped her shake the humiliation she'd felt.

She'd informed Mrs Brown of what had happened, wanting to get in before Mrs Muldoon. The cook had taken in Jane's trembling hands and mottled complexion and had taken pity on her. She'd told her off for not taking more care but had left it there much to Jane's relief because she really could not have taken much more.

She'd no idea just how much more she was going to have to withstand.

As for Sidney, he'd tried to talk to her later that awful evening as he smoked a cigar in the drawing room, as he had the first evening he'd engaged her in conversation. She'd cleared away the detritus left behind in silence ignoring his overtures. She didn't want his pitying comfort.

She'd been trying to redeem herself to both Mrs Brown and Mrs Muldoon by working herself to the bone ever since. It helped not to give herself a moment to think.

This particular day, she was carrying down the last of the lunch dishes when a sharp knocking sounded on the side door.

'Come in,' Mrs Brown sang out. She was expecting the fish man to call.

It wasn't the fish man Jane saw before depositing the dishes on the worktop but rather a telegram boy. He was backlit by the afternoon sunlight but she could make out the dark uniform, the satchel slung over his shoulder, and the envelope he was holding in his hand.

'I've a telegram for Miss Jane Evans,' he said stepping down into the kitchen.

'For me?' She was puzzled. Her mam wrote to her but she didn't have the money for telegrams. Telegrams were for emergencies. She bit her lip and hung back feeling frightened.

'I don't see any other Jane Evans here do you, Sabrina?' Mrs Brown said unperturbed as she pressed the lattice pastry down on top of her apple pie before beginning to crimp the edges.

Sabrina, filling the sink with water, shook her head.

Jane took the envelope from the boy who looked no more than seventeen, remembering to thank him. He nodded his head in acknowledgement and said he'd be on his way.

She'd have liked to have gone off to the privacy of her room but as that wasn't an option she'd no choice but tear the envelope open there in the kitchen.

She read the bold type and it swam before her eyes not making any sense.

Blinking rapidly, she waited for the letters to arrange themselves properly so she could re-read the urgent message. This time there was no mistaking the words and as they sank in she grabbed hold of the kitchen table, the scent of cinnamon and apples in her nostrils as her legs buckled and the colour seeped out of her world.

'Jane, girl, what is it?' The cook looked over at the table barely holding Jane up and barrelled over to help her sit down.

'There, there. You're alright now. What is it? What's happened? Sabrina fetch the girl a cup of tea, she's had a shock.'

Jane was still clutching the telegram. She handed it to Mrs Brown who pulled a pair of spectacles from her apron pocket and quickly scanned the text.

A terrible accident yesterday. Mam, Dad hit by motorcar way home from doctors. Both killed at scene. You must come home. Frank Evans.

'Oh, my. Oh, dear. What a thing. You poor, poor girl.'

Sabrina put the tea in front of Jane and Mrs Brown whispered the tragic news before urging Jane to have a sip. 'The sugar will help with the shock, luv.'

'Oh my God, Jane.' Sabrina pulled a chair over to sit next to her before wrapping her arm around her shoulder. She was in turmoil at the horror of the news her friend had received.

Jane did as she was told on automatic pilot, uncaring as the hot tea scalded her mouth and unable to make sense of what had happened. Her mam and dad were gone? It couldn't be true. But it was there in front of her in bold black typeface. Poor Frank, her poor, poor sisters.

As the sugar seeped through her veins she looked at Mrs Brown. 'I must go to them.' The thoughts as to what would happen to them all now jumbled in on top of one another.

The cook retrieved a hanky from her pocket and dabbed Jane's cheeks. She hadn't been aware of the tears sliding down them.

'They'll need me to take care of them, Mrs Brown. Sabrina, they'll need me.'

'Of course,' Mrs Brown soothed.

'You must go,' Sabrina said tightening her grip on Jane's shoulder.

Jane had to make sure they were alright. Her mind was spinning and she lowered her head onto her hands as her body was wracked by sobs.

Sabrina rubbed her back while Mrs Brown clucked over her.

Jane was too overwhelmed by her grief to hear her say to Sabrina, 'Fetch the kitty, take out two pennies and go to the phone box down the road and telephone Doctor Houghton.'

Sabrina didn't want to leave Jane but she could see the sense in the cook's instructions and she did as she'd said.

The next thing Jane was aware of was a strange man giving her a sleeping draught.

'It's veronal, Mrs Brown. She'll sleep soundly and then tomorrow arrangements can be made for her to return home when her body has had a chance to recover from the trauma of the news.'

'Yes, Doctor Houghton. Thank you for coming.'

Mrs Brown and Sabrina steered Jane to her quarters and as the sheets were pulled up over her, blackness fell like a curtain.

THE KNOCKING ON THE door woke Jane as it did every morning. She had a blissful second or two of not remembering the events of the previous day but then realised a warm body rested against her with an arm slung across her protectively. It was Sabrina and the memory of the telegram slapped her around the face and her throat tightened. She forced herself upright, her eyes feeling heavy and her head woolly and as Sabrina stirred she repeated yesterday's sentiment. 'I've got to go home.'

'Yes. I'd better get dressed too. Mrs Brown will have a cup of tea waiting for you, Jane,' Sabrina said, swinging her legs off the bed. Reluctant to leave her friend alone for even a second, she paused to hug her before padding back to her room. She would be expected to carry Jane's load today and she'd do so gladly.

Jane went through the motions of getting dressed, the splash of cold water to her face shaking away the inertia whatever she'd been given yesterday had left behind.

Opening her door, she could hear voices in the kitchen and as she walked towards them the stone flags beneath her feet felt precarious, but then everything she'd held dear and familiar had been ripped away from her, was it any wonder the earth no longer felt stable?

Sidney was there, Mrs Brown speaking to him in hushed tones. She stopped on seeing Jane appear.

'I'm so terribly sorry, Jane.' Sidney stepped toward her as though to take her in his arms but Jane, despite everything, was still conscious of where she was and stepped back.

'Thank you, sir. I can't believe it. It doesn't seem real.' She looked to Mrs Brown in a vague hope she'd tell her it was all a nasty dream but her face was soft with sympathy.

'I don't suppose it will, Jane, until you get home.'

She nodded. It was a prospect she desperately wanted but dreaded with equal measure.

Sabrina was nowhere to be seen and Jane could only assume she'd been sent upstairs to see to her duties.

'Mister Sidney has volunteered to take you home, Jane, isn't that kind?'

Jane looked at Sidney through heavy lidded eyes and thanked him. 'It's very kind.'

'Not at all. It's the least we can do. I've spoken to mother and you're to take as long as you need. There'll be a place here for you to come back to when you're ready.'

Jane dipped her head in thanks.

'If you get your things we can leave straight away.'

Chapter Twenty-four

The drive to Wigan was a quiet one. Sidney concentrated on the road, driving at a sedate pace while Jane sat alongside him. Her hands twisted in her lap as she stared dully out the window.

It was a motor car like the one she was sitting in now that had killed her parents. How had it happened? Frank would fill in the blanks soon enough, she supposed. The sentence, you, Frank, Mary and little Emma are orphans, ran over and over in her head and the thought was terrifying.

Sidney parked Harold in the same spot as when he'd brought her to the Evans family's stone cottage on that first occasion. She couldn't believe it was less than a month ago. She'd been so happy to see them all and them her.

It was a different scene altogether today as her brother peered out the window before opening the door and coming to meet her, his gait stooped, his shoulders slumped.

'Oh, Frank,' she sobbed falling into his embrace.

''Tis terrible, Jane, terrible.'

Sidney held back to let them share their grief in private.

When her brother released her, she looked past him to see her sisters in the doorway, their little faces sombre and frightened. She ran to them and they clung to her fiercely.

Jane took her sisters inside and Frank ushered Sidney into the cottage. Already, Jane thought it felt forlorn with the life force of her mam and dad no longer filling it.

Little Emma insisted on sitting on Jane's knee even though she was too big and Mary sat at her feet as Frank relayed what the policeman had told him when he'd come to find him at the mine with the news of what had happened in town.

'Mam and Dad had been to see Doctor Jones in town. They'd just left the chemist with Dad's medicine. The motorist was driving too quickly,' he said, his voice flat. 'He rounded the corner as they stepped into the road.'

Jane's hand was to her mouth, with the horror of the imagined scene and she pulled little Emma who was sucking her thumb in close.

'Have the children eaten?' she asked her brother wondering what on earth she'd find in the cottage to feed them.

'Marie came last night with soup and sat with them while I saw to things in town.'

Jane didn't want to ask what things but she guessed he'd had to confirm it was their mam and dad. She reached out and rested her hand on his arm briefly. It must've been a terrible task for him.

'They've not eaten today though, said they weren't hungry.'

'They must eat, Frank. We've all got to keep our strength up. It's what Mam and Dad would have wanted.'

She was dimly aware of Sidney having left the room and when he reappeared he had a basket, again filled with supplies. She managed a grateful smile and thanked God for small mercies like a meal to put on the table.

SIDNEY SET OFF BACK for Allerton Road shortly after their packed lunch of leftovers. The girls, despite their protestations, had eaten well. Frank too had made light work of the meal but Jane had only picked. Sidney, she'd noticed had barely touched a thing. She didn't know whether it was because he didn't feel like eating or because he wanted to ensure there was plenty for them.

She opened the door to the cottage to wave him off despite his telling her there was no need. The sunshine was bright after the dim light inside the cottage and it was at odds with the sombre mood of the day.

They walked down the path and Jane said, 'I can't thank you enough for bringing me today,' she hesitated, sir suddenly seemed wrong.

'Sidney,' he said softly.

'Sidney.'

Her hand reached out to open the wooden gate but Sidney stopped her and took both her hands in his. He squeezed them tightly. 'You will get through this, Jane, you're stronger than you think.'

She shook her head. 'I'm not but I don't have a choice, do I? The girls need me.' A sudden panic filled her. The girls, what would happen? Frank had his sweetheart, Marie. They'd wed soon enough and set up a home of their own. How was she to support her sisters? Emma was too young little to be left on her own while she went out to work and where would she even find work here? It was all too exhausting to think about.

'I shall wait for you, you know.'

Jane looked up at him squinting into the light. She could see that he meant it and she was too tired to argue because right at that moment she was so very grateful.

Chapter Twenty-five

The day of the funeral was suitably dull with a persistent drizzle. So many tears had been shed in the preceding week that Jane was startled to find there were still more. She dabbed her eyes and heard Frank blowing his nose. Jane, her sisters and Frank sat in the front pew of the packed stone village church where she'd spent every Sunday morning of her life until she'd left home for Allerton Road.

The familiar feeling of her bottom growing numb set in and she recalled how her mam would frown as she began fidgeting, just as Mary and little Emma were now. A smile played at the corner of her mouth at the memory of her mam lamenting as they walked home from the church one morning. 'Why he can't just say what he has to say, let us sing our hymns and say a prayer is beyond me. I've never heard a man talk so much as Father Arnold.'

It was heart-warming to see so many of the townsfolk had come to see them off.

She tuned Father Arnold's intoning out, her eyes fixed on the simple boxes containing the broken bodies of her parents. Soon they'd form a procession out of the church and into the yard outside where Jane's grandparents also lay to say a final goodbye to them. Her parents would be laid to rest with the burble of the stream that ran alongside the churchyard singing to them.

Behind the huddled group of four sat Aunt Phyllis and Uncle Carl, her mam's sister and husband, who'd travelled up from London as soon as the news had reached them. It had been decided in an around the table discussion that her sisters were to return with them to London. Their own children, three girls, were all married now and they could devote themselves to seeing right by Mary and Emma. 'It's what our Elsie would have wanted.' Phyllis had said.

It was true, Jane had thought, even though her heart was breaking at the thought of her sisters growing up so far away. She was in no position to support them and Frank would struggle as it was to look after himself and Marie.

Aunt Phyllis and Uncle Carl had a comfortable life in the capital, far easier than the one her parents had forged here in the north. Theirs was a generous and kind offer and to let them go was the right thing to do.

Frank would stay in the cottage and Marie would join him after they were wed. She liked to think this would please her mam and dad. The cottage at least was something to show for all their hard graft. As for her, she'd return to Allerton Road. Sidney had said her position would be held open. The thought that she had nowhere else to go filled her with loneliness.

Father Arnold told them to stand and she closed her eyes as a final prayer was said.

———————— ◉ ————————

IT WAS AS SHE FILED out of the chilly church with her sisters' hands firmly in hers that she saw him sitting near the back. Sidney. He'd come to bring her back to Liverpool.

He met her watery stare and offered her a smile.

It was possible, Jane thought, stepping outside into the drizzle to wait for her mam and dad to say so much without words. In that smile, she'd been warmed by his sympathy and sorrow at her loss and by his obvious love.

The townsfolk filled the churchyard with its moss-covered headstones. Aunt Phyllis and Uncle Carl had kindly offered to pay for a headstone for the family's plot. They'd also organised the tea and cake back at the cottage following the burial.

The hole the two coffins were lowered into gaped and then handfuls of soil were scooped up and tossed down onto the twin boxes lying side by side just as they had been in life. Jane said her final goodbye.

SIDNEY HELD BACK DURING the funeral tea back at the cottage giving Jane and her family the space to accept condolences and listen to the reminiscing of their fellow mourners.

It was over an hour before the last of the townsfolk trickled away leaving just the family, Marie who was as good as family, and Sidney alone in the cottage.

'Girls, go and get your things,' Phyllis said, faux joviality in her voice. 'We've a long journey.' They'd agreed it would be best to leave at the first opportunity.

Little Emma scampered over to Jane and grabbed hold of her leg. 'Don't want to go.'

Traitorous tears sprang at the sight of the imploring face staring up at her. 'I want to stay with Jane.'

Mary came over and tried to prise her little sister off her. 'Come on, Emma, we have to be brave. You know that.'

'No, I don't want to go.' The little girl's voice climbed an octave and Jane's throat felt as if it were closing over.

'Emma, listen to me. Aunt Phyllis and Uncle Carl are going to look after you very well,' Jane said, bending down to look her in the eye.

Little Emma stole her chance and snatched at one of Jane's curls, further anchoring herself to her as she twirled it around her finger just as she'd done when it was three to a bed.

'You won't ever have to go to bed with pains in your tummy again,' Jane cajoled.

Aunt Phyllis looked aghast at the thought of members of her own family going to bed hungry.

Her mam had been a proud woman, Jane thought. Never letting on how dire things had become after their dad had become ill and Frank's hours cut back.'

'I'll come and see you as often as I can. And Mary will look after you. Won't you, Mary?' Bless her Jane thought, seeing Mary's pale face and frightened eyes as she pushed past her own feelings to reassure her sister that she would indeed take care of her.

Mary held her hand out to her sister once more and this time little Emma took it.

Jane swallowed the sob lodged in her throat. As Mary had said, they had to be brave for all their sakes. Histrionics would not help.

Her sisters retrieved the cases that had been brought up by Aunt Phyllis for both of them to fill although their scant belongings would have easily filled one.

'You'll always be welcome at our home, Jane, Frank,' Aunt Phyllis said and Uncle Carl nodded agreement.

'Phyllis, the train leaves in twenty minutes. Best not to drag things out, eh?'

The two eldest Evans children murmured their agreement and gave their younger sisters one final embrace.

Uncle Carl took Mary's hand and Aunt Phyllis little Emma's and with their cases held in their free hands, the foursome filed out the door.

Jane, Frank and Marie moved to the door to wave them off, Frank pulling his sister in under his arm in a comforting embrace.

'Smile, Jane. Don't let them see you get upset.'

Jane sniffed and made her mouth curve upwards. It took all her will not to break down when little Emma turned and looked over her shoulder a fat tear rolling down her cheek before they disappeared out of sight down the lane.

Jane turned then and buried herself in her brother's jacket.

When she was spent, she stepped back releasing her brother.

'Frank,' Marie said, giving Jane an apologetic glance, 'My mam and dad are expecting us. We're to have our dinner with them. Frank doesn't like eating alone and you'll be heading back to Liverpool soon.' She indicated her head toward the open door where Sidney had hung back to let them say their farewell.

Already she was staking her claim on her brother, Jane thought, but then dismissed the uncharitable thought. She was grateful he had Marie and her family.

Frank ducked inside to say goodbye to Sidney and to retrieve his hat.

'I'll look after him, Jane.' Marie said and Jane summoned up a grateful smile. 'And you'll always be welcome in our home too.'

Our home, she thought, eyeing the stone walls that had been her home for so many years. How strange that in a few months when Marie and Frank exchanged vows she would from thereon in be a guest inside those four walls.

She waved her brother and his fiancée off with a promise she'd be back for the wedding, before venturing inside the cottage to find Sidney had taken his suit jacket off and rolled up his shirt sleeves. She watched as he took the pot of water he'd heated on the stove and poured it into the tub in order to make a start on the dishes.

The sight of him standing where her mam had once stood made her freeze momentarily but as he put the first of the upturned saucers on the worktop to drain she spoke. 'You shouldn't be doing those, Sidney. Let me.' She moved alongside him but he didn't step away.

'I want to.' He scrubbed industriously and Jane watched the smattering of dark hair on his forearms.

'Thank you for coming today. I wasn't sure how I'd get back to Liverpool.'

'How could I not have come. I only met your parents once but I could tell they were good people. They had to have been to have raised you and, I wanted to be here for you.' He didn't turn his head from his task.

'That's very kind, thank you.'

'Kind? There's nothing kind about it.' He took his hands from the water, drying them on a cloth he pulled from the stove handle. 'My reasons are completely selfish. I wanted to see you. I've been desperate to see you. I never believed in love at first sight but I fell in love with you the very first moment I saw you. I want to marry you, Jane, and I know you said—'

Jane silenced him by pushing her body against his. She wanted to take comfort from his nearness, to forget the horror of the past while, and just be in the moment with him. Life was too short, too fragile and too precious not to squeeze everything you could from it.

His arms encircled her and she raised her head to meet his mouth as it closed over hers. She wanted the blissful escape from all the misery. She wanted Sidney, she loved him too and knew she wouldn't push him away.

Chapter Twenty-six

'It will pass quickly. I promise,' Sidney assured Jane as she stood wrapped in his arms in the drawing room. She'd been lighting the fire when he'd come looking for her.

Resting her head against his chest she felt the steady rhythm of his heart beneath his shirt. She breathed in the cigar smell and that unique sweet, spiced scent that was his alone and wished she could bottle it. That way she could bring it out when she was missing him most, inhale and feel as though he were there with her instead of miles away trawling the Yorkshire countryside in search of treasure.

His words didn't reassure her. She knew how these stolen moments between them made the drudge of her days bearable. How they eased the grief that lurked so close to the surface. Those snatched embraces in the shadows throughout her working hours gave her the promise of a brighter future.

She'd sensed Sidney's need in the way he'd pressed his hardness against her but she would not skulk about his home. What they'd done together that afternoon after the funeral was something she refused to be ashamed of but, the next time they made love, she would be his wife.

A brighter future was what her parents would have wanted for her. There was comfort in that. She refused to think what they'd have to say about her having consummated hers and Sidney's partnership without a wedding ring on her finger.

She'd confided in Sabrina just the night before as her friend sat hunched down the bottom of her bed how Sidney made her feel. She told her of their lovemaking after the funeral knowing she wouldn't be judged. She confided too how it had hurt at first but how she sensed the next time they came together it would be wonderful.

'I don't want him to go,' she'd said.

'He'll come back, Jane,' Sabrina replied, the wistful note not escaping Jane's attention.

'Just like you'll get back to your Adam.'

'But I'm not even sure he's mine to get back to anymore.'

Sabrina's shoulders had slumped and Jane had been uncertain what to say so in the end, she'd simply told her she'd added her to her prayers of an evening.

Sidney and Jane had been circumspect since her arrival back at Allerton Road. There was to be no whiff of impropriety by either of them until they could announce their engagement. This they'd do upon Sidney's return in three weeks. He wanted to wait until then as he felt it unfair to leave Jane to manage his mother with the news of their engagement on her own.

It was a thought that had filled Jane with terror too and she'd readily agreed to wait.

She'd been dreading this morning though. With Mr Thompson, Sidney's business partner, now fit and well and ensconced in the shop on Bold Street once more, Sidney was headed to Yorkshire and beyond on an overdue buying trip.

He'd spend his days hunting for hidden treasures tucked away in old farmhouses or gathering dust and forgotten about in country manor houses.

Now, he kissed her on the tip of her nose. 'I hate the thought of leaving you slaving away here. It isn't right.'

Jane didn't say anything; there was no point. She'd continue to toil for Magnolia Muldoon until his return. It was the way it had to be for now.

Neither of them was aware as they lost themselves in a lingering kiss goodbye of the woman lurking outside in the hallway.

Magnolia Muldoon's breath came in ragged bursts. She was raging. Sidney was being taken advantage of by a money-grabbing harlot. She regretted holding the girl's position open now but at the time it would have seemed heartless not to.

Her insides churned as she slunk silently back down the hall to the library from where she'd emerged a few minutes earlier having chosen a volume to read in the drawing room. She'd woken early and, frustrated by her inability to get back to sleep, had opted to search out a book and read until her breakfast was ready.

Her heart as she retreated to her bedroom was banging and her blood boiling at the knowledge her son planned to make the trollop in her employ his wife.

———◦———

JUST AS JANE HAD KNOWN they would, the days stretched long in Sidney's absence. He'd been gone over a week and she missed him dreadfully. The house was overwhelming with him not filling the vast spaces and the silence unsettling. She yearned for the evenings when she could chat with Sabrina.

Then, there were the watchful eyes of Magnolia Muldoon following her around in the daylight hours. Her soon to be mother-in-law's steely gaze as Jane moved about her duties was making her feel more and more ill at ease.

She'd the uncanny sensation the older woman knew about her romance with her son and was biding her time as to what she would do about it.

She tried to take comfort from Sabrina's comments that there was no way she could know and it was her angst at how she'd react when she and Sidney shared their news that had her feeling like so.

It wasn't the only unpleasantness. The kindness Mrs Brown had shown her in the aftermath of her parents passing was wearing thin as she grew more annoyed each passing day with Jane's absentmindedness.

Jane was trying her hardest but her mind was so full of Sidney she was constantly making silly mistakes and instructions needed to be given twice or even thrice before she'd grasp what she was to do.

It was, Jane thought, bone tired as Sabrina went to her own room and she dimmed her light at the end of a long day, a miserable existence. It was only Sabrina's company and the thought that in a few short weeks when Sidney returned things would be altogether different that spurred her on each morning.

CLAUDIA MONROE WAITED until Jane's afternoon off to do her worst.

Magnolia Muldoon was sitting in her favoured armchair in the drawing room attempting needlepoint work when Sabrina announced Miss Monroe's unexpected arrival.

She raised her chin and, trying not to squint, told Sabrina to see her in as she put her embroidery to one side. It hadn't been going well. She was finding her eyes bothersome these days. Her sight wasn't what it once had been and such close work was becoming a strain. She refused to wear the awful spectacles she'd been prescribed because they added, in her opinion, ten years to her. Ten years she could ill afford!

Magnolia pushed herself up to greet Claudia who was looking particularly fetching today in pink and as she kissed the girl on her cheek she wondered over the fool her son had been.

'We'll take tea and cake in here, thank you,' she directed at Sabrina who disappeared to do her bidding.

Claudia settled herself down and engaged her mother's friend in idle chit-chat as to who had been wearing what at the luncheon she'd attended the day before while they waited for the refreshments to be served.

Sabrina eyed the young woman with distaste as she set the tea things out a short while later. She'd have liked to have lingered in the hall to listen to the conversation between the pair but Mrs Brown had given her strict instructions not to dally as she was needed downstairs.

Claudia watched as Magnolia played mother, accepting the cup of tea from her with a gracious smile and hoping the generous slice of pound cake would offset the festering bitterness she'd felt since the evening she'd encountered Sidney and his servant girl at the Grafton.

'Magnolia, I wondered if I might confide something in you only it's rather delicate you see as it concerns Sidney.'

Magnolia put her tea down. 'Of course, you may, my dear.' She was all ears. The day had been panning out extremely dully until now.

'My conscience has been keeping me awake and I've mulled over whether it was my place to tell you this or not but in the end, I've concluded I simply must. For your and Sidney's sake. People talk you see.'

Magnolia wanted to scream at her to get on with it but she kept her concerned façade firmly in place.

'What it is, Magnolia, is your housemaid, Miss Evans I think her name is, she's been behaving inappropriately by stepping out with Sidney. I saw them with my own two eyes at the Grafton. She was dancing the Charleston no less.'

This elicited a satisfactory shocked intake of breath from Magnolia and Claudia stole a glance at her. Displeasure had crept in around the corners of the older woman's mouth and her lips had tightened.

'Of course, it's not my place to question Sidney but you know what people are like. Let's just say tongues were wagging about the spectacle she was making of herself and I didn't feel it was fair on you not to know what's been going on under your own roof.'

'Quite. It's not.' Magnolia's voice was clipped.

Claudia wasn't finished yet though. She'd planted the seed and now it was time to water it. 'I wondered too how a girl on a housemaid's wage could afford such a dress as the one she was wearing. It's been bothering me. It was rather beautiful and obviously quality you see.'

Magnolia's eyebrows shot up at this. Here it was handed to her just like the afternoon tea had been on a silver platter. A perfectly legitimate reason to let the girl go. Stealing! She had to have because Magnolia was aware of her impoverished background. The timing was perfect with Sidney being away.

When he returned home Jane Evans would be long gone.

Chapter Twenty-seven

It was Monday and Jane's morning had started out like any other in the week since Sidney had left. She'd been about to take the lady of the house's breakfast up and was filling the milk jug when Magnolia Muldoon herself blew into the kitchen like the eye of a bad storm without having knocked.

Her thunderous sights were set firmly on Jane as she insisted she take her to her quarters right that very minute. 'I've good reason to believe you've stolen from me.'

Mrs Brown, whose hand was up a chicken's backside as she made an early start on the luncheon went white with the shock of this impromptu appearance and accusation.

'Mrs Muldoon, what on earth is going on?' she managed to splutter.

Sabrina and Jane locked eyes in silent acknowledgement of the dress Jane had worn to go dancing. Somehow she'd found out about it.

All Jane could think of was that Claudia must have decided to tell Mrs Muldoon about her sighting of her and Sidney at the Grafton that evening and Magnolia had resolved to accuse her of theft. How she'd decided on that she didn't know. She'd known Claudia would strike. She'd been biding her time was all.

Now, with her legs feeling like a quivering jelly, she knew she'd no choice but to do what the imposing woman was demanding. Sabrina shot her a panicked glance but there was nothing she could do now. The wheels were in motion and hearing the authoritative clip-clopping of Magnolia Muldoon's heels following behind her Jane forced herself to walk down the corridor to her room. She felt as though she were walking the plank.

Mrs Muldoon went straight to Jane's drawers and began to rifle through the contents of the top drawer.

Cowering in the doorway, Jane tried not to feel violated. The mementoes the woman was defiling were all she had left of her home. She jumped as Mrs Muldoon slammed the drawer shut and she held her breath waiting for the inevitable as she wrenched the second drawer open.

Sure enough, as she pushed Jane's undergarments aside, a triumphant look settled on Magnolia Muldoon's paunchy features. She pulled the silvery fabric out and waved it at Jane with such vehemence she shrank backwards.

'You can pack your things. I'll not have a thief under my roof!'

Jane opened her mouth to explain but registering the satisfied gleam in Sidney's mother's eyes she knew she would be wasting her breath. She didn't want excuses. She wanted her gone. She could see plain as day the woman was pleased to have found a reason to get rid of her.

The uncanny feeling she'd had of Magnolia Muldoon knowing about her and Sidney's romance these last weeks since she'd returned to the house had been well-founded. Just as she'd worried she would, she'd deemed her precious son's relationship with her unacceptable.

Jane threw her things into her case and through the blurred vision of unshed tears at the unfairness of it all, walked through the kitchen murmuring her apology to Mrs Brown before taking the stairs to the servants' entrance for the very last time. There'd been no sign of Sabrina but she didn't dare hover longer to say goodbye.

She was halfway down the driveway when she heard the crunching of footsteps hurrying after her. 'Jane, wait!'

It was Sabrina, the case Mrs Brown had given her banging against her leg as she hurried to catch her up. 'You didn't think I'd leave you on your own did you?'

Jane didn't think she'd been so grateful to see anybody in all her days.

Both girls turned at the sound of another shout only this time it was Mrs Brown.

'I'm so sorry, Mrs Brown,' Jane mumbled as the portly woman, panting and red in the face, caught up to them. 'Sidney asked me to a dance and I wanted to look nice for him. It was wrong to take what wasn't mine.' She would not apologise for going to the dance in the first instance. There would be no more apologising where she and Sidney were concerned. Why should she apologise for being in love?

'You'd not be the first girl to make a silly mistake for a man.'

'It wasn't Jane's mistake,' Sabrina interrupted. 'It was me who was to blame. It was my idea not Jane's I talked her into it. I tried to tell Mrs Muldoon just now but she wouldn't listen.'

'It was me she wanted rid of Sabrina because of Sidney. It wouldn't matter what you said.' Jane said.

Mrs Brown's head swung from one girl to the other, trying to keep up with what they were saying. She shook her head. It was a cliché was what it was. A romance between the master of the house and the servant. Sadly, it was always the servant who paid.

'Will you go home?' she asked.

'No, it's not my home anymore. It belongs to my brother and his soon to be wife.'

'Where then?'

'I've managed to put a little aside these last few weeks with not sending money home. I shall find lodgings in the city I suppose and wait until Sidney returns. We're to be married, Mrs Brown. It will all be alright when Sidney gets back.'

Mrs Brown looked at her, surprise in her eyes which quickly faded to sympathy. 'I'm sure you are, dear.'

Jane wouldn't allow the doubt in the cook's voice to crush her faith in Sidney. He'd keep his word.

'And what do you think you're doing?' The cook turned to Sabrina.

'I won't leave Jane on her own, Mrs Brown,' Sabrina said. 'But I want you to know I'm grateful to you for taking me in and trusting in me enough to take me on here.' She gestured toward the crumbling big house. 'I'm sorry if you regret it now.'

Mrs Brown shook her head. They were so headstrong the youth of today. 'I don't regret it and I'm glad you are a faithful friend, Sabrina. That to me speaks volumes as to your character.'

She reached into her pocket and retrieved a pen and the notebook she usually kept in the bureau in the kitchen for writing the day's menu. Opening it she scribbled something down and then tore the page out.

'You'll both need a roof over your head. I've a cousin, a respectable widow who runs a boarding house on Upper Parliament Street. I dare say she'd be glad of extra hands to help her about the place if you tell her I sent you. If you strike her on a good day you might be able to come to an arrangement.' She pressed the paper into Sabrina's hand.

Both girls murmured their thanks, touched by the cook's concern for their welfare.

'Will you tell him where I am when he returns? Please, Mrs Brown,' Jane asked.

The portly woman nodded, knowing she'd do no such thing. Enough damage had been done. Jane thanked her and Sabrina gave her a spontaneous hug.

'Thank you, Mrs Brown, for everything.'

They didn't look back as they walked through the iron gates and set off towards the city.

———— ◦ ————

THEIR FEET WERE THROBBING and they were beginning to suspect they'd taken a wrong turn somewhere along the way because the street Sabrina and Jane found themselves on was a far cry from leafy Allerton Road or anywhere they'd find a respectable boarding house.

Here, red terraces looked in danger of crumbling, and they could hear shouts of conversation in a language neither of them understood floating down through open windows. They trudged past a drain emitting a smell that saw them both hold their hands to their mouths in an effort not to gag.

Sabrina pulled Jane to one side to allow a horde of children running wild to pass.

As they rounded a corner, the bricks rising either side of them seemed to close over them claustrophobically. There was only a sliver of sky visible above them although the sheets billowing overhead could be mistaken for clouds.

A cluster of women stood around a water pipe at the end of the dead-end in which they'd found themselves and several children whose pallor was ghostly and with arms and legs protruding from their grubby clothes like twigs, were playing on the cobbles with an old rope.

The stench here was overwhelming and Jane and Sabrina exchanged panicked glances as to where they were. Sabrina, who knew her city like the back of her hand didn't recognise this version of it.

Jane wished right then she'd swallowed her pride and used the little savings she had to take them back to Wigan. She'd been a fool choosing instead to walk away from all that was familiar and look where they'd wound up. She'd no right to lead Sabrina into danger either.

She could have made a story up as to why she'd returned to Wigan with her friend in tow. She'd as much right to the cottage as her brother. But it was dishonesty that was responsible for her current predicament and so she'd baulked at the idea of telling a lie. Besides, she doubted she could have convinced Sabrina to come with her. She'd not want to be far from Bold Street.

And so they'd resolved to walk to Upper Parliament Street, go cap in hand to speak to Mrs Brown's cousin and ask if she'd take them in. It wouldn't be forever they'd explain.

Sabrina held onto the conviction that she would return to where she'd come from and Jane to the strength of her love for Sidney and her faith in him coming to fetch her.

He would understand why she'd done what she'd done. He had to because she needed him more than ever. There was another reason Jane wouldn't go back to Wigan, one she'd not confided in Sabrina as she was still trying to come to terms with it herself. It had dawned on her over the weekend when the sickness stole over her again late in the afternoon.

She was pregnant.

Oh, it was early days but she knew the signs right enough from when her mam had been carrying little Emma. It had explained her weariness, her absentmindedness and the sickness these last weeks.

Weariness hit Jane now and she sat down in a doorway and put her head in her hands. She was lost, pregnant and to all intents and purposes destitute and she'd put her dear friend in the same position.

Sabrina draped an arm around her in an effort to reassure the younger girl they'd be alright. She wished she felt reassured herself and she quashed her rising panic at the thought of never returning to the life she'd known. This was not the time for wallowing.

Both were oblivious to the women at the end of the courts into which they'd wandered, staring at the strangers in their midst. Jane's head lurched up as she felt a hand on her knee and she found herself looking into an enormous pair of blue eyes. A solemn face stared back at her, far too solemn on one so young.

A little girl with a tangle of brown hair had come to stand alongside her, offering her comfort and Jane blinked the salty tears away managing a smile.

The little girl smiled back, 'All better now.' She parroted her mam no doubt before re-joining the other children playing their skipping games.

Sabrina and Jane watched her go.

One of the women who'd been fetching water made her way over and pausing beside the two girls said in an Irish accent so broad they struggled for a moment to understand what she was saying. 'I see you met our Angela.'

They both nodded and made to stand, it was clearly the woman's doorstep they'd plonked themselves down on and now she wanted to pass.

'A cup of tea will fix whatever's ailing yer both, come on inside with yer.' She smiled.

She was young to be missing a front tooth but right then Sabrina and Jane thought she'd the most beautiful smile they'd ever seen.

The room they found themselves in wasn't much. The door had been taken off and was serving as a bed. It wasn't fit for one let alone all the bodies the bedding piled up in the corner suggested occupied it each night.

'I'm Deirdre,' she said gesturing to a chair at the table. 'Sit yerselves down.'

'My name's Sabrina and this is Jane. Thank you.'

Deirdre bustled about making the tea and chattering on all the while. 'There's six of us live here. My husband Colm and our children. Fiona, she's our eldest, Finbar and Darragh and you met Angela.'

The chatter settled over the two girls like a warm blanket and when the tea was placed in front of them they sipped it gratefully.

Deirdre seemed content to let them drink it in silence while she told them about what had brought her family here.

'Colm had work on the docks but he lost his job. He's a good man but he's got a weakness in him when it comes to the ale. We look after each other here though. Sure, there's worse places we could be.'

Jane and Sabrina caught one another's eyes. They weren't so sure but then they were hardly in a position to pass comment or judgment. Jane finished her hot drink and decided it was true, tea really did have a restorative effect as did a kind gesture.

'You've a littlun on the way?' Deirdre directed her question to Jane.

Sabrina's head spun toward her friend.

'I've only known a short while,' Jane said by way of explanation. She glanced down at her stomach under her dress but it was too soon to see any physical signs of hers and Sidney's baby. How did she know? She looked at Deirdre with a questioning gaze.

'You don't bear four of your own without recognising the signs.'

Sabrina reached over and took her friend's hand giving it a comforting squeeze.

The gesture pushed Jane over the edge and it all poured out. Losing her mam and dad, falling in love with Sidney and the consequences of that love growing inside her.

'He'll come for me, my Sidney,' she said.

Deirdre wondered what the other girl's role was in all of this but didn't ask as she said, 'I hope he does, luv, for your and the littlun's sake.'

Jane looked at the woman who was only a few years older than herself and for whom life had dealt a hard hand. She'd no right to complain or feel sorry for herself. Everything would be alright. She got up then. 'Thank you for your kindness, Deirdre. We must push on. Could you tell us how to get to Parliament Street?'

Deirdre explained how to wind their way back out to the main thoroughfare and where to go from there before sending them on their way. 'Best of luck to yer both.'

She stood on the same steps Jane and Sabrina had been sitting on an hour earlier and watched them go, shaking her head. The young lass had a hard road ahead of her if that fella of hers didn't come for her.

Chapter Twenty-eight

Mrs Brown's cousin was as thin as the cook was round and about the same age with a similar set of spectacles. The only difference was Mrs Page rarely took hers off and when she did they left behind a deep red indent on either side of her sharp nose.

Like her cousin, she was kind but could also be tough especially with those that failed to obey the house rules, messed her about with their board, or didn't keep their lodging to an acceptable standard.

Jane and Sabrina had arrived at the three-storey Lismore House, named after a previous owner, dead on their feet. Jane's face had been streaked with dried tears. Sabrina's expression stoic and hopeful at being taken in.

They could smell the promise of a meat and cabbage dinner wafting from the kitchen at the back of the house.

'I'm famished,' Jane whispered and Sabrina murmured her agreement. From where they were standing in the hallway the runner looked swept and the bannister rail following the stairs, polished. It was a clean establishment just as Mrs Brown had said.

Mrs Page would have taken pity on the duo regardless of her cousin's recommendation. She'd a soft spot for waifs and strays and as it happened, she told Jane and Sabrina, she was in need of help with the cleaning and cooking.

They struck an arrangement whereby in exchange for their grafting and sharing a room with another young lass, they'd pay a fraction of the going rate. Meals were inclusive.

'It will only be for a few weeks, Mrs Page,' Jane said as she and Sabrina followed her up to the third floor. Mrs Page had batted the remark away, busying herself with pointing out the doors to the other rooms as she told them who to keep an eye on and who'd give them no cause for bother.

The room they were to share was biblical in its sparseness with a picture of Jesus looking skyward, hands clasped in prayer, along with a crucifix hanging from a nail over the neatly made bed closest to the door.

'I don't abide holes being put in the walls but when it comes to the good Lord, I make an exception.'

Jane and Sabrina were to share the bed by the window. The room had a chest of drawers in it and a mirror on the wall along with a handbasin. The only difference from their quarters at Allerton Road was the extra bed and the window.

'There's a bathroom on the second floor I expect kept to a high standard and you'll find the privy out the back. There tends to be a rush for it first thing in the morning so I supply all my lodgers with a chamber pot under their beds,' she'd informed them before leaving them to unpack and to rest.

She paused in the doorway as their cases were tossed down on the end of the bed. 'Dinner's served at six o'clock sharp and we'll start tomorrow as we mean to carry on. I'll expect you downstairs in the morning at seven o'clock sharp, dressed, washed and ready for the day. After breakfast, I'll give you a list of chores for the morning. The afternoon's yours to do what you want with.' She closed the bedroom door behind her and, too tired to unpack, they kicked off their shoes and collapsed onto the bed.

They must have gone out like a light despite the rumblings in their stomachs because they awoke to hear an Irish lilt. Jane thought in her fuggy state they were still with Deirdre.

She prised her eyes open to see a girl about her own age, with hair the colour of a carrot, freckles across her nose and cheeks and a dancing pair of brown eyes. She liked the look of her immediately. Beside her, Sabrina sat up too and was rubbing her eyes.

'I'm Ciara. We're to share. Tis lovely to make your acquaintance, Jane and Sabrina. I'll be glad of the company so I will and the drop in my lodgings! Mrs Page sent me up to tell you dinner will be ready in ten minutes and that you're to wash yourselves up. I've fetched clean flannels for yer.'

She smiled, taking note of their sleep befuddled expressions before adding, 'A word to the wise,' she tapped the side of her nose. 'You'll be grand here so you will so long as you're punctual. Mrs Page can't abide any of her guests being late for meals. Tis the only time you'll see her lose her rag.'

Jane and Sabrina exchanged a glance. They'd neither of them any wish to see that and with a smile of thanks, the bed creaked as Jane got up and took the washcloths from Ciara with a thank you. The Irish girl turned and disappeared out of the room as Jane tossed a cloth to Sabrina and crossed the threadbare carpeted floor to the sink.

JANE AND SABRINA WERE happy at Lismore House with Mrs Page, Ciara and their fellow lodgers. The arrangement suited Sabrina well as she'd the afternoons free to return to Bold Street.

Jane would wait for her familiar, 'It's only me,' sung out as she came back to help serve the evening meal with bated breath.

Sabrina hadn't mentioned her unusual circumstances to Ciara and she'd asked Jane not to as well. It wasn't that she didn't trust or like their Irish roommate, it was more she couldn't see what difference Ciara knowing would make. It wouldn't change the fact she was stuck.

Jane respected Sabrina's wishes and was vague if Ciara ever inquired about Sabrina's background. She'd her own secrets to keep having decided no one needed to know she was in the family way with the exception of Ciara. She had faith in their new friend not to breathe a word of her condition and it meant that when their bedroom door was shut the trio could speak freely.

There was no need to share her pregnancy with the others and possibly garner their disapproval. She'd be gone before she began to show and a respectable married woman once the baby arrived. Sabrina, she'd decided, without having told her would live with her and Sidney until she managed to return to her time.

She'd a far easier life here at Lismore House than she was accustomed to and felt they'd landed on their feet. She was immensely grateful to Mrs Brown for that.

Given she was increasingly tired during the day, Jane relished the time when the housework was done and the dinner set to simmer on the stove. It meant she could climb the stairs to the peace of their bedroom for a few hours.

The silent house had a different rhythm of an afternoon and she'd grown used to its creaks and groans as she lay with her stocking clad feet up on the bed, her hands resting on her belly murmuring softly to the little dote growing within.

Ciara was under an apprenticeship at a milliner's and along with Sabrina, Jane looked forward to her arrival home each evening. The Irish girl had a talent for telling stories and her anecdotes of working under the austere Madame Le'Reve who was permanently grumpy on account of being permanently hungry because French women were elegantly thin, not like zees frumpy English puddings, had both Jane and Sabrina in fits.

The two weeks until Sidney was due to return rolled around surprising quickly and the day Jane knew Harold would once more be parked in the shed at Allerton Road, she finished her work in record time in order to sit in the window of the front room eagerly awaiting his arrival.

'I don't have to go out this afternoon, Jane. I can stay and wait with you if you like,' Sabrina offered, poised in the doorway. The hopeful expression on her friend's face worried her. She'd so much pinned on Sidney coming to fetch her.

'No, it's important you go. Today might be the day. Not that I want you to leave of course.'

'I don't want to leave you, Jane, but—'

'This isn't your time. I know that, Sabrina. If you don't come back today I want you to know you've been a dear friend to me and I shall miss you terribly.'

Sabrina fought the threatening tears as she crossed the room and hugged her friend tightly. 'And I don't know what I'd have done without you.'

Jane pushed her away gently. 'Go. You know you must and staying here with me won't make him come any quicker.'

Sabrina went, feeling the tug as she did each day to go to Bold Street.

Sometimes she'd walk, sometimes she'd sit but every afternoon she'd hope that day she'd find her way back.

From her window vantage point, Jane could observe the comings and goings up and down the industrious street. She played a game to while away the hours whereby each time she spied a figure in the distance that could be Sidney she'd hold her breath. She'd only exhale when it became clear it wasn't.

When he didn't come for her that first day she was disappointed but as she lay in the bed that evening she explained his absence away to Ciara and Sabrina breezily. 'I think he must have arrived back at Allerton Road late in the day. I'm certain he'll come first thing in the morning.'

She didn't see the glance Ciara and Sabrina exchanged. A silent communication of their hope that Sidney Muldoon wouldn't prove fickle in his affections.

He didn't come the next morning or the day after, or the day after that and when a week had slipped by apathy set in. Jane no longer sat in the front window of an afternoon but took herself off to her bed to lie there, staring unseeingly at the ceiling until dinner was ready.

She had to face the fact that Sidney had chosen to believe whatever it was his mother had told him about her. It was the only explanation.

'Jane, you've a wee one to be thinking about. You must go and see him, try and talk to him. It'll be altogether different when he knows you're in the family way,' Sabrina urged, and Ciara, sitting on the edge of her bed, unpinning her long fiery hair concurred.

'I don't want his pity, Sabrina.'

But it's not just about you now, is it?' Sabrina said sensibly.

Jane remained silent, staring up at the ceiling cracks she'd grown familiar with these last few days.

Ciara tried next. 'Sure, how're you going to manage on your own? You can't work and look after a baby. How are you planning on eating and putting a roof over your heads? Mrs Page is a kind woman but she's a businesswoman too. She won't have the scandal of an unmarried woman lodging here. You don't want to wind up in one of those homes.' Ciara shuddered then. 'It's too high a price to pay, Jane.'

'What homes?' That had grabbed Jane's attention and she turned her head to look at her.

'The ones the nuns run. The girls go in and never come back out. I've heard they're no more than slaves and their babies are given away to rich couples from America.'

Sabrina was as horrified by this as Jane. It was exactly what Ciara was hoping for. Jane needed to be shocked out of her inertia and into doing something, for her baby's sake as much as her own.

'I can't face going to the house,' Jane said, panicking at the very thought of facing down Magnolia Muldoon.

'I could go with you,' Sabrina suggested gently. She'd nothing to lose in going back but Jane shook her head.

'What about the shop then? You said he's an antique business in town here.'

'Bold Street, yes.'

Sabrina had walked past Muldoon's Antiquities that very afternoon trying to catch a glimpse of Sidney but she'd not seen him. If Jane wouldn't talk to him, she would. He was responsible for the predicament her friend found herself in and he would be made to face it.

'There you go then, that's settled,' Ciara said brightly. 'You'll go to the shop tomorrow and tell him face to face that he needs to take responsibility for the bit of fun he had.'

A bit of fun, Jane played the sentence over in her head as a tear trickled out of the side of her eye. Was that all she'd been? A bit of fun. Ciara was right it was too high a price to pay to be thrown on the mercy of others because he'd had his fun. She would go tomorrow she resolved, squeezing her eyes shut.

━━━◉━━━

JANE FINISHED HER CHORES about the place and then tidied herself up before setting off for Bold Street, her arm linked through Sabrina's. She was determined she wouldn't lose her resolve. She needn't have worried. She wouldn't. She had to do her best by the baby and forget her pride because to date it hadn't got her far in life.

It was the first time Jane had visited the street Sabrina frequented daily. She pulled her friend to a halt to soak in the bustling scene with the grand church, where Mrs Brown had encountered Sabrina, presiding over it. There was no sense of mysterious goings-on. Or at least none she could grasp hold of.

She wondered which side of the street they should walk down but Sabrina steered her down the left-hand side. She was glad of her coat warding off the stiff autumn breeze upon which she could catch the scent of salt and soot.

As they walked past the various businesses, Jane's stomach began churning with both anticipation at seeing Sidney and apprehension as to his reaction when she'd said her piece.

'This is it, Jane,' Sabrina said, gesturing to a shop slightly ahead of them with a blue door above which the sign Muldoon's Antiquities was displayed. As they approached it the door opened and there he was, larger than life, Sidney!

Jane's face broke into a smile, despite her anxiousness, at the solid sight of him. She and Sabrina stopped in their tracks to hear a woman's muttered annoyance as she side-stepped around them.

Jane was poised to call out lest he stride off in the opposite direction without seeing her when a woman emerged behind him.

She watched with creeping horror as Sidney locked the door and the woman who was clad in purple threaded her arm through his with an air of propriety. Sabrina's grip tightened on her arm holding her steady as bile rose in her throat. She swallowed hard feeling her nerve desert her.

She was about to tug Sabrina's arm and tell her she wanted to turn and go when the woman glanced toward her. There was no mistaking those sharp features and jade eyes.

It was Claudia Monroe.

Chapter Twenty-nine

The sight of the woman staring smugly at her galvanized Jane. A surge of righteous anger at Sidney's fickle behaviour crashed over her as without thinking she unhooked herself from Sabrina and whirled toward them.

'Sidney!' she called.

He stopped dead, the key still in his hand as he drank in the sight of her. Claudia pulled at his arm, eager to get away from the scene she sensed was about to unfold on the busy street.

'I must talk with you, Sidney. It's important.' Her voice shook as anger and emotion at seeing him again swelled. She would do right by their child. She would not wind up living a hand to mouth existence like poor Deirdre. Or shut away in a convent working her fingers to the bone while nuns cracked the whip and her baby was stolen from her.

Claudia Monroe jerked him away more firmly. 'Sidney, dahling, ignore her, remember what your mother said. You don't owe her the time of day. Besides, we've a booking. It would be terribly rude of us to be late.'

The note of desperation in her voice empowered Jane and she faced the other woman down. They weren't in a formal dining room now. She wasn't a servant any longer and she would not be dismissed.

'I'll have you know, Miss Monroe, that I might come from working-class stock but I'd never belittle others the way you do. Or resort to underhand tactics to get my way. My mam raised me to be better than that.' She arranged her features into a sneer.

Claudia's face contorted and she looked as though she were about to retort when Sidney disentangled his arm from her.

'You go on ahead, Claudia.'

'But Sidney...'

His voice brooked no argument. 'Go on ahead, Claudia.'

Still she hesitated, not liking the way she was being dismissed. 'Well, don't be long. What should I tell your mother?'

'Apologise to her and to yours and tell them I won't be able to make the luncheon after all.'

Claudia Monroe's face went various shades of pink as, with nostrils flaring in a most unbecoming way, she rounded on Sidney. 'You're making a very poor choice, Sidney Muldoon. A very poor choice indeed.'

She shot Jane a venomous look and then turned heel and stalked off down the street.

Jane was not a vindictive girl but nor was she a saint and she wouldn't apologise for the smile that twitched as Claudia caught her heel in a cobble and wrestled with her shoe in a most unladylike manner.

Her gaze flew to Sabrina who was grinning from ear to ear.

Jane grinned back.

'I'll meet you back at the house later,' Sabrina said, stepping forth and saying hello to Sidney who looked surprised to see her. She set off for Cripps, her usual destination, with high hopes of them working things out. She'd seen the way Sidney's face had lit up at the sight of her friend.

Sidney and Jane watched her go before he put the key back in the door he'd just locked. 'Come inside the shop, Jane, we can talk in the office out the back.'

Jane followed him inside, barely registering the Aladdin's cave of antiques as he threaded his way around a tall vase and a handsome dining table and chairs to a small room out the back. He gestured to a chair in front of the desk before bringing another out from behind the large oak desk upon which a ledger lay open.

He tossed his hat down on the desk and sat down opposite her, rubbing at his temples before leaning forward with his hands clasped.

'Jane,' he sighed. 'You broke my heart. Why did you do it? I never trusted anyone with it before.'

Jane felt shame prickle as she told him the truth of all that had happened right down to having seen Claudia Monroe at the Grafton, explaining she'd known she meant to cause trouble and so she'd made out she felt unwell so as they could go home before she could cause a scene. As it worked out she'd done so anyway later at that awful dinner when she'd stuck her foot out causing Jane to humiliate herself.

Sidney was shaking his head. 'But I don't understand.'

'I've just laid it out for you plain as day, Sidney, please don't make me repeat myself.'

'Oh, I heard what you said alright. But it's a far cry from the story I was told when I returned home.' He stood up then and paced the space, a lion in a cage looking for a place to put the indignation and anger at the realisation his mother had lied to him.

'Mother told me you and Sabrina had stolen jewellery from her and that you were planning to pawn it so as to start a new life in the south close to your sisters. She told me you were long gone.'

'But, Mrs Brown, she promised.' Jane's voice caught, distraught at the thought of what Sidney must have thought of her. 'Sabrina insisted she come with me and Mrs Brown was kind to us. She sent us to her cousin's boarding house where we've been staying. She said she'd tell you where we'd gone. Why would she betray me by not saying a word?'

'I dare say she was told to go along with whatever Mother said if she wanted to keep her position. Survival of the fittest and all that.'

'I'm very sorry for what I did, Sidney. It was wrong and I know that. I'm not a thief.'

Sidney made a dismissive sound. 'For God's sake, it was a dress that mother wouldn't have even known existed if it wasn't for Claudia. Between them, they've both more dresses than sense. It was hardly the crime of the century. No, Jane, I think my mother has proved how narrow-minded she is. She's a snob of the highest order and I'm not sure I can forgive her for this.' He sighed heavily. 'I don't want to waste my energy thinking about Mother. You're what matters. I love you. You know that, don't you?'

'If you love me, then why were you so quick to step out with Claudia Monroe?' Anger sparked at how quickly she'd been put aside.

'I was not stepping out with Claudia.' Sidney was indignant.

'It certainly looked as though you were.' She tilted her chin challengingly.

'Mother arranged a luncheon here in the city and Claudia showed up, uninvited I'll have you know, to walk to the restaurant with me. It's you my heart belongs to.'

He pulled her up onto her feet then and into an embrace. 'I've missed you every waking hour and in my sleep too.'

Jane's body melted at his touch.

He released her then, cupping her face with his hands and tilting her head towards him before searching for her mouth.

Her lips moved to his rhythm and she didn't want the kiss to ever end but there was something else she needed to tell him and breaking away she took a step back and tried to catch her breath. How should she word what she needed to say? She only pondered it for a fraction of a second before blurting, 'I'm to have a baby, Sidney.'

She trembled, waiting for his response.

'A baby?' he echoed. 'But we only—'

'Once, yes I know.'

Jane watched as the news sank in her and delight lit his dark features. She gasped as he swept her up and twirled her around. The angst of the last weeks disappeared.

Everything was going to be alright; she'd just needed to keep her faith in him.

Sidney put her down and taking her hand in his, he said, 'Come with me.'

She followed him out into the shop, coming to stand in front of a locked glass cabinet. Inside it was an array of rings, watches, brooches, bracelets and necklaces.

'Choose a ring any one you like.'

She looked to him for confirmation and he urged her on. 'Any one you like.'

She chose a sapphire, falling in love with the luminous, deep glow of the precious stone.

Sidney retrieved the key from a drawer behind the counter and opening the cabinet he plucked the ring from the velvet stand. He got down on one knee and taking her hand in his raised his eyes to hers and said, 'Jane Evans, would you do me the honour of agreeing to marry me?'

'I will.' Jane thought she might never stop smiling as he slid the proof of his love onto her finger.

He stood up and they looked at one another utterly pleased with themselves.

'We need to make it official as soon as we can for the sake of appearances,' Sidney said, placing his hand gently on her belly.

Jane placed her hand on top of his and agreed, yes they should.

'I've an idea.' He retrieved his hat and then, holding his arm out Jane linked hers through his wondering what he had up his sleeve. She let him lead her outside and waited while he locked the shop once more before they set off down Bold Street as a newly engaged couple.

'Where are we going, Sidney?'

'A bride has got to have a wedding dress, doesn't she?'

Jane nodded slowly, realising they'd come to a stop outside a shop. She gazed at the beautiful froth of lace in the window before looking to the sign that read, 'Brides of Bold Street'. It was Sabrina's shop. Her home.

'Shall we?' Sidney held the door open for her and Jane stepped inside.

Evelyn Flooks stepped forward to greet the happy couple.

Chapter Thirty

The afternoon of Jane and Sidney's wedding was gloriously autumnal. The sky was clear and cloudless and it was just hot enough if you stood in the sun to make you forget winter was around the corner. A breeze was blowing with enough gusto to send the sort of leaves children rush to pick up and admire floating down from the treetops overhead like confetti.

Jane, Sabrina and Sidney had piled into Harold and driven to Wigan at first light that Sunday morning. The girls' wedding finery was draped on the back seat beside Sabrina.

Jane had wanted the service to be held in the parish church she'd attended all her life until she left for Allerton Road. She'd wanted to feel the presence of her parents nearby as she said her vows and for Father Arnold to bless their marriage because she knew it would have made her mam and dad happy.

Sidney had no wish for his mother to attend their wedding despite Jane's urging that he should give her the chance to make amends. He was her only son after all. It would do no good to hold on to hurts and bitterness she'd said but he wouldn't be swayed in his decision.

The wedding, once the wheels were set in motion had come about very fast. It needed to, given Jane and Sidney's bun in the oven as they referred to her burgeoning bump.

There'd been no time for banns to be read and as such Jane had fretted there would be nobody in the little stone church to admire hers and Sabrina's dresses on the day. Sidney had been adamant she should have the wedding dress of her dreams and Jane had wanted to know Sabrina was there supporting her on this, the most important day of her life. As such, she was her bridesmaid.

Sidney had organised the purchase of a wedding certificate and Father Arnold, given Sabrina's family ties with the church had agreed to hold the service. Mercifully, he'd not asked any probing questions as to why there was such a need for expedience.

They'd pulled up out the front of the Evans family cottage when most would be sitting down to breakfast and were greeted by Frank and Marie. How strange it had been not to see her mam and dad but rather Frank and his new bride Marie standing at the gate.

She was sorry she'd been unable to make it back for their wedding. Poor Frank had no one from their side of the family to help him celebrate his nuptials. She was here now though and she was so very grateful her brother and his wife were to be a part of hers and Sidney's day.

How strange to be shown to the small room her parents had once occupied and told she and Sabrina could get ready there. Sidney, dashing in the morning suit he'd travelled up in, would meet them at the church.

Jane took comfort in knowing her parents would be pleased the cottage had passed to her brother and his bride. She'd tried not to think of her sisters whom she missed terribly. The cottage was so silent without their incessant chatter.

Today would be a happy day after so much sadness, she resolved, turning her attention to Sabrina who'd slipped into her dress. It was white, something Jane had reassured her was perfectly acceptable given her own gown was pale pink. The bridesmaid dress had a satin fitted bodice with long sleeves and a full taffeta skirt in two layers. Ciara had made the cloche hat with its flower ornamentation on the side.

'You look beautiful, Sabrina.' Jane steepled her hands to her mouth.

Sabrina smiled at her friend standing there in her pale pink crepe de chine slip. 'Aunt Evie's a wonder.'

'She is. 'I'm only sorry she didn't believe you.'

'I don't blame her.' Sabrina shrugged.

Evelyn had recognised her when Jane had brought her to the bridal shop but she'd been wary of her after their previous encounter.

With Jane's support, Sabrina had tried one last time to convince the seamstress she was part of her future but knew her aunt well enough, even this young version of her, to stop pressing when she saw the shutters of her eyes close. She'd let it be for Jane's sake not wanting anything to cast a cloud over her special day.

'I'll always be grateful you believed me though. I don't know what I would've done if you hadn't. Now come on.' Sabrina tutted. 'We can't have your Sidney waiting at the altar.'

Evelyn had done a wonderful job with Sabrina's gown but she'd excelled herself with Jane's. The dropped-waist dress and the blush pink colour brought out the roses in her cheeks. The satin was dreamy to the touch and sparkled with the embroidered crystal bugles, pearls and silver thread.

Sabrina helped Jane into it and then stood back to appreciate her. 'I've lost count of how many wedding gowns I've made, Jane, but you are the most radiant bride I've ever seen.' She meant every word of what she'd said. Her friend was glowing.

Next, she helped her affix her veil before letting Jane admire herself in the looking glass attached to a chest of drawers Marie must have brought with her.

'I'm so happy, Sabrina.' Jane sniffed.

'Then stop crying.' Sabrina smiled handing her a hanky.

Jane dabbed at her eyes and put the damp lace-edged cloth on top of their belongings on the bed before embracing her friend. 'I pray you'll get your happy ending too.'

'This is your day, don't think about me.' Sabrina was touched. 'Come on, it's time we went. We've a wedding to go to.'

They were to walk the short distance to the church but as they stepped out of the room, to Jane's surprise Marie was sitting at the table. She'd thought she'd be seated at the church with Frank by now.

She got up from the table, picking something up as she did. It was a bunch of deep pink, almost red, Autumn Joy tied with a lace ribbon.

'An autumn posy for you, sister.' Marie thrust the bouquet out shyly and Jane blinked back more tears at the gesture.

'It's perfect, Marie, thank you.'

'Your Sidney will think himself a most fortunate man when he lays eyes on you. You're a picture.'

Marie kissed her sister-in-law on the cheek and then said she'd see them at the church as she set off at a pace down the road.

Sabrina and Jane with Sabrina holding Jane's veil to ensure it didn't trail along the dusty road set off behind her.

Now, Jane stood next to her Sidney at the altar bathed in the prisms of light from the stained-glass window behind them. Father Arnold was in his element with a full congregation as he intoned his wordy service, pausing for prayer now and again.

Jane didn't mind, she'd expected nothing less, even though she was desperate to say her vows and to become Sidney's wife in the eyes of God.

To her delight, as she'd walked down the aisle amazed to find the pews full with villagers all come to wish her well, she'd spied her sisters near the front. They were tucked in between their aunt and uncle. Their faces pink, round and happy as they fidgeted in their seats desperate for her to notice them.

At last, it was time for Jane and Sidney to turn and face one another. He took his hand in hers.

'I, Sidney James Muldoon take you Jane Annabel Evans to be my wife.

To have and to hold from this day forward;
for better, for worse, for richer, for poorer,
in sickness and in health,
to love and to cherish, till death us do part;

according to God's holy law. In the presence of God I make this vow.'

Sidney let go of her hand and then it was Jane's turn to take his hand in hers.

Her voice rang out clearly in a church so quiet you could hear a pin drop as she said her vows.

Sidney's eyes never once left Jane as Father Arnold said a prayer before leading them through the exchange of the rings. And then, at last, the words, 'I now pronounce you man and wife,' were said and Jane fancied she heard a collective sigh from the congregation as she and Sidney knelt for their blessing.

A cheer went up as the new Mr and Mrs Muldoon made their way back down the aisle and into the sunshine.

There was to be no reception. Sidney was keen to whisk his new wife back to Liverpool because, as he'd confided in Jane, he had a surprise for her. He'd bought a house. A perfectly ordinary house, in a perfectly normal street upon which to start a life together he knew would be extraordinary.

'I'm going to toss my bouquet, Sabrina,' Jane said over the top of the babbling stream as leaves danced downward.

Sabrina helped arrange the veil over her arm before moving back to stand alongside the young village girls, all eager to catch the flowers and perhaps be the next to stand in front of Father Arnold to say their vows.

A count went up amongst the milling villagers.

'Three, two, one!'

Jane tossed the bouquet high over her shoulder and Sabrina squinted up into the dappled light her hands grasping upwards wildly. A split second later a cheer went up as she held the bouquet jubilantly overhead beaming from ear to ear.

Jane smiled back at her. 'Well, it's official then, you'll be next'.

Sabrina glanced down at the autumn posy she was holding and her mind flitted to Adam. Would she ever see him again?

Part Three

Chapter Thirty-one

Sabrina stood stock-still in the middle of the busy pavement feeling the whoosh of people passing by her. Something was different. Overwhelmed, she closed her eyes feeling her body sway at the sudden blackness. She'd been parading up and down past Cripps fancy shop front as she did every afternoon when she'd felt a frisson of something she couldn't put her finger on. It had made her feel peculiar though.

'You ahright there, queen?'

She opened her eyes to see a man with a multi-coloured head of spikes and earrings in places where earrings didn't belong.

Don't judge a book by its cover ran through her head. It was one of Aunt Evie's favourite sayings.

'I think so.'

The fella gave her a searching look and, satisfied she wasn't about to keel over, went on his way.

It was noisier, busier, Sabrina realised as her senses were assaulted with exhaust fumes, cigarette smoke, the honking of a horn and a shouted insult. She could almost taste the waft of fried food and spices the sources of which she couldn't locate and Bold Street was awash with the colour of the fashions its hustling patrons were decked out in.

She swung round to look at the shops. Cripps with its specialist ladies dressmaking services was gone and in its place was the bookshop, Hudson's, advertising Stephen King's latest offering, *Cujo*.

The cars streaming past were different too; faster, sleeker, familiar.

'Excuse me,' Sabrina moved toward a woman with big hair clad in an all-in-one pantsuit, the waist of which was cinched in tight. 'What year is it?' Her makeup was loud with two slashes of blush highlighting her cheekbones.

'What are you on about, girl? It's nineteen eighty-one.' She snapped her gum and narrowed her eyes as she swept over Sabrina's dress. 'Is this some sort of joke?'

'No, no joke. Thank you!' Sabrina set off at a trot. *It was 1981. She was home!*

She burst in the door of the shop, which was empty but, nevertheless, exactly as she remembered it. Her decorating touches jumped out her, the painted table come counter, the velvet fitting room drapes! She called out. 'Aunt Evie, it's me!'

'Sabrina?' The whirring of the old Singer stopped and Evelyn, her heart in her mouth, ventured out to the shop. 'Sabrina, sweetheart! I've missed you.'

Sabrina burst into tears as she found herself wrapped in the familiar embrace. She sniffed, 'You must have been so worried. I'm so sorry. I couldn't tell you where I was. I couldn't get back. I tried so hard whenever I could but today and I don't know why but it happened.' The words tumbled over one another as her breath juddered.

'Shush, luv. It's alright. You're home now. How's about I make us a nice brew?'

That sounded like heaven, Sabrina thought, watching as her aunt hung a closed sign in the window and locked the door. She followed her upstairs and looked about her warily, wondering if anything had changed. She'd no clue as to how long she'd been gone.

Everything was just as it should be and she exhaled slowly.

'Sit yourself down, Sabrina,' Evelyn bossed, opening a cupboard in the kitchen. 'I had faith you'd be back so I made sure I had these in.' She waved a packet of garibaldi biscuits at her.

The glow of the familiar settled over her as she felt the spring of the antwacky sofa dig into her thigh. She watched her aunt move about the kitchen and tears welled once more as she saw her pour the tea into her mishappen mug. She was home, she repeated to herself.

Evelyn handed Sabrina her brew and settled herself into her seat. The biscuits were on a plate on the table in front of them. Sabrina helped herself and nibbled on the currant filled garibaldi relishing the sweetness. She'd so many questions. She didn't know where to start but as it happened she didn't have to. It was Evelyn who began as she picked a biscuit up and put it on the side of her saucer.

'You've been gone a week, Sabrina.'

'But it was months. I was there months.' She shook her head not comprehending.

'Time moves to its own rhythm,' Evelyn said, dunking her garibaldi into her dainty teacup.

'You must have been frantic, Aunt Evie. Did you go to the police?'

Evelyn shook her head as she popped the sodden biscuit in her mouth replying a moment later. 'I knew where you were, Sabrina.'

Sabrina stared at her. 'How?'

'You came to see me remember? More than once. You tried to tell me.'

She remembered alright. It had been an awful moment when it had dawned on her she was a stranger to her aunt. 'You didn't know me.'

'I didn't, Sabrina, but I never forgot you. There was something about you that haunted me and I always regretted not taking on board what you were trying to tell me. I was too practical to accept it you see.' Evelyn's cup rattled in its saucer.

'I imprinted what you'd said to me to memory. Then, when I met you as a little girl and you said your name, I finally understood what you'd been trying to tell me back then. I knew you and I were destined to be together.'

'But you still looked for my mam?' Sabrina held her breath unsure how she'd feel if what her aunt had told her about her fruitless search wasn't true.

'Of course I did even though I doubted we'd find her. You'd told me you see, back in nineteen twenty-eight that I'd raised you. You told me you'd come from nineteen eighty-one too, which gave me hope you'd be back. I just didn't know when exactly.' Evelyn put the cup and saucer down on the table in front of them.

Sabrina shook her head. It was all so much to take in. 'I don't understand any of it.'

Evelyn donned her wise old owl persona as she gazed thoughtfully at her from behind the thick lenses of her glasses. 'I've tried to make sense of it but there are some things in this life of ours that are beyond our understanding or control, Sabrina. Time is one of them.'

'My poor mam.'

'Yes.' Evelyn's sigh was weighty. 'My gift came at her cost and I think of her often. I hope one day time will catch up to wherever it was you came from and you'll find each other again. She deserves to know the truth of what happened to her girl.'

They sat, each lost in their own thoughts until Sabrina jutted her head up once more. 'What about Flo? She'll have been wondering where I was.'

'Poor, dear Florence was beside herself. I telephoned her when you didn't come home the first night you were gone and she was as worried as I was. She mentioned how your visit with Mystic Lil—'

'Lou.'

'Wherever, had gone. I came clean about you coming to see me in nineteen twenty-eight and what I suspected had happened to you. It was a lot for her to take in but we've both been holding on to the hope you'd find your way home.'

'I'll phone her.' Sabrina made to get up.

'Finish your tea first and have another biscuit. Sugar's good for shock and it has been a shock.'

Sabrina never needed to be asked twice when it came to having another biscuit.

'Aunt Evie, a fella didn't happen to call while I was gone did he?'

Evelyn's eyes twinkled. 'By the name of Adam perhaps?'

Sabrina nodded, knowing her aunt was deliberately teasing.

'He did as a matter of fact. I wasn't sure what to tell him and in the end, I was vague. I said you'd gone to visit a friend for a few days and I'd get you to telephone him when you got back.' Evelyn pointed to the sideboard. 'His number's in that dish there.'

Sabrina's heart gave a little leap. *He had phoned just as he'd said he would!*

Evelyn shifted in her seat, pushing her glasses up her nose. 'Where did you go? After I—'

'I understand, Aunt Evie,' Sabrina interjected softly, laying her hand on her forearm. She was still wearing her shop coat. It was lilac with a deep purple stripe running through it which meant it was Friday. 'You didn't understand. How could you have?'

Evelyn dipped her head and Sabrina noticed her hair was in need of doing. She must have cancelled her standing weekly appointment with Dee her hairdresser, afraid she'd miss her if she came back.

'It's been some adventure though,' Sabrina said, settling herself down to tell her aunt her story from the beginning.

SABRINA'S VOICE WAS hoarse when she came to the end of her story and exhaustion was creeping in. Still, she itched to telephone Adam just to hear his voice but her loyalty lay first with Florence.

Evelyn, satisfied Sabrina wasn't about to vanish on her again, had gone back downstairs. It was nearly closing time and she would see to that before putting a pan of soup on for their supper.

Sabrina picked the telephone up and dialled the number of the shipping firm where Flo worked, smiling from ear to ear upon hearing her bezzie mates posh 'I'm at work' voice answer.

There was nothing at all posh about the squeal erupting from Flo when she heard Sabrina's voice; she had to hold the receiver away from her ear.

'I've so much to tell you, Flo,' she said, once her friend had calmed down.

'And I want to know everything, queen, but firstly, you're ahright?'

'I'm perfectly fine apart from feeling like I've run a marathon for some reason.'

She visualised Flo flapping that comment away as she demanded, 'Where've you been? Was Aunt Evie right?' She was choosing her wording carefully given she was in the office.

'I've been in nineteen twenty-eight and so much has happened. You won't believe it when I tell you.'

'Oh my God, girl, that's where she said you were.'

'It was so weird, Flo, meeting Aunt Evie when she was our age and her not recognising me.'

Florence's voice dropped to a whisper. 'Mr Steel's giving me daggers, he hates us having personal calls. Can I come around when I finish work?'

'Flo, I'm knackered. I'm going to go to bed.' Sabrina was apologetic.

Nevertheless, she received a huffy sigh. 'It's Saturday tomorrow. Is it business as usual in the shop?'

'Yes.' Sabrina stifled an eye-watering yawn. She was keen to get back to her normal routines as soon as possible. 'How about I pop round to yours after?'

'How am I supposed to wait until then?' Florence's whisper whined.

'Sorry, Flo.'

'You do sound done in. I'll manage, I suppose. What about Adam, have you spoken to him?'

'No, I wanted to talk to you first.' Sabrina pictured her pleased grin.

'I'm so glad you're home.'

'Me too, Flo.'

'I've got to go. I'll see you tomorrow. Ta-rah.'

She put the phone down and retrieved the number Aunt Evie had jotted down. She dialled the digits for Adam's home phone watching them spin back with a nervous excitement replacing her tiredness. Taking a deep breath as the last number, eight, spun back she listened to it ring, one, two, three. By the time she reached nine she knew she was wasting her time and disappointed she put the receiver back in the cradle. He wouldn't be back at work yet, and she wondered where he might be.

Sabrina must have drifted off because the next thing she knew, Aunt Evie was calling her to the table for a bowl of tomato soup and toast which she devoured.

'Aunt Evie, do you mind if I head off to bed?'

'No, I thought you were going to fall asleep with your head in the soup yawning like so. Off you go.'

Sabrina got up from the table, pausing with her hand on the back of the chair as a thought occurred to her. 'You haven't seen Fred while I've been away have you?' A surge of panic over what he must have thought when she'd stopped bringing him his morning porridge surged.

'Don't you be worrying about Fred. He hasn't missed out while you've been gone.'

Sabrina moved around the table to kiss her aunt on her soft cheek. For all her tough talk she was as soft as butter beneath it all.

Chapter Thirty-two

Sabrina slept the sleep of the dead, waking at six am after nearly twelve hours of solid slumber. She didn't feel groggy or fuddly headed though, she was alert and keen to start the day, or at least she was once she'd had her cup of tea. She slipped back into her familiar routine, making the porridge, eager to go down and check on Fred.

He was pleased to see her but as Aunt Evelyn had said he'd not gone without his hot cereal in her absence. She'd said ta-rah with the praises he'd been singing where her aunt was concerned still ringing in her ears. She was left with the impression he was a teeny bit taken with her.

It had filled her with joy to complete the simple tasks she'd taken for granted before opening the shop. She'd polished the fitting room mirror, tidied the pattern books away and dusted the counter, barely having turned the sign to open when the door rattled open.

'Am I early?' asked a pretty woman in her mid-twenties with red hair, who immediately made Sabrina think of Ciara. It wasn't Ciara however, it was Tara Newton and remembering she was supposed to have finished her dress this past week, Sabrina went hot wondering how she'd explain it not being ready for her final fitting.

'You're right on time, Tara,' Evelyn spoke up from out the back. 'I've your dress here.'

Sabrina swallowed the remnants of the strawberry Opal Fruit she'd been chewing and turned to where Aunt Evie was carrying through a weighty, sequinned affair. She should have known she'd manage in her absence.

Their customer was shifting about excitedly and Sabrina took the dress from Evelyn, carrying it carefully through to the fitting room. She hung it up and waited for Tara to follow her in before pulling the curtain shut and telling her to call out if she needed help with the dress.

Tara kept up a running commentary from within. 'Me boss isn't happy about me taking time off to come and try my dress on but I don't care. I could've come in my lunch break today I suppose but it would've been an awful rush. Besides, I couldn't wait, not knowing it was ready and once I'm married I'll be saying goodbye to that old dump anyway.'

Sabrina recalled Tara having mentioned she worked in the office of a car dealership.

'My Scott doesn't want me working there after we're wed.'

It was how they'd met. Sabrina remembered the story. Scott was a car salesman for the company and had taken a shine to the office girl, asking her out. Sabrina held her breath as she caught sight of her aunt's gin-soaked prune expression. She knew what was coming. She'd heard it many times before.

'Young lady, no woman should be reliant on a man to keep her. It always comes at a cost.'

Tara poked her head out from behind the pink drapes, her blue eyes widening at the little woman's outspoken remark.

'Well I'm looking forward to being a housewife,' she replied snippily, pulling the curtain back to reveal her bridal glory. 'I'm proud to be marrying my Scott.'

Sabrina coughed to try and cover up her aunt's, 'Well more fool you then.'

Tara floated out onto the floor in her princess gown where Sabrina was ready to make a fuss of her. As it happened not a single tweak was needed and so, once Tara was back in her civvies, she'd carefully wrapped the dress placing it in one of their namesake bags before ringing it up.

Tara had barely exited when the phone began to shrill and Sabrina was just finishing the call when she looked up to see Ray Taylor walking in. She said her goodbyes and put the phone down.

'Good morning, Mr Taylor.' She beamed. 'What can I do for you today?'

'Hello, Sabrina. Are you well?'

'Very thank you.'

Ray tugged at his suit jacket where it was straining across his middle. He was a natty dresser with a penchant for quality. Sabrina could almost smell the Italian leather of his shoes as he tapped his foot. 'I wondered if I might have a word with Evelyn.'

Sabrina was certain Evelyn, who heard everything, was well aware Ray Taylor was out the front but the steady hum of the Singer continued.

'I'll just get her for you.'

He nodded and smoothed the hair he meticulously combed over to cover his bald spot. Sabrina bit back a smile at the futility of the gesture given the wind howling down the street outside.

'Aunt Evie, you've a visitor,' she sang, ducking out the back.

Evelyn glowered overtop of the machine confirming what Sabrina suspected. 'I'm very busy, Sabrina,' she muttered shooting her a pleading glance.

'I'm not making excuses for you,' Sabrina whispered. 'He knows you're here. Don't be rude, go and say hello.'

Evelyn sighed, her annoyance clear as she stopped sewing and stood up, smoothing her coat before traipsing out behind Sabrina.

'Hello, queen! You're looking fetching in blue,' Ray exclaimed delightedly as she appeared in her Saturday blue shop coat hands thrust in her pockets.

Sabrina busied herself tidying away a roll of fabric and watched the unfolding scene with blatant curiosity.

'You always were one for the flattery, Ray. What can I do for you? I've a lot to do. There's always a bride in need of a dress you know.'

'You work like a Trojan. You always have. That's why I'd like to whisk you away for an evening. I wondered if I might interest you in a show I happen to have two tickets for. You always enjoyed big band music.'

Sabrina's eyes were wide and she'd forgotten she was trying to look busy. There was definite history between these two, she thought, wondering exactly what sort it was.

'It's been years since my dancing shoes had an outing, Ray. I'm not a girl anymore you know.'

'You'll always be that girl to me, Evie sweetheart.'

'Evelyn! Don't take liberties.'

Ray was unrepentant. 'What do you say? It's next Friday.'

Sabrina let out a sigh, guessing exactly what her aunt would say.

'I couldn't possibly, Ray. I go to Bingo with Ida on a Friday. Now, you'll have to excuse me, I can't stand around gasbagging all morning.'

Sabrina emerged from behind the roll of dupioni in time to see a dejected Ray Taylor take his leave. Once the door banged shut behind him she poked her head into the back.

Evelyn was arranging herself behind the sewing machine once more. 'Don't you say a word, Sabrina. Not a word, my girl.'

Sabrina rolled her eyes. Things were back to normal, alright.

The machine began to hum again and Sabrina returned to her Saturday morning duties eager for closing so she could head to Flo's and tell her everything that had happened while she'd been away.

Chapter Thirty-three

Sabrina tried Adam again before she left for Flo's but to her disappointment, there was no reply. The day was chilly and she shivered despite her jacket as she waited for the bus. It didn't take long and she sat downstairs, her nose pressed to the window, watching the world go by until she reached her stop. Calling out a thank you to the driver, she jumped off and walked at a clip down the street to the house she considered a second home.

The door of the pebbledash two-storey house was unlocked and pushing it open she called out a hello.

'In here, Sabrina luv.'

Sabrina followed her nose through the living room to the kitchen overlooking the back garden. A quick glance out the window gave her a glimpse of Mr Teesdale, a look of steely determination on his face as he tried to get his lawnmower going.

'It smells gorgeous in here, Mrs Teesdale.'

'Our kid told us you were coming round.' The older, plumper version of Flo finished buttering a plate of hot scones and passed it to her. 'Go on, take it up with you. She's had a right cob on all week. Seeing you might perk her up.'

'Ta. I think she'll be alright now though, Mrs T.' Sabrina smiled, pausing to ruffle the top of Shona or Teresa's hair, she never could tell them apart, before taking the stairs. She nearly tripped on Mittens who was sprawled across the top step his gingery colouring blending in with the carpet. The old moggie mewled his indignation but didn't move.

Tapping on Flo's door, she pushed it open to find her pal sitting at her dressing table an open magazine in front of her and an eyeshadow brush in her hand. She'd one eyelid coloured blue the other bare.

'Sabs!' she shrieked standing up. 'Bog off, you.' Her sister, peering around the door, scarpered down the stairs before Flo could get her in trouble with their mam.

Sabrina put the scones down on the dresser and hugged her pal tight, breathing in an unfamiliar fragrance. 'What's that you've been spraying.'

'Mystique. I'm a stress shopper. You being away was not good for my getting out of home fund. I bought this new eyeshadow set too.' Flo released her and gestured to the open blue-colour palette. 'I was trying to keep myself busy until you got here so I thought I'd copy her look.' She pointed to the glossy picture of a Cheshire cat grinning Christie Brinkley.

'Well, you'd best do the other eye or I won't be able to concentrate on what I'm telling you.' Sabrina laughed.

Flo obliged and once she'd matching eyelids they made themselves comfortable on her bed hoeing into her mam's offering.

'Mam keeps baking even though she knows I'm on the Weight Watchers. She's sabotaging me,' Florence mumbled, her mouth full of scone.

Sabrina grinned and polished her own off before saying, 'Are you ready to hear this?'

'Definitely,' Flo brushed crumbs off her midriff.

She launched into her tale, leaving nothing out, and every now and then Florence would open her mouth wanting to butt in with a question or to pass comment but then, not wanting to interrupt the flow, she'd close it again.

'I was so scared I wouldn't get back and then it just happened. I have no idea why,' Sabrina said, having reached the part where she'd unwittingly stepped forward in time.

'I was scared you wouldn't get back too.' Flo gave her a weak smile and reached over to squeeze her hand.

Sabrina squeezed back. 'I believe what Mystic Lou told me now, Flo. I think my mam and I got separated in a timeslip and I got stuck for some reason. I think I must be susceptible to whatever it is that causes the slip to happen. I mean for it to have happened to me twice and yet other people who walk past that spot on Bold Street never experience anything untoward.'

'I think you're right.'

'She didn't abandon me. She's looking for me and I have to keep looking for her.' Sabrina angled her head on the pillow toward her friend.

Flo looked back at her alarmed. 'You don't mean what I think you mean do you?'

'I'll try and go back to another time.' Sabrina nodded, the idea had been lurking but she'd not formed it properly until now. 'Imagine not knowing what happened to your child?'

'I can't, it's too awful.'

'Exactly, which is why I have to try and find her to tell her I was alright. Although Adam told me a story the night I stepped back which is why I went sniffing around outside

Hudson's in the first place about how his uncle encountered a woman claiming to be from nineteen eighty-three who'd lost someone. She said, 'Her, I've got to find her'. Maybe she was looking for me? She could have been my mam.'

'Oh my God,' Flo said, her shadowed eyes enormous. 'That would mean time catches up to when you got separated in two years.'

Sabrina nodded. 'Or she didn't make it back to nineteen eighty-three and she's lost in another time. I have to know, Flo.'

'Have you told Aunt Evie what you're planning?'

'No.'

'She won't like it you know, Sabs.'

'I know.' Sabrina was torn. She didn't want to put her aunt through her disappearing to who knew where it might be next time if it even happened a third time but she had to for her mam's sake.

Florence sat up then. 'I don't want to think about it. I've only just got you back. I wonder what became of Jane and Sidney?' She stretched.

'I'd like to find out. She was a good friend to me. It shouldn't be hard to find them. I could always go to where the antique shop used to be and ask the people in there now if they know what happened to the previous owner.'

'Good idea.'

'We've been lying here so long my legs have gone to sleep. I think we should go for a jog, Sabs. Wake ourselves up.'

Sabrina dabbed at the crumbs on the plate. 'I'm awake.'

'Come on, girl. I'm the poster girl for the Bootle Weight Watchers remember? Bossy Bev's put a lot of responsibility on my shoulders and I need to work those scones off. You said you'd come with me next time,' she wheedled.

That's right, Sabrina thought, regretting the impetuous remark. It seemed a lifetime ago now. But first, let me try Adam one more time.

This time he picked up.

———⊙———

FLORENCE LUNGED FORWARDS, hands on hips, resplendent in her lemon tracksuit ensemble complete with a towelling headband to prove she meant business.

Sabrina watched her for a moment before following suit. She'd borrowed Flo's blue tracksuit bottoms pulling the cord as tight as it would go to ensure they didn't wind up around her ankles as she jogged along.

'We've got to warm up or we might pull something,' Florence informed her friend, straightening and grabbing her ankle before bending her leg behind her. Clearly an expert in her field given this was her second time doing a circuit of the park.

Sabrina nearly fell over as she attempted to do the same. She steadied herself and took a moment to admire the shades of gold, orange and red in the canopy above them. She smiled remembering the beautiful perennial posy Jane had carried.

Autumn was certainly making its presence known, she thought, knowing too that it would be dark soon but if they set off now they'd make it around the park and back before it set in.

'Ready?' Flo said, now jogging on the spot, keen for the off so she could find out what Sabrina and Adam had talked about.

Sabrina had refused to give her the low-down until they were running. She reckoned relaying their conversation mid-run would take her mind off the fact she was doing something unnatural like jogging.

Sabrina pumped her arms and hummed the theme tune to the Bionic Woman. 'Ready.'

They set off at a sedate pace somewhere between a fast walk and a run. Sabrina soon picked up on the secret language of their fellow joggers giving what Flo informed her was the jogger's nod as they passed by one another.

Flo puffed, 'Right, Adam, you promised.'

'I told him I'd been away seeing my cousin, Tess in Wales.'

'You don't have a cousin Tess in Wales.'

'I know but it was all I could think of on the hop like. I wasn't expecting him to answer.' She didn't know why she hadn't told him the truth. He was openminded when it came to the unexplainable, he'd said so when she'd visited him at the hospital. Still, it was a lot to get in to over the phone. She needn't have lied though, and she promised herself she'd put him straight when she saw him. Hopefully, that would be sooner rather than later. 'He asked if he could take me for a spin on his bike.'

'And what did you say?' Flo panted, her cheeks turning pink with exertion.

'I said I'd like that.'

'Did you make a date?'

'No.' She'd not realised until she'd put the phone down that they'd not organised a specific time.

'I'm surprised he's keen to get back on a motorbike after what happened.'

'He loves it, Flo, his bike's his passion.'

'Well just make sure he doesn't put you before his wheels. Remember that right divvy I went out with for a while who talked to his car like she was his girlfriend?'

Sabrina nodded, keen to conserve her breath.

'What will Aunt Evie say about you going on the back of his bike?'

'Probably pretty much what she'll say when I tell her about my plan to find my mam.'

Flo agreed and then gasped. 'Oh my God, girl, the state of those shorts!'

There, jogging towards them in the skimpiest, tightest pair of shorts was Mr Tight Trousers from the Swan.

He swerved into their path, jogging on the spot as he panted, 'Ahright there, girls, you drink at the Swan, don't you? Fancy meeting you here.' He pulled one of the earplugs out of his ear. He'd a Walkman hooked onto his shorts and the tinny sound of Queen's *Another One Bites the Dust* emanated from the dangling plug.

'Me name's Tony.'

'This is Flo and I'm Sabrina,' Sabrina said, all but elbowing Florence who mumbled hello. She cast about for something to say. 'Great night for a run.'

'It is. Are you coming down the Swan tonight?'

'We're not sure yet are we, Sabs?' Florence found her voice.

'Well, if you are, maybe I can buy you a round of bevvies?' He'd included Sabrina in the equation but he only had eyes for Florence, Sabrina noticed, thinking he was making her dizzy with all that dancing about in one place.

Flo gave him an evasive smile and glanced at her watch. 'Sabrina, we've got to get going. Me mam's got tea on the go and she hates it when I'm late.' She got to her feet.

Tony appraised her lemon outfit and it was obvious he liked what he saw. 'I'll hopefully see you tonight then?'

'Mmm, maybe. See you then,' Florence mumbled, taking off at a sprint.

Tony put his plug back in his ear and giving Sabrina a wave jogged off. Sabrina took off after her friend.

'Wait up, Flo!'

'Don't you say a bloody word,' Florence said as Sabrina, red in the face and breathing heavily, caught her up.

Sabrina smirked. It was exactly what Aunt Evie had said to her earlier that afternoon.

IT WAS A GOOD ALBEIT uneventful night that had ensued at the Swan which suited Sabrina just fine. She'd be happy with uneventful for the time being. Flo followed Tim around with Bambi eyes for the best part of the evening.

He'd not ventured onto the dance floor this time, much to her disappointment, instead spending the evening trying to get over Liverpool's football loss that evening by laughing bawdily at the table where he was sat with his posse of mates.

Flo had muttered into her pint glass upon seeing him track Sally Wanderley's sway to the bar. 'She's all fur coat and no knickers that one.'

Sabrina snorted hearing that. 'Aunt Evie says that sort of thing.'

Sally, with whom they'd gone to school, had the looks of a fashion model but when she opened her mouth she was pure Scouse.

'Well it's true,' Flo said, a smile creeping across her face despite herself.

Tony minced over to their table; it was impossible to do anything else in trousers that tight. He was carrying two glasses as promised. He flicked his sandy hair away from his face as he deposited the drinks down in front of the girls.

'Mickey told me what you were drinking.'

'Ta very much,' Sabrina said, nudging Flo's foot under the table.

There'd been an awkward silence then as he waited for an invitation to join them. Sabrina's insides had scrunched up as her pal, who didn't have it in her to be rude but couldn't be seen to encourage Tony in front of Tim said, 'I'd ask you to join us but Sabrina here's telling me about her aunt's woman's troubles. It's a nasty business the change of life. A nasty business indeed.'

He'd beat as hasty a retreat as his trousers allowed back to the others at that.

'Aunt Evie went through the change long before I happened along!'

'He doesn't need to know that though, does he, Sabs?' Flo had said, pleased with herself.

Chapter Thirty-four

Sabrina finished stitching the lace sleeve onto Lucy McGowan's gown. Her eyes flicked about looking for scissors because she refused to ask Aunt Evie to pass hers over. She wasn't in the mood for an 'if you wore a shop coat' lecture and she grabbed the pair she spotted peeking out from under a bolt of fabric she'd been showing a customer earlier. Snipping the thread off she eyed her work with a sense of satisfaction before standing up and holding the dress up against her.

'Voila! What do you think, Aunt Evie?'

Evelyn took her foot off the treadle and pushed her glasses back up her nose to inspect Sabrina's handiwork. For a moment, she visualised her walking down the aisle in the gown and was in danger of becoming emotional as her throat tightened. She'd make a beautiful bride she thought, swallowing hard and knowing she was being silly. It wasn't Sabrina's dress. She was a way off marching down the aisle especially given she was back to her fidgety telephone watching once more. She appraised the dress once more with a critic's eye.

'The eyelet lace was a good suggestion, Sabrina. It works a treat on the sleeves. The perfect choice for an in between season. Lucy should be very happy with it I'd say. You've made a lovely job of it.'

Given her Aunt Evie had been a thorough and uncompromising teacher not shy in telling her when her work wasn't up to standard as she apprenticed under her, Sabrina was chuffed.

'Thank you. I hope she's pleased.' Retrieving a padded hanger from the rack of other dresses waiting to be picked up, she slid the gown carefully onto it before hanging it in between the Vicky and the Sarah gowns.

Job done, she thought, swallowing a yawn and stretching. She'd a crick in her neck from being hunched over sewing this last hour.

It had been a quietish afternoon on the shop floor and the uninterrupted few hours sewing meant they wouldn't have to put in any late nights toiling in the workshop to meet their commitments. Commitments that had fallen a little behind in Sabrina's absence.

'I'll try Lucy and tell her her dress is ready.'

Evelyn mumbled an 'mmm' intent on the panel she was sewing.

There was no answer and with one hand rubbing the stiff part of her neck, she glanced at her watch. Another five minutes and she'd close for the evening.

A frown puckered her forehead once more as she heard a rumbling coming from outside. It sounded like a motorbike but then Adam was never far from her thoughts. Crumbs, now she was even hearing phantom motorbikes!

She'd been doing her cat on a hot tin roof impersonation waiting for the telephone to jangle into life each evening since she'd spoken to him from Flo's on Saturday afternoon but so far nothing.

'A watched pot never boils, Sabrina.' Aunt Evie had remarked the night before.

'I'm not watching a pot, I'm waiting for the telephone to ring,' Sabrina had replied mutinously and when the adverts came on she got up and fetched a packet of biscuits down from the cupboard. She'd have preferred it if they were chocolate but beggars couldn't be choosers she thought, offering the Jacob's fig rolls to her aunt who took one from her and promptly dunked it in her tea.

Sabrina was working her way through her fourth when Aunt Evie had told her she'd best quit while she was ahead because if she ate much more fig the telephone not ringing would be the least of her problems.

The rumbling grew louder.

'Is that thunder?' Evelyn called out. 'They didn't mention that on the weather last night.'

Sabrina knew she wasn't imagining it then and she rushed over to the fitting room mirror to check she'd not got the Opal Fruit she'd been chewing stuck in her teeth or crumbs down her front from her afternoon tea bicky before hastily trying to fluff some life into her hair.

The rumbling had stopped and when the door opened she was pretending to straighten the fitting room drapes. She looked over, her heart jumping, to see Adam clutching two helmets and a bunch of pale pink and yellow dahlias.

'They're an autumn flower apparently,' he said, holding them out with a boyish grin on his face. 'I hope you like them.'

Sabrina wouldn't have cared if they were dandelions. 'They're beautiful, thank you.' She took the flowers from him. A tingle where her fingers had brushed his shot up her arm as she buried her nose in the blooms. She felt foolish coming back up for air as she realised they didn't have a scent.

'Eh-hem.'

Sabrina swung around to see Aunt Evie standing in the doorway.

'Oh, erm, Aunt Evie, this is Adam.' She willed her aunt to behave herself and not drop any clangers about telephone watching and fig roll stuffing.

'Hello, Adam, it's nice to make your acquaintance.' Evelyn gave him the once over. He reminded her of someone, she thought frowning, but it wouldn't come to her.

'And yours—' Adam looked apologetically at her and then to Sabrina for help. He couldn't very well call her Aunt Evie.

'Miss Flooks,' Evelyn cut in. It was far too early for first names, she thought, eyeing the helmets he had hold of and hoping they didn't mean what she guessed they did.

Adam tracked her gaze. 'I wondered if I might be able to take Sabrina for a ride on me bike? I'm very careful and I promise to go easy. If you want to that is?' He looked questioningly at Sabrina and then hopefully across to Evelyn once more. She was quite intimidating for such a little lady. But then, he already knew that.

'A ride on your motorbike?' Evelyn said this in a tone that might as well have said, 'On yer bike, son.'

'Yes. I'll be very careful.'

It was a good job her aunt didn't know about his accident Sabrina thought seeing her mouth working in that way of hers that signalled she was about to come up with one hundred and one reasons why Sabrina would not be going for a ride on his motorbike. She headed her off. 'Aunt Evie, I'm twenty-one.' She did not need her permission and reaching forward she took the helmet from Adam. 'I would love to go for a ride, ta very much.'

Adam was hesitant, he didn't want to get off on the wrong foot with Sabrina's aunt.

Evelyn sized him up. He didn't look like your James Dean *Rebel Without a Cause* type and Sabrina was right, she was an adult. 'I want you to pretend you've the Queen Mother herself on the back of that bike. Do you understand, young man?'

'Aunt Evie!'

'I understand.' Adam gave her a reassuring nod.

'You'd best put those flowers in water then, Sabrina, and get your jacket. I take it you'll want to put trousers on too.' She eyed Sabrina's knee-length skirt.

Sabrina put the helmet on the counter. She was hesitant about leaving Adam alone with her aunt while she raced upstairs to get changed but she couldn't very well hop on the back of his bike in what she was wearing. Her skirt would be billowing out like a parachute if she did, giving anyone who cared to look a good goggle at her knickers.

'I'll be back in two ticks.'

When Sabrina came back downstairs she half expected to find Adam gone, frightened off by an overprotective Aunt Evie. Instead, they were chatting amicably about her second favourite subject after wedding gowns, football. She zipped her jacket and smiled eagerly at Adam. 'I'm all set.'

'I'll have her back by ten at the latest, Miss Flooks.'

Evelyn nodded. There was something about him but for the life of her, she couldn't put her finger on what it was.

Chapter Thirty-five

Adam pulled the helmet down on Sabrina's head and she tilted her chin upwards as he did the strap up, pulling on it to make sure it was tight enough. He straddled the bike, kicking the stand back before gunning the engine and gesturing for her to climb on the back.

The bike was the sort that garnered admiring glances from the foot traffic; that or annoyance over the thunderclap of sound. Either way, Sabrina felt as if she were starring in her very own Calvin Klein jeans advertisement as she swung her denim-clad leg over the seat of the Triumph and squished up behind him.

'Brooke Shields, eat your heart out,' she said to herself, wrapping her arms around his waist and breathing in the rich leather of his jacket.

He half turned and said, 'Ahright.'

She nodded, unable to stop the excited grin that spread all over her face as he swerved out into the early evening home-time traffic. She was trembling at the thrill of it all and wished she'd see someone she knew so she could wave out. Not that they'd know who she was with a helmet on her head anyway.

Remembering he'd not long since had surgery, she hoped she wasn't hurting him with her vice-like grip around his middle but she was too worried about flying off the back to loosen it.

He dodged the bike expertly around the pootling rush hour traffic and she could feel the wind whipping her face and stinging her eyes as they rode through the streets. She pressed her face into his jacket to stave it off as her eyes streamed, wondering where they were going.

She didn't have to wonder long because he slowed before nudging the bike in between two cars parked outside Clive's chippy. Sabrina smiled. She should have guessed. They were going to have that fish 'n' chip supper they'd talked about up at the hospital.

'How was that?' Adam asked, taking his helmet off and running his hand threw his hair. 'Are you ahright?'

He undid the buckle under her chin and she pulled hers off, wincing at the thought of her helmet hair.

'Great! I loved it.'

He pushed open the door to the chippy, yet to get busy given it was still early, which was a little disappointing as Sabrina would have liked an audience for her cool, biker's girl swagger. *Oh, if only Flo could see her now!* They placed their order and sat down to wait.

Sabrina picked up the salt shaker toying with it as she spoke first. 'I was surprised to see you. You're supposed to be taking things easy, aren't you?'

He nodded. 'I feel okay though. I'm a fast healer and it was driving me mad kicking about at home. I had to get out. The bike's therapeutic.'

Sabrina smiled. 'I wonder what Nurse Ratched would say if she knew what you were up to?'

Adam laughed. 'I don't think I want to know. The Royal Liverpool won't have to worry about not having enough beds while she's on the payroll. The lads on my ward couldn't get home fast enough.'

They both looked up as the door opened and a scruffy fella whose hair looked in need of a good scrub mooched in, the stub of a cigarette threatening to burn his yellow fingers. He stared at Sabrina for a moment before heading up to the counter. She didn't think anything of it as she asked, 'What about work?'

'Light duties only, paperwork, boring stuff I can do from home.' He waved his hand dismissively. 'It's not worth talking about. How was Wales?'

'I didn't go to Wales.'

Adam tilted his head quizzically.

Sabrina lowered her voice and dived straight in. 'I'm sorry I fibbed. I just didn't want to get into it over the telephone and Wales just sort of popped out of my mouth. Do you remember what you told me at the hospital about your uncle and the girl he met who was looking for someone, who said she was from a different time?'

'Of course I do.

'That's where I've been.'

Adam's dark eyes widened and he leaned closer to her across the table as Sabrina gave him a brief run-down of where she'd gone after she'd been to the hospital that night to see him.

'That's flippin' amazing,' Adam said, shaking his head.

Sabrina was relieved there was no doubt at what she'd told him in his voice.

'My God. I can't get me head around it. So it was true all along what me uncle Eddie said?'

Sabrina nodded. 'If what happened to me is anything to go by, then yes. And who knows, maybe the woman he met that day was my mam.'

Adam reached across the table and grabbed her hand. Sabrina tried not to jump at the jolt his touch sent through her. 'I'm glad you made it back.'

'Two fish, one chips.'

'That's us.' Adam let go of her hand and got up, taking the newspaper parcel from the counter.

'Are we not eating here?'

'No, I've got somewhere else in mind. Will you be alright holding on that?'

Sabrina nodded, curious as to where he'd take her next.

Chapter Thirty-six

The newspaper package was still like a hot water bottle when she handed it to Adam before clambering off the bike. They were at Everton Brow and taking her helmet off herself this time she fluffed her hair up.

There was an empty bench seat on the side of the grassy hill of Everton Park and they made their way over to it, sitting down.

'Not too cold?'

Sabrina shook her head. 'It's gorgeous.' She looked at the rich autumn glow from the trees punctuating the sloping greenery. The vibrant hues were made more intense by the sun's last hurrah. Lights flickered on in the park like the first stars twinkling in the sky.

Adam did the honours, unwrapping the newspaper and sending up a tummy rumbling waft of fried food and vinegar as he did so.

'That smells so good,' Sabrina said, helping herself to a chip. 'I don't think I've ever sat up here.'

'I come here a lot just to sit and clear my head.' Adam went straight for the fish.

Sabrina pointed out the various city landmarks whose shadowy shapes she could make out, spread below them in between munching.

'I can see the coastline.' She'd always loved a day out at Crosby beach, squealing and running away from the encroaching waves with Flo as the family picnicked on the sand. Nobody ever minded the fact there was always sand in their tomato sandwiches.

'On a good day, you can see as far as North Wales,' Adam said.

'I've never been to Wales,' Sabrina said sheepishly.

Adam stared at her, chip halfway to his mouth. 'You've never been to Wales at all? Not even on a school trip?'

Sabrina shrugged. 'No, and Aunt Evie isn't one for going far. She hates closing the shop and she wouldn't trust anyone other than me to run it if she were to have a holiday. I always spent my holidays with my bezzie mate Flo's family. They liked the Isle of Man.'

'Flo would be the lass me mate Tony fancies?'

Sabrina nodded hoping he wouldn't ask what Florence thought of him in order to report back to Tony. She decided to change the subject. 'We had some good times on the Isle of Man.'

'I love the Isle of Man, me. I want to compete in the TT there next May.'

'What's that?' She listened with her head tilted to one side as he filled her in about the motorbike sport race.

'It's been an annual event since nineteen oh seven,' he said, offering her the last chip.

'No, ta. I'm full.' She was in danger of popping the top button of her Calvin's something she was sure Brooke Shields had never experienced as she lounged about in her brand-name jeans. She supposed it would take more than one half-hearted jog to loosen her belt. 'It sounds dangerous.'

Adam's eyes sparkled, 'It's not for the faint-hearted but then neither's time travel I'd say. What are you going to do?'

'About my mam do you mean?'

He nodded. 'I don't see you as the type of girl who'll let something like that go.'

'I'm not.'

She relayed what she'd told Florence about how she planned on trying to find her mam. 'The woman your uncle saw may or may not have been her. If it was then perhaps I'll find her in two years when we reach the time she came from.' She shrugged. 'Who's to say she didn't get lost in another time though. I can't do nothing for the next two years. I have to look for her.'

'But what if you don't come back?'

'It's something I have to do, Adam, besides, I got back this time, didn't I?'

He nodded. 'It's a risk though, isn't it? There're no guarantees but I understand your need to try. I know you were small but it's a hard thing losing your mam. I lost mine a few years ago now and it leaves a hole here.' He put his hand on his heart. 'If there was a chance, any chance of seeing her again, I'd take it even if it meant travelling through time.'

He scrunched the empty newspaper and got up, 'Sabrina?'

'Yes.'

'I want you to come back. Promise me you'll come back if you go again?'

She couldn't promise. 'I'd never stop trying.' It was the best she could come up with.

He looked at her for a beat and then walked the short distance to the bin near where he'd parked the bike, tossing the balled up paper in it.

It was nearly dark now and Sabrina watched as a mist-shrouded, evening luminosity settled over her city. Adam came back and held out his hand, 'Shall we get a pint to wash that down?'

She nodded and took his hand but as he helped her up his other arm reached out and pulled her in to him. The gesture took her by surprise and her heart thudded with exhilaration at what was about to happen. She wondered if he could feel it pounding like she could feel the heat of his chest through his sweater. His hair fell into his eyes which were half closed as she raised her head to meet his mouth. His lips were soft and she could taste salt on them and as he gently parted hers with his tongue her whole body began to tremble inside. She pressed herself harder against him and melted into that kiss.

They only pulled apart when a car pulled in above them, spearing them briefly with its headlights.

'C'mon,' Adam said, taking her hand and leading her back up the hill.

Chapter Thirty-seven

Sabrina floated through the next couple of days. There'd been hers and Adam's first kiss overlooking the city and then he'd kissed her again as they said goodnight outside the back entrance of the shop on Wood Street.

She was in a bubble of happiness and the world had seemed different when she got up the morning after their date. The smells were sharper, the colours brighter, things even tasted better. It could be called love she'd thought, remembering how it had felt to be in his arms, the taste and smell of him which sent a quiver coursing through her where Aunt Evie would say no woman should quiver.

The only thing she'd like to forget about their evening was how, when she'd paid a visit to the Ladies once they'd arrived at the Swan she'd nearly died. She had mascara streaks down either side of her face and if she were to run through the pub emitting a war cry she'd very much look the part of a psychotic warrior rather than cool biker girl. She'd use a waterproof mascara next time she was going on the back of his bike!

She'd stared in the mirror horrified that she'd sat in Clive's chippy—no wonder that fella had stared at her—gazed at Adam with love struck eyes up Everton Brown—and walked through a heaving pub looking like that.

Flo would have a field day she'd thought, rubbing the streaks away. Her mouth twitching at the thought of her pal's giggles. It was funny and Adam, God love him, had been too polite to say a word. What must he have thought? And how had he kept a straight face homing in to kiss her?

She'd thumped him playfully when she sat back down and he said he was sorry for not saying anything but he thought she looked beautiful anyway. She'd had to forgive him.

Now, as the double-decker chugged in alongside the bus shelter where a young girl was busy grinding out her cigarette, the driver turned and called over his shoulder, 'This is the Peterborough Street stop, luv.'

Sabrina got up from the seat, 'Ta very much.' She stepped down onto the pavement, narrowly missing stepping into a fresh blob of chewed gum some charming so and so had deposited there. She turned the corner onto Peterborough Street and looked down the long row of perfectly normal red brick houses on either side of the road. Her hand reached into her jeans to retrieve the address she'd dug out of the phone book. It was number forty-two she was after.

It wasn't in the first block and crossing the side street running through she received an indignant, 'Oi, look where you're going,' from a young lad on a bike. She'd been too busy focusing on where she was headed.

A dog let the neighbourhood know a stranger was in their midst and she said, 'Oh, shurrup, you,' to the black and white collie whose paws were resting on the front gate as he barked for all he was worth.

And then, there it was. She double-checked the number, yes forty-two. The house was tidily kept and the front door painted a cheery red with the shiniest brass knocker she'd ever seen.

Taking a deep breath and with a building excitement, Sabrina unlatched the gate and walked the short distance to the door. She lifted the knocker and rapped.

She was jiggling from foot to foot with anticipation when the door opened a few seconds later and she found herself looking into a pair of silvery eyes she'd once known well.

The two women stared at one another and Sabrina was oblivious to the black cat who'd also come to the door and was brushing against her leg in a bid for attention.

The woman held the door open wider. 'I always hoped you'd come, Sabrina.'

The years fell away from the woman's face and Sabrina smiled. 'I wanted to know if you and Sidney got your extraordinary life, Jane.'

'Oh, we did, Sabrina. Come in we've so much to catch up on.'

THE END...

Read on for an excerpt from The Winter Posy, Book 2 in the Liverpool Brides Series

Chapter One

Liverpool, 1952

Patty

IT WASN'T THE DAMP and the rats that scuttled about the walls that killed her, Patty Hamilton thought, watching as her dear mother's body was carried from the squalid room they occupied in Osbourne Court, Toxteth. No, it was despair.

She was certain if there'd been a glimmer of hope their circumstances would improve then her mam would've found the strength to shake off the rumbling cough that had turned sinister as the winter months stretched long and the cold crept into all their bones.

Patty, who was ten and her eight-year-old brother, Davey were sitting at the table that had come with the room. The tea things were still laid out because their mam liked things to be nice. Aside from the two mattresses she'd insisted they drag into the middle of the room of a night to be away from the scratching sounds and rising damp in the walls, it was the only furniture in the room. The one-ring cooker pushed into the corner didn't count as furniture in Patty's opinion. It was as useless for cooking as it was for heating.

Patty's blue eyes, which were mirror images of her mam's, had once shone brightly. Now they were dull as she looked at her mam's mattress where she could see the indent her body had made in it along with the damp patches left behind by her feverish sweats. Her breath caught and her throat tightened to the point where she felt as if it were closing over as the reality of what was happening hit her.

She'd never see her mam again. Geraldine Hamilton who'd left Ireland with her family as a fourteen-year-old girl for a brighter future in Liverpool had not lived to see in her thirty-third birthday.

The unfairness of it all weighed down on Patty but she knew thinking like that would get them nowhere and grieving was a luxury she couldn't afford. There'd be time for that later once she and Davey were safely settled. She'd made her mam a promise so she could pass peacefully and she intended to keep it.

Now, she needed to gather their things and go. Mam had told her what she was to do. She'd mustered what strength she'd had left to clutch Patty's hand as she rasped, they weren't to linger after she'd gone or she'd find herself in a children's home, likely separated from Davey. She'd made Patty promise they'd stick together and that she'd look after her brother come what may. Then, she'd pressed a piece of paper with an address she said they were to make their way to.

It was their father's.

Mrs Maher from next door had poked her head around the door to give a sanctimonious tut when Mr Maher and kind Mr Finnegan, who lived downstairs, had come to take their mam away not fifteen minutes earlier.

She'd no right, Patty had thought, with a scowl at the hard-faced woman who was known for being quarrelsome. She was no better than them. Her flat, while marginally larger and with more in the way of homely furnishings, was no palace and it reeked of onions. She was slovenly.

Mam had done her best by her and Davey but it was hard when you had nothing; even harder when you had no hope.

Patty didn't like Mrs Maher and this feeling was cemented as the woman's eyes, pushed into a fleshy face like currants in a bun, had feigned concern over where'd they go now they were orphans.

'We're not orphans, Mrs Maher,' Davey had replied indignantly. He was the spitting image of his father with his brown hair and grey-green eyes. He shared the same ski ramp nose as his mam and sister though. 'We've a father and that's where we'll be going.'

Mrs Maher had raised a disbelieving eyebrow, her dimpled hands resting on fat hips, 'And what makes you think he'd want you? He hasn't done much for you up to now has he, young Davey? Leaving your poor mam to fend for youse both on her own, like.'

It was a good point, Patty had thought with a stab of uncertainty at what lay ahead but Mam had assured her the man she'd married wouldn't turn his own flesh and blood away. Not when he heard what had befallen them. He was a weak and arrogant fella she'd said but he wasn't cold-hearted.

'Because he's our daddy,' Davey replied simply.

With the speed Mrs Maher had thudded down the stairs after that, Patty surmised the meddling woman had decided to hotfoot it around to the powers that be to notify them the Hamilton children from Osbourne Court were orphans and what were they going to do about it?

It was with this in mind she told Davey to gather up his things and not to mess about doing so as she retrieved the battered case with which they'd arrived. Back then, Mam had assured them it was only for a little while as she'd surveyed their grim surroundings. Patty shook that memory away and scooped up her own scant belongings depositing them in the suitcase.

There'd been no wake for their mam but she and Davey had said their goodbyes and that was what mattered. Patty had sung to her as she'd done to soothe her when she was alive and the pain got bad. Mam had always said she'd the voice of an angel. It was a gift she'd said and she must be sure to use it. She hoped her mam was with the angels now.

There was no family to contact because she'd been estranged from them since before Patty was born. There was nothing of hers to keep either. The engagement ring with its red-pink ruby Patty used to enjoy gazing at had been pawned long ago to pay the rent. It was still at the shop and would have to stay there. She'd have liked that ring as a keepsake.

The children's mother hadn't been fit to work at Cadbury's where she'd worked on the factory floor for some months now. Patty had wanted to leave school to help out but Geraldine Hamilton wouldn't hear of it.

'You'll finish your schooling, Patty, and find yourself a decent job. Don't leave yourself beholden to a man like I did,' she'd choked out. 'You must make your own way in the world.'

It was the closest she came to talking about their daddy, who'd gone to apply for a job one morning and never come back.

They weren't to worry about what would happen to their mam now, Mr Finnegan had said, giving them a reassuring smile as he'd wrapped their mother's body carefully in the sheet she'd lain on. Father Sean would look after her. She'd not have to suffer anymore.

He was cut from the same cloth as his wife, Patty had thought, grateful for his kindness. Mrs Finnegan had a soft heart too. She'd often sent up an extra bowl of whatever she'd cooked for dinner, stretching it out somehow because she'd known the Hamilton children were in dire straits with their poor mam not fit for earning.

Patty pulled herself back to the here and now. 'Have you got teddy?'

Davey sat down cross-legged on the floor by the case pushing his thumb in his mouth. Their mam had told him he was far too old for that sort of carry-on and he'd catch germs putting his thumb in his mouth like so but Patty figured if it gave him comfort so be it.

The little boy nodded and pointed to where the grubby worn toy he refused to sleep without was nestled between their meagre assortment of clothes.

Patty scanned the room once more, reassuring herself there was nothing more to go in the case. Then, she closed it. The click echoed in the empty space that no longer felt like any sort of home now their mother was gone.

She'd not miss this place, she thought, casting her eyes about one last time. It didn't hold happy memories and she doubted she'd ever get the smell of damp and decay from her nostrils.

The Hamilton family hadn't always lived hand to mouth picking their way through the parts of the city still pockmarked by bombsites. Once they'd lived in a terrace house with a front room, a proper kitchen, and a bathroom on Lowry Lane. It hadn't been the smartest of addresses but so far as houses went it had been happy and it had been home.

Patty and Davey had shared one of the two upstairs bedrooms. The wallpaper had not been hanging off the wall and they'd had a proper front door to come and go through. They'd not been cold and they'd not gone to bed hungry either.

Patty had thought she'd live in that house until she was old enough to get married but then one evening their father stormed in waving his P45. She'd only been eight at the time but she remembered him spouting off about having told that bunch of woollybacks he worked under at the English Electric he'd had enough. 'Anthony Hamilton won't be told what to do by the likes of them,' he roared in a manner that made Patty and Davey's eyes pop. He was a senior salesman who knew his domestic appliances better than any of the others on the payroll he went on to lament, saying it was their loss.

He'd seen his children watching on from the doorway wide-eyed and had given them a wink telling them not to worry he'd be moving on to bigger, better things.

Even at her young age, Patty would never forget the way the light had seemed to go out in her mam's pretty blue eyes that evening.

Patty couldn't understand why because she'd believed every word her daddy said but then he was her hero. She worshipped the ground her handsome father walked on and if he said not to worry, well then she wouldn't. Davey was too young to know what was going on and so long as he was fed and watered he was a happy lad.

The weeks had ticked by though and with each day that passed without their father walking through the door with a spring in his step and news of his new job, the atmosphere in the house shifted. It became oppressive and their mam always seemed to be crying.

Patty had been told often enough she was a sensitive child but the evidence that things had changed was stark. The reminder was there each evening in the lack of meat in the stew and the watery soups Mam was presenting them with.

Patty had asked her mam when Daddy would find work and to her surprise and horror she'd set her mam off on a fresh bout of crying.

Geraldine had sniffed out that Patty's father was a dreamer and she should have seen beyond his good looks and listened to her auld mam because dreams were all well and good but they didn't put food on the table and provide a roof over the head.

'He came from wealth,' she sniffed. 'He thinks he's destined for grander things than selling on the shop floor. Your daddy,' she carried on, her mouth forming a hard flat line, 'sees himself at the top of the ladder. He wants to sit up there lording it over all those below without doing any climbing first. It's not the first job he's thrown to the wind,

Pats. Selfish is what he is. He doesn't think about what he's doing to me or you and Davey.'

She'd gestured to the stack of letters that had been pushed through the letter box at a steady rate of knots these last few weeks. All had big red angry letters jumping off them.

Patty had wanted to put her hands over her ears. She didn't want to hear any of this but her mam had kept going wiping her hands on her pinny.

'Your father thinks he knows it all you see. It's not a good trait to have and if I ever see it in youse children I'll be snuffing it out.'

Patty didn't like her mam talking to her like she was an adult. Nor did she like hearing her talk about her daddy like this. The sun rose and set over him where she was concerned and her bottom lip had trembled with the urge to bite back but she wasn't a child to give cheek by answering back and anyone could see her mam was on the edge.

Geraldine had sighed, picking up the knife once more to return to the spuds. 'I was like you once, luv. I believed all his pie in the sky big talk and let my head be turned by a handsome face but my dreams died the day your dad walked out of English Electric. I should have listened to me mam,' she repeated, half to herself and half to Patty.

'He'll find something else, Mam. You'll see.'

'He won't, Pats. He's marked his cards. The word's spread he's difficult.' She'd begun to peel the potatoes then and the set in her shoulders had told Patty she wasn't about to say anymore. The conversation had left Patty, feeling unsettled as though her life as she knew it was an eggshell that had cracked.

Things had gone from bad to worse after that, and one day she and Davey had arrived home from school to find Mam and Daddy waiting on the front path, suitcases by their side. Their father's expression frightened Patty. It was one she'd never seen before. It was of defeat.

The two Hamilton children were bewildered by what was happening but their mam had jollied them along with how it was a big adventure going to live somewhere else.

'Will I have to go to a new school, Mam?' Patty had asked, clambering aboard the bus behind her.

'You will.'

'But what about my friends? I haven't said goodbye to any of them.'

'Now, now none of that. You'll soon make new friends. You can't dwell on the past, Pats. You must look forward.'

Patty's head was spinning as she sat down on the seat and the bus pootled away from the street she'd called home.

Their new home was a flat above a newsagent with no front entrance. Patty and Davey hadn't liked it. Davey found the boys his age who played in the street rough and Patty had come home from school crying to her mam that she was scared the nit nurse would shave her head like some of the other girls.

Their daddy had found temporary work in a menswear shop but he wasn't happy with the wages and they'd hear their parents hushed whispers as Mam told him he'd have to put it up with it and he hit back that he deserved more. The hushed voices had grown louder in intensity each evening and Davey would ask Patty to sing to him to block out their arguing. Then, one morning, their daddy set off for work and never came back.

That had been over three years ago now and they'd had to move again to the room in Osbourne Court and their mam had found work in the Cadbury factory.

She'd never offered an explanation as to where he'd gone or what had happened despite her children's confusion and tears over his disappearance. It was only when she knew she'd not long left that she'd pressed the handwritten address near the sea into Patty's hand and made her promise to go there with Davey when she passed.

Now, Patty felt in her pocket for the fare Mam had put away for them. She closed the door on their old life and hefted the case down the stairs, holding Davey's hand with her spare hand. It was time to go.

The Winter Posy

ONE LITTLE GIRL LEFT ON THE STREETS OF LIVERPOOL. A MOTHER VANISHED INTO THIN AIR.

In an utterly gripping tale of two loves from very different times, a young woman's quest for answers could see her lose the man she's just fallen for...

Liverpool 1981. Sabrina Flooks can barely remember her mother. Abandoned when she was three, she longs to understand what happened. But when she searches the mysterious pocket of Bold Street where she was found, she unwittingly leaves those she loves behind and embarks on an unimaginable journey back to 1928.

Taking a position in the kitchen of the arrogant, Magnolia Muldoon's manor house, she befriends a house maid with starry-eyed dreams. And when she agrees to assist her new acquaintance in winning the heart of the mistress's son, she has no idea of the repercussions their romance will cause or, how she'll get back to Adam, the man she loves.

The Autumn Posy is the heartfelt first book in the Liverpool Brides historical women's fiction series. If you like charming characters, delightful humour, and intriguing mysteries, then you'll love Michelle Vernal's captivating tale.

★★★★★*"I absolutely loved this well-written time travel story. Not only great characters and a well thought out plot, but it's set in the best city in the world.'* **Pam Howes** bestsellling author of The Factory Girls of Lark Lane

Acknowledgments

Firstly, I couldn't have written this novel if it weren't for the stories my mum tells of what it was like growing up in Liverpool. They spark my imagination. Thank you Mum and I like to think if Dad was here with us, he'd be super proud of this Liverpool story.

Thank you to the supremely talented Helen Falconer for her structural help with this novel and Melanie Underwood, Editor for always squeezing me in and ensuring I've got my commas in the right place.

I'd also like to thank Mandy Vere, from Bold Street's News from Nowhere for her amazing help with location information. I plan on visiting one of these days, Mandy.

Thank you too Gel Kevin Creighton for your photographs of Bold Street. They were a big help.

As always a huge big thank you to you, my readers for your ongoing support. I so, appreciate all the lovely comments you send me and our Facebook chats x

Lastly, thank you Paul for all the cooking and hoovering and to our boys for accepting when Mum is sat on the sofa with her lap top she is actually working. I love you guys.

Lightning Source UK Ltd.
Milton Keynes UK
UKHW010636220522
403341UK00002B/148

9 780473 576²